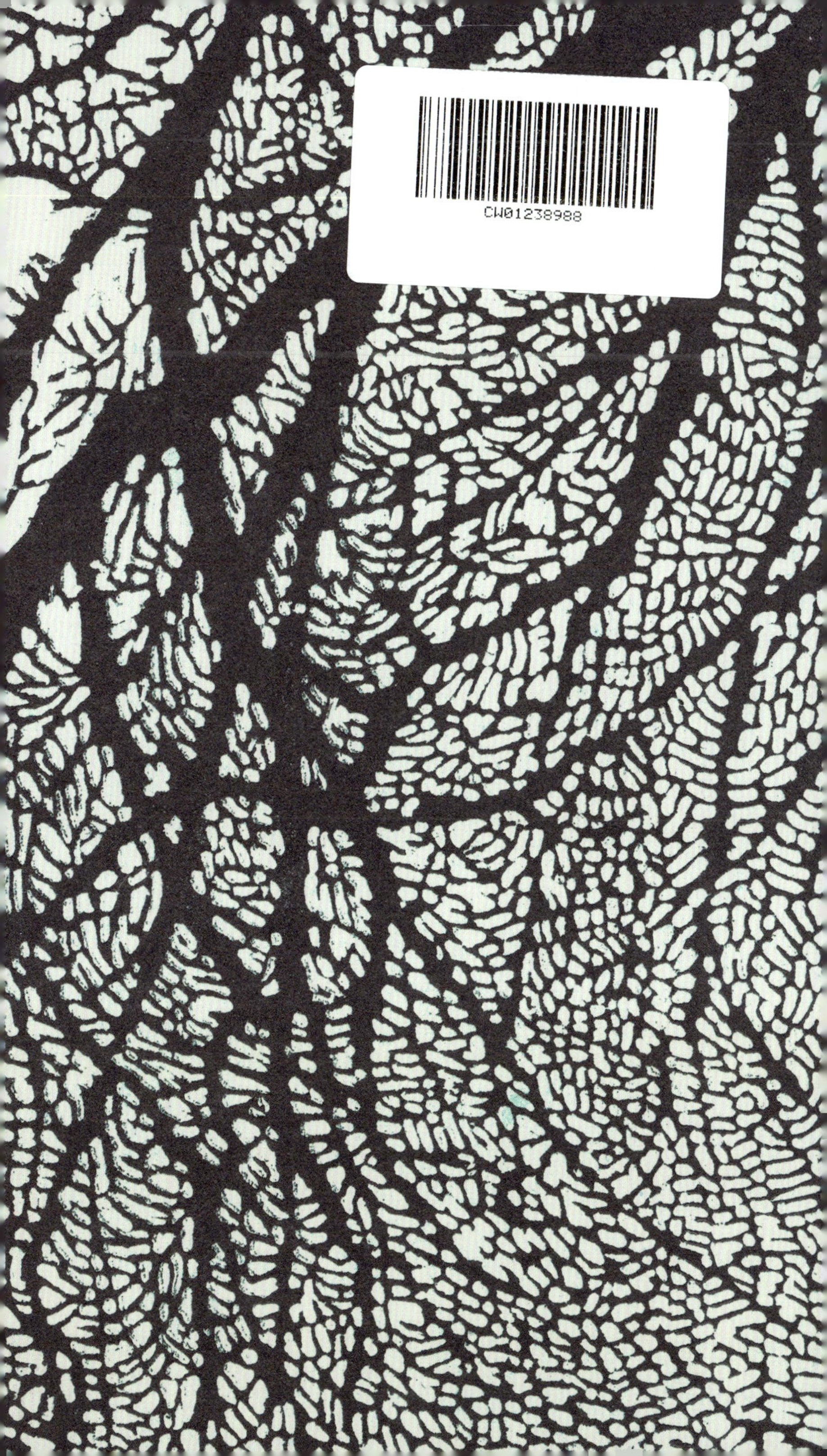

LIFE CYCLE OF A MOTH

LIFE CYCLE OF A MOTH

ROWE IRVIN

CANONGATE

First published in Great Britain in 2025
by Canongate Books Ltd, 14 High Street, Edinburgh EH1 1TE

canongate.co.uk

1

Copyright © Rowe Irvin, 2025
Chapter illustrations by Rowe Irvin

The right of Rowe Irvin to be identified as the
author of this work has been asserted by her in accordance
with the Copyright, Designs and Patents Act 1988

No part of this book may be used or reproduced in any manner
for the purpose of training artificial intelligence technologies
or systems. This work is reserved from text and data mining
(Article 4(3) Directive (EU) 2019/790).

British Library Cataloguing-in-Publication Data
A catalogue record for this book is available on
request from the British Library

ISBN 978 1 83726 245 8

Typeset in Goudy by Palimpsest Book Production Ltd,
Falkirk, Stirlingshire

Printed and bound by CPI Group (UK) Ltd, Croydon CR0 4YY

The manufacturer's authorised representative in the EU
for product safety is Authorised Rep Compliance Ltd,
71 Lower Baggot Street, Dublin D02 P593 Ireland
(arccompliance.com)

MIX
Paper | Supporting
responsible forestry
FSC® C013604
www.fsc.org

For Bill and Susy

Part I

Larvae

1

A red-brown shadow, loping to the scent of a wound. A lugged bellyful of twitching cub, the teats already swelling sore. Behind the trees the fox stood, one dewed paw lifted, muzzle sharp towards what had been discarded there.

The body interrupted the ground like a stone. It lay in the stains and spillings of itself, slack as the hares whose thrashing the fox stilled with a bite.

When the men had come, it had been dark. The noise they brought with them had sent the fox panting for the mud sky of the whelping den. Cowered under it had listened to the cries, the grunts, the thuddings of flesh. It had heard the quiet that came after, the men's silence as they moved away, their feet hurried. And the body left behind, its sound pinched out.

Now it was morning. Now the fox had emerged, nose-first from the dug earth to skulk in the thicket. It smelled what had been spilled. It smelled the scents of the men, strewn thick and heavy like the reek of dog-fox.

The fox paced a wide circle. It sprayed its musk on a bush. It killed a vole and ate it. It padded to its den and back, trailing scent on its paws to say that this ground was the fox's ground. It sat for a while and scratched, and it listened to the furtive creatures darting in the undergrowth, and at the centre of all those scurryings still the body lay limp and quiet.

Crows thickened the sky. Below, the fox left the trees and went low-bellied in the open. Fat teats skimmed the earth. Around the body the dirt lay scuffed. Pieces of the ground and of the men were caught under the fingernails. The face was hidden by some covering that had been wrapped round and round to make a lumpy bundle of the head. The fox touched its nose to the folds. Dog-fox.

Close now, the fox caught a new scent muddied with the others, that hairy under-scent particular to this body, a scent worn against the skin like the fox's own pelt. Its head tilted. A whine came from the white throat. Then the fox stiffened. The long red back bowed upward, tail pulled tight to flank.

From the covered head, a moan that flinched the fox backwards, flattened its ears. Limbs stirred. The torso expanded. A cough heaved up to shudder the ribcage.

The fox fled.

Maya spat ground.

She opened her eyes and found that she was blind. In her blindness she believed herself dead. I have been buried, she thought, and my head is now a part of the earth's darkness. The thought was calm and without fear.

But pain pierced the calm, so she knew she could not be dead. Her mouth sucked air through the cloth that wrapped her. Her hands found her head. The cloth stuck at her eyebrow when she pulled. It came away with a crust of hair and blood. She touched the warmth that trickled and the tips of her fingers turned red. She thought, I am not blind then. I see there is red on my hand, so I am not blind.

The sky was grey, brightening.

Her whole body was an ache. She sent herself into its parts to fetch the hurts and bring them back so they might be separately felt. The jut of stones into her back, her calves. At her toe, the sting of a torn-off nail. The fingerprint pulse of bruises at her hips and jaw. A tightness to her face, her lip swollen and a coin taste on her tongue.

The smell of urine from her thighs hitched in the dried-blood crackle of her nostrils, and with it came another smell of salt and slick and seep, but when she reached for where it came from, for the wet beating heart of the pain, her mind spoke firm and the word it said was no. Not yet. Do not go there.

I must get up, Maya thought. She sat upright too quickly to a pounding in her head and a yellow surge of sickness. Bile rose and she thought she would vomit, so she lay back down. She did not have to get up after all. She could stay here, yes. She would lie still and silent. She would wait for animals to come and take her apart piece by piece and carry her in chunks to their young. She heard the hoarse laughter of crows, the yipping of a fox. She imagined the satisfaction of having her body torn and dispersed, all the cartilage and gristle of her chewed and swallowed and softened and shat. What relief to be scraped and stripped of herself, an itch scratched to the bone.

Maya waited. Her jaw throbbed. When nothing came to tear at her, she thought, Well, there it is, and she hauled herself up, slowly. She felt her split places. She held those parts tight.

Her t-shirt hung tattered from one shoulder. She bent to pick up the thing that had wrapped her head. The shirt stank of its wearer, a stale residue of sweat and something else, something almost rotten. She put her arms into the sleeves and buttoned it up to the neck. She looked about for her trousers but found only her overalls, bunched and filthy, the front ripped open. She drew them on and tied the arms at her waist.

One boot lay nearby, the other some distance away beneath

a hawthorn. Inside the left boot, Maya's foot met a cold hard edge. She remembered sliding the shard of mirror in alongside her ankle, and she almost laughed. She had not had the chance to pull it out.

Maya listened for the fox but heard only wind, leaves. Even the crows had quieted. She began to walk.

Myma Calls Me Daughter

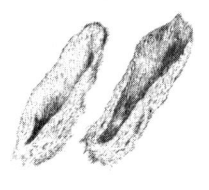

Myma calls me Daughter but that is not always my name. What are you now, Daughter? she asks, and I tell her I am Stone or Vole or Twig or Finger or Worm. She laughs at my names and calls me Little Stone, Little Sniffler-Daughter, Crawly-Kin, Wriggle-on-the-Belly-Daughter, Branchling, Finger-Daughter.

Now I am Mud, the clotting that rain makes of dirt. I carry it with me as I tread the forest, a bottle of wet earth tucked into the pouch slung across my bare chest. I think I will be Mud for a while before the feel of the name turns dry and gritty in my mouth and I have to spit it out. Then the bottle of mud will go into the Museum with all the other names I have carried.

In my fifteen season-cycles I have been many names. But Myma is always just Myma. I asked her once if she used to have other names too and her eyes sort of emptied, then she pinched the skin of her neck and twisted so I knew not to talk of it again.

Late-summer air cooling now about me, nipples hardening on my chest like the drops of resin on the pine trunks. Sweat dries in the furry unders of my arms. My pouch hits against my ribs. The sack hangs empty at my side. This my last chore before dark-come, to check the traps and bring the food.

As I step between the trees I am thinking of Myma, of how she was strange this light-come. How I woke at the just-arrived of the light and the gone of Myma beside me, the door to the house open and bumping in the warm breeze. How I called and heard her just outside, speaking low and not to me. She often talks to herself so that wasn't the strange part. Not strange even that she came inside with a sliced palm because she said the blood was needed for strengthening the Keep-Safes. The thing that bent me funny was the sore red colour around her eyes. The puff of her lids as if she had been crying, the way I used to when I was a small Daughter but not so much now. Yet in this I cannot find sense, because Myma does not cry.

Swipe my knife at a nettle and send the difficult thoughts flopping to the ground with its head. A leaf catches me on the wrist and raises a pink tingle.

Nine pairs of traps in the forest. Each pair marked by Myma's piles of stones balanced one on top of the other on low stumps. Back when my fingers were short and clumsy I would try to make my own stone piles but could never stack more than three before they toppled. Myma would crouch beside me to pick up the fallen stones and I would watch with jealous twitching fingers as the pile heaped up under her careful hands. I no longer need the stone markers to find the traps but always the sight of them is firming, a press of Myma's hand at the base of my back.

The light will not stick in the sky much longer. Soon dark will come and peel it away. I move quick along the trail our feet have trod so often that the undergrowth is worn thin, a sleeve razed through at the elbow by a bending arm. Our trudge-beaten path spiralling out from the house and around between the trees until it meets the fence, where walking must stop.

I pick up a flattish stone, turn it over in my fingers as I go.

With the other hand I feel for the place in the hem of my shorts where Myma has sewn a Keep-Safe. A scrap of skin from the roof of her mouth, folded up and tucked away in the scratchy cloth.

Protect you against Rot, Daughter.

Shudder with the thought of it, that worst thing. Rot like the gone-bad-on-the-inside of fruit, like biting into an apple without checking for holes and my mouth filling with a rancid brown mush. Worse than a foul mouthful the Rot that comes from outside the fence. If that kind of Rot got into me or Myma then we would be the gone-bad apples. Us Rotters. Everything inside us eaten away. I wouldn't be Mud any more. I wouldn't be any name at all. I wouldn't even be Daughter.

Those Rotters out there, they look like you and me, Daughter, but they're all empty on the inside. You can see it when they turn their backs, see right the way in. They're hollow, like dead trees.

I have never seen a Rotter, even when I've stood right up close against the branches and bones and hair of the fence and watched into the forest on the other side. This is a good thing, I know. It means Myma's Keep-Safes are working. I do not want a Rotter to come here but a part of me would like to see one, just once, just to know. I imagine how they might smell. Something like meat gone sour, and the reek of left-wet clothing.

Myma says that as long as we stay inside the fence the Rot cannot get into us. But sometimes when I do something bad like lying or not finishing my food, or when I have a thought that is red and angry, I worry that maybe the Rot is already in me, growing like a clump of hair behind my navel.

I reach the first marker and place the stone on top. It trembles then settles, perfectly balanced. Nothing caught in either snare. One loop is broken. Touch my thumbs to the ends where the braided grass has split. Our snares do not usually break. We make them tight-woven and tough. Too tough to be snapped by a flimsy rabbit. The break is clean, sharp through the fronds, as if sliced by my own knife. I frown. Myma and me are the only things in the forest that carry knives.

The broken snare gives me a scuttling feeling that I can't quite grab hold of, a leggy insect crawling down my back. Judder my shoulders to shake the feeling loose. Some animal must have used its sharp teeth to bite through. A fox maybe. Yes, a stealing skulkering fox that snapped the grass cord and took our rabbit for its own belly.

I'll catch you and eat you, I say into the trees, then your belly will be inside mine, and the rabbit with it.

If the fox is listening it doesn't move.

I check nearly all the snares before finding one dead rabbit. Untwist the loop from the neck and the soft head flops backwards, long yellow teeth hanging out stupid. The rabbit is thin. Small bones rolling under my fingers. Spine knuckling up through grey fur. I stuff it into the sack and crouch to reset the snare. Open out the grass loop to rest in the crook of branch stuck into the ground. The snare stretches wide, a mouth without a throat.

Thickening of the undergrowth as I move towards the last marker. Sharp twigs drag red lines across my chest. I slash at the quick-growing brambles that have narrowed the way.

Get out of my path, I say to them.

I am always fighting brambles.

A rabbit bucks in the trap ahead. Hind parts snared up. Forepaws scrabbling at the ground. It kicks and kicks as I step towards it. I kneel beside the trap and the rabbit goes very still. Ears flat to back. See my face tiny inside the watching black eye, black as Myma's eye. Under the threadbare fur the pumping lungs. I take the legs in one hand, feel tendons and cartilage moving under slack skin. The rabbit twists. High-pitched keening shriek of it. Draw it close to my chest and grip firm the neck. Sharp pull on the back legs. Pop of bone from bone. The rabbit stops making noise and stops moving so I know that it is dead. That's what dead means. No noise. No moving. I drop the limp body into the sack and adjust the snare.

Squat and wee on some foxglove. Pull my shorts up, start back through the trees.

I reach the edge of the clearing as the light is leaching from the sky. Myma's tooth is still there with mine, in the hole on the cleft post. So I am back before her. I take my own tooth from the hole and put it into my pouch alongside the bottle of mud.

A small knot loosens in my stomach. Myma's mood is always better when I am the first back. If I stay out in the forest too close to dark-come she gets the worry-itch on her left inner arm and has to scratch it. Sometimes she scratches it so hard it bleeds. I do not want to make Myma bleed so I always try to come back before the light has gone.

Across the clearing, to the house. Row of crow beaks strung up with hair over the doorway. Click-clack of them. I sit below on the step, back against the door.

My feet ache hot. Tug off my boots. Mends of resin and gut-thread. Before my feet lengthened I wore only skinshoes. Now my feet are bigger than Myma's though still not quite long enough to reach the toes of my boots, these stuffed with rags. I would like to go barefooted always but Myma says I must be booted in the forest because if I step on a thorn or wasp or if a worm goes burrowing up into my foot then she'll be the one to have to deal with it and that'll mean both of us missing out on our chores, won't it, and where would we be then, eh, Daughter, eh?

Daughter. Mud-Daughter.

Her call quivers the hazy light, pulls me up from the step. Above my head, the black beaks clatter. Myma comes striding round past the woodshed. Sinews in her thin arms taut with the weight of her sack. Her breath cracked and shallow in her open mouth. She stops by the water tank, sets down the sack and palms the handle to set gushing the tepid water. Splatter up her dusty legs and a handful scooped to her lips. I watch the muscles in her neck moving back and forth.

Myma wipes her sleeve across her chin. Turns then and stretches her wet mouth wide at me, teeth bared right to the pink gums. The smile carries no flecks of that strangeness I sensed in her at light-come. It is clear and whole and happy. Shiver with the joy of it, of her. Scrunch my eyes, wrinkle my nose, roll back my lips.

Mud-Daughter, says Myma. Dirtling. Loam-Kin.

The residue of her doings clings to her like a scent. Chore-smock grimy with soil. Long grey-brown braid all raggled. A strip of cloth, rusty with blood, tied across her cut palm. Through these things I see her, and she comes back to me, she comes back.

Her black eyes hold me, take in all of me. Me seeing her seeing the thorny hatching of red lines on my chest and arms. Green-brown scuds of dirt on my shorts. Nettle-spot on my wrist. Sweat-stiff hair above my ears. This returning, this slipping back into each other's skins.

She comes close and puts her thumb to the underside of my chin. The past few summers and winters have grown me taller than her, stretched my limbs longer than hers. My eyes now can see over her head. She has said I came from inside her but she is so small I do not know how her body contained me. I think I must have been folded tight like a leaf before it unfurls, tucked behind her breastbone, or else splayed thin and flat under her skin. Hairlike roots and tendrils of me twisted around her bones.

I breathe her nutty earth smell, sweet and fetid. Feel the rough of her skin.

Her thumb draws away. Her eyes graze my slumped sack. Disappointment there, in the pressing of her mouth, the creasing of her brow.

Slim pickings then, she says.

They are small, I say, but there are two.

I think of telling Myma about the broken snare, about the ungripped feeling it put in me, but I do not want to deepen the groove between her eyebrows. She rubs the scar that splits the left one, a jaggy white path between the dark hairs. I do not know how she got it and the pinches she gives herself when it is mentioned keep me from asking.

Have to make do I suppose, she says. Lots of potatoes to bulk out a stew anyhow.

She nudges her own full sack with her foot.

Alright then, she says.

She breathes in, out. Pats her stomach.

Fetch a board and lamp, she tells me. I've got a hankering.

We sit together on the step. The skinned rabbits stretch across the board on Myma's knees the way they must have stretched when they went leaping in the forest. Rag wick burning in a tin of resin. Gleam of red muscle and white bone in the flickering. I scrub soil from the potatoes and hack them to chunks. Then I am twitchy so Myma gives me a long furred ear for fiddling.

She slits the bellies and rips out the innards in one pull. Slippery coils steam in the cooling air. Myma separates the liver, heart and kidneys from the bowels, those rank parts that spoil the meat if accidentally split. The bits that aren't for eating join the two heads and eight paws in the waste bucket between Myma's feet. A soggy jumble of used-to-be-rabbit. The skins are scraped and folded neat beside her, ready for hanging and stitching.

Myma sets down her knife. Rabbit blood mixes with Myma blood on the rag around her hand. She gets to her feet.

Chuck the waste will you, she says.

The lamp goes inside with her. Hear the dull splash of meat and potatoes hitting water in the pot. I sit for a moment in the gloom, thumb and forefinger rubbing the rabbit ear, its blood-spiked fur.

Mud-Daughter.

Myma's shout comes through the open door and jabs me in the back. I drop the ear among the waste parts. Heft the bucket to the edge of the clearing. The dark now is thick, is black. The packed earth cool under the bare pads of my feet. White sting of stars over my head, tiny and round like the bone tips of needles.

I shake the waste at the foot of a tree. Flip-flop of guts on the ground.

A shift in the blackness. My head flicks towards the movement. Two eyes, yellow between the black trunks. Pale red fur and a ragged tatter of a tail. I bare my teeth at the fox and snarl. It slicks its ears and slips off among the trees. I know it will return for the waste when I am gone. I glare it into the dark before turning and padding back across the clearing towards the warm light.

2

She dragged herself the way a hunter drags the body of an animal. Her hand went ahead of her, gripping the mirror shard.

The going was difficult, the ground broken up by rocks and by the pieces of farm machinery dumped at the edges of the long-neglected woodland. Maya stepped between rusted plough blades and seed drills, bent wheels, hay rakes and harrows, gutted cars and tractors with nettles and ivy bursting up around the seats. She passed a worn stone gatepost, the iron joint wrenched loose, the gate lying crumpled and grown over with brambles, a corroded sign just visible between the vines: No Public Access.

On her belly she pulled herself under a tangle of barbed wire and went tumbling down the scree of a dried-up riverbed. Trees had fallen across and some had sent up new growths that branched above and blocked the light. Maya had to clamber over trunks and push through bracken to reach the slope on the other side. When she turned around, she could no longer see where she had come from.

The forest was dense. She felt it closing behind her as she waded into it, thorns knitting at her back.

It might have been that she walked a very long way, or it might have been that she walked very slowly. Her only thought was to keep walking. Away, away. Her bruises ached. Night passed, followed by day and another night, and the forest began to seem to Maya impossibly large, as though it were endlessly sprouting up ahead of her as she passed from thicket to thicket. It rained and she lapped water from bark. When she tired she scraped a shallow bed into the earth and lay under a blanket of dirt. Once, she was woken by a scrabbling, two paws and a sharp nose digging for the blooded stench of her. She hissed and spat from the ground until the animal streaked away.

Exhaustion and hunger put pricking spots in her eyes. She saw things. Thin grey fingers slipping around the flanks of a beech. A long pale back between the birch trunks. The grey heel of a foot swinging up into the branches. She stood staring at where the foot had disappeared and saw only leaf, twig.

Then, a thinning, an openness of space. A gap that broke the trees like the patch of skin left behind when a clump of hair is torn out.

The hut crouched at the centre of the clearing. Moss clung to the stone walls. The tiled roof was spored with lichen. A smaller, wooden structure with a slanted metal roof leaned brokenly at one side. The door was closed and quiet, a shut mouth. Maya watched it from the cover of the trees and she did not move until the sun sank and the trees loosed their shadows into the clearing.

There was a water tank beside the hut, fed by guttering that hung loose in places, the moss heavy where rainwater had leaked. Maya worked the stiff handle of the tank. Water coughed brown from the spout.

The door whined when she pushed it. Inside, an animal musk blurred with the smells of stale smoke and mildewed air. She saw a table with two stools. Iron pots and a pile of wood in the blackened hearth. Above the hearth, a rack that looked as if it had once held guns. A metal bucket, a shovel, a broom. Hooks and nails on the walls, from which hung an axe, a pair of shears, a stiff-looking brush with a handle, a wooden mallet, stained sacks, a moth-pocked coat. Tins with faded labels stood on sagging shelves. The lowest shelf had collapsed, a rubble of glass and earthenware spilled to the floor. In one corner, a bowed drinks cabinet. To the right, an empty doorway into a second room gaped like an eyeless socket.

It was the mugs that made Maya wary. Two mugs, on the table. Were it not for the dust, she might have thought them only just set down. She picked up the closest by the handle and traced the flower design on its surface, the chipped rim. The other was yellow, a rabbit painted on one side and a letter R on the other. The bright colours seemed at odds with the wear of the place.

A sound then that coiled her tight. From the other room, a scuffling. Maya stepped towards the open doorway and felt something splinter underfoot. The door that must once have filled the empty frame, now lying flat on the floor, hinges rent.

She saw the small room, the low cot of a bed bundled with filthy sheets, the squat wood burner. She saw the dusk light coming through the window. She saw the disturbance of dust, the frenzied movement of what had startled her, and she let the hand holding the mirror shard drop to her side.

The bird flapped and beat itself against the wall at Maya's approach. Stunned, it dropped to the floor and lay crooked. Maya stuck the piece of mirror back in her boot and wrapped a hand around the bird. The tiny heart stuttered. It was a blackbird, a mud-coloured female, the feathers on one side shredded to the quills. Maya had seen that kind of wing-stripping in hens. She knew it could mean mites or stress. This sudden thought of the poultry farm slicked her throat with bile. She felt the dark wound that had opened in her between there and here. Her mind lurched from it. No.

With the heel of her hand she hefted open the stiff window.

The blackbird flopped from her palm to the ground. It heaved itself into flight and Maya watched it careening away among the trees. It would have been better, she thought, to snap its neck. It would likely die anyway.

She turned back to the room. The grey shell of an abandoned wasps' nest hung in the corner above the bed. And there, on the bed, something tangled in the stained sheets, some huddled shape. Maya went close and pulled back a corner. Her breath stumbled.

She could not tell how long it had been there. The bundle of withered limbs lay like a sleeping child, knees drawn to chest. It was grey, the same grey as the wasps' nest, the same grey as the hair that spilled around it, the grey rag of a dress that seemed part of the body itself. The flesh was not rotted away but dried, leathered stiff around the bones. From its slightness, Maya guessed that the body must be female.

Looking at the hair, she felt as if she was in the presence of something still living. It swathed the body, thick and tough-looking. The face was small, skin pulled tight against the cheekbones, lids empty. Maya looked at the hands, at the feet, their fanned bones like the spokes of wings.

She felt no repulsion as she knelt there. Only a settling, a calm. It reassured her, the thought of the quiet grey body lying there for years, undisturbed and alone.

Maya lay down on the dusty stone floor beside the bed, and she slept. In the night, she had the sense of a slim-fingered hand stroking her hair. It comforted.

We Slump

We slump around our stomachs, rabbit-fed. Full-bellied weight of us on our stools. Leftover tumble of bones stripped clean in our bowls and the sharp ribs plucked out to pick the stringy meat from between our teeth. Greasy splash on the table, me the messy eater. I lower my mouth to the puddled spill and lap-lap. Then take up my R-for-rabbit mug and hop it about to make Myma laugh.

No pudding because pudding only happens once each season-cycle, at First Frost to mark when, fifteen winters ago, Myma pushed me from the hole between her legs and called me Daughter. All that comes from between my legs is wee, and blood with each moon, and sometimes a sticky white stuff that goes crusty in my shorts.

Instead of pudding we read the labels from the empty tins. Ultimate Creamy Chocolate Pudding, a brown-and-white label, faded where our thumbs have rubbed.

Deliciously smooth. No added colours. Natural flavours. Store in a cool dry place. Once opened keep refrigerated. Serve hot or cold. To enjoy hot, empty contents into a saucepan and place over medium heat. Stir frequently.

When Myma showed me how to read the words on the labels she told me that not all words have meanings. Some are only shape and sound and feel in the mouth. Re–fri–ger–a–ted pushes up under our tongues. Crea–my slides down our gullets. Cho–co–late we stretch out between us, spit it back and forth, that memory of sweetness in the pockets of our cheeks.

I have already chosen which pudding I will guzzle when the First Frost comes. Caramel Treat Ready-To-Use Dessert Topping. The picture on the label is the yellow colour of a scab. I think how I will press the tin to my lower lip and tip the sweet sludge into my mouth, how I will keep the dried smears in the corners of my lips to lick up later.

Myma slides the Ultimate Creamy Chocolate Pudding label back behind the row of tins on the shelf. Six full tins left. I do not know what will happen when they are all empty but now isn't the moment for worrying about that, when I am warm and fed, so I tuck the thought away into the place for things that do not quite matter yet, along with thoughts of the cut rabbit snare. Those skin-creeping uneasinesses. Flick them into the dark.

Willow bark, chewed to keep our teeth from blackening. Spit my woody pulp into Myma's open hand and wipe the dangle of saliva on my wrist. Myma adds our chewed bark to the wad she is storing up in a tin for new Keep-Safes.

Then through the doorless doorway and into the room where we sleep. The wood burner in the corner, left cold through summer, though in the winter we will keep it burning light and dark. Opposite the burner, the glass-front cupboard that holds my Museum. The lamp in Myma's hand flings orange across the drawings covering walls and ceiling. Trees and stones and all the shapes of leaf. Muddy fox, stoat, rat. Charcoal crow, pigeon, jackdaw, owl. Ripple and shift of them in the lamplight. Myma's drawings are closer to the actual solid things than mine are. I have never been able to make a thing leap between my mind and my hand the way she can. It always changes as it comes out, and I get impatient and fumble it to a mess. My lumpy creatures struggling after her swift and sure-footed ones.

Myma sets the lamp beside the bed. Black streak up the wall from all the flames that have burned there.

I am too tired for dancing, Myma says.

It is her turn to choose This-and-That.

My legs are too heavy, she says.

She bends and rubs her calves. If it were my turn choosing This-and-That I would have liked to dance. To stamp and beat, to jerk my limbs and spin.

We will do hair-brushing, Myma decides.

I do not complain because it is Myma's choice and she says it is important to respect each other's choices. I go across the room tiptoed to see how it feels walking fox-like. Crouch by the This-and-That crate, knees bumping against collarbones. There the blindfold, there the brush, the quiet shoes, the wishbones, the masks, the copying crown, the tin of coal and dirt and chalk. Grab up the brush by the handle and push my nose into the tough bristles for the smell of Myma, her salt-reek. I go back to her, now walking only on my heels.

A blanket spread on the floor. Me sitting with my back to Myma. Her fingers firm at my shoulders and under my jaw, arranging me. Her breath warm at the back of my head. She drags the brush through the short rabbity fuzz on my scalp and down to the base of my neck where the hair tapers into a bird tail. My hair is cut close so that it will not tangle or dirty when I am doing chores. Myma's hair stays long. She only trims it when the ends begin to fray, or when she needs a hank of it for a Keep-Safe. She says her hair is a cloak. She says her hair keeps us both wrapped safe. But I have my winter cloak of rabbit fur and that keeps me warm enough.

Close my eyes while Myma brushes. One hundred strokes then I turn to face her and she turns to face the doorway. She looses her hair from its plait. It flexes like a limb, thick and muscular. A thrumming thing of blood and sinew.

Pull the brush from the top of her head down the curve of her back. Myma shivering at the feel. I imagine I am combing through long strands of grass, the small mound of Myma a hillock full of roots and earth and worms. Brush hard to make the grass crackle.

After, Myma lifts her arms in a stretch that looks like it feels the way Ultimate Creamy Chocolate Pudding tastes. Her hair bristled huge by the brushing. Her hands smoothing it.

Bed, Daughter. Mud-Daughter.

I tuck my head between my knees and roll backside over nose, then jump-roll-flump into the raggy nest of our bed. My legs sprawl long. Myma turns her chore-smock inside out over her head. Little hanging folds of her breasts that once fed me. Small hard knots of muscle in her arms. Her worry-itch a scabby patch below the crook of her left elbow. Furrows in the skin of her belly, like beetle tracks in bark. I touch my own stomach, disappointingly smooth, no interesting markings or textures except the nub in the middle, the cut stem where I grew from Myma. Lift my hand to skim my fingers over the mossy clump of hair in the part of her legs. She bats me away and bends to fetch her bed-smock.

See as her arm swings forward, the hooked scar at the top of her ribcage. The rabbit in my belly flops with guilt, though it's been seven whole summers now since I left the tap on the tank open and all the water gushed into the dirt and Myma had to teach me a Lesson by rolling herself sideways off the roof. It wasn't high but a jut from the woodshed caught her under the arm. I helped pick the splinters out while she told me slowly that this is why, Daughter, this is why we don't leave the tap open. And I am always careful now to close it all the way. Twist it so hard it dents my palm.

I shuck my shorts to my ankles and pull my own bed-smock

over my head. Moment of panic as the cloth presses at my eyes, at my nose and mouth. Relief as I burrow into the light.

In the bed our foreheads press together. She taps her own chest, then mine.

Thank you, Mud-Daughter, for fetching the rabbits and chopping the potatoes. Thank you for the hair-brushing.

Thank you, Myma, for digging the potatoes and stewing the rabbits. Thank you for the hair-brushing also.

I don't have any sorrys, Myma says.

I have one sorry, I say.

Okay.

Sorry, Myma, that the rabbits were small.

Pause.

One more actually.

Yes.

Sorry, Myma, for leaving the tap open and spilling all the water.

Pause.

That was a long long while ago, Little Mud-Daughter. You already said a sorry for it. And you learned not to do it again. You don't need to think about it now.

I am still sorry, I tell her.

Okay.

She pinches the lamp and I take her hair into my mouth and suck on it until I sleep.

3

Something like it had happened before. There was a girl and a boy. They were young. They wore grey-and-white school uniforms. Under hers the girl wore a thin-strapped thing her mother had bought her though she did not yet need it. Under his the boy wore father-shaped bruises.

The boy gave the girl a wrapped sweet.

'I'm going to hunt rabbits at the back of school,' he said. 'My dad says there's too bloody many. He says they need a good culling. I'll show you how to shoot them if you like.'

The two went with sticks to the burrows. They beat on the dirt roofs and called out.

'You're being culled. You have to leave.'

But the rabbits stayed holed under and so the boy said, 'Little buggers', the way his father did, then he pointed his stick like a gun and muttered, 'Boom–ch–ch–boom.' He pelted stones into the burrow and together he and the girl listened for the sound of them hitting the earth inside. Then they both stamped until the clods of soil began to fall inward. They pushed the dirt into the mouths of the burrows so the air couldn't get in. After, the girl stood still and held her breath for as long as she could and the boy ran up and down the grass mounds to keep himself from crying.

They were uncertain then and a little sad. They crouched on the flat grass with the honeycomb of burrows underneath. The girl found a piece of rabbit bone. Then the boy told her to lie on her back, and he showed her what his parents did by lying on top of her and moving. The girl did not like the weight of him there. She told the boy this and he answered her with a word that the girl did not know, but which sounded spiked and nasty, so she rolled the boy off sideways and stood hard on his fingers. He cried then. She told him not to worry, that the buried rabbits would probably dig their way out anyway.

When the girl got home, she picked the grit from the wrinklings of her knees. There were muddy grass stains up the back of her uniform. A thread trailed loose at the hem of her skirt. The sweet the boy had given her was warm in her pocket next to the piece of rabbit bone. The girl imagined how it would feel to be buried alive and she hoped the burrows had been empty. Then she thought about the skin around the boy's right eye, a purple swell to it, like the eye of a rabbit sick with myxi. She had wanted to touch her fingertip to that tenderness, perhaps to stroke it, perhaps to press inward until it whitened.

The girl stuck the sweet to the piece of rabbit bone and wrapped the grey thread from her school skirt round and round to bind them. She did this to make sense of the thing that had happened with the boy, the thing that had made her feel as if her body didn't belong to her, as if she might pitch backwards into the earth and be trapped there. She did it to thrust the feeling out of herself and into a thing that could be held. It went under her bed and whenever the girl felt her grip loosening she would look at it and think, There – there is the thing I am afraid of. I keep it under my bed.

Everything Sounds

Everything sounds, even the air when there is no wind in it. I am always hearing. All murmur, all patter.

The objects in the Museum sound different to other things in the forest. The Museum is an apple pip, dried-grass plait, acorn cup, alder catkin, big grey stone, bottled puddle, squirrel tail, birch leaf, thistlehead, finger-shaped root, finch nest, smooth black pebble, owl feather, moss, pine cone, dried worm, black beetle, shiny conker, large dead spider, coughed-up owl pellet, crow foot, millipede, dried sap blob, blue egg, dandelion stem, shrew nose, mouse tail, bracken frond, badger claw, rusty metal ring, seed pod, rat spine, crispy dead wasp, rabbit paw, hazel twig, rook beak, white garlic flower, bramble thorn, bent nail from the doorway, scab of lichen, vole skull, oak leaf, hawthorn bark, snail shell, walnut shell, splinter from Myma's heel, apple bark, muntjac hoof, dried redcurrant, hedgehog spike, rabbit rib, dead woodlouse, pigeon wing, weasel foot, sycamore seed, holed fox tooth.

These things have names hidden inside them.

When I finger-thumb-plucked the pip from the apple pit the sound it made was full and round, like a humming in the throat or a whomph of wings. I felt the thrum of it behind the bone of my breast and knew that it was my name, my first.

I said to Myma, Now I am Pip, and she looked at me a moment then said, Pip-Daughter, okay, yes, and she wrote it in the dirt with a stick and showed me it was an unusual word because it reads the same both ways. But when I held the apple pip to her ear so she could listen to its hum, she shook her head and frowned.

I don't hear anything, she said. Must be for your ears only, Pip-Daughter, Seed-Kin, Little Soon-Grow.

She tugged at my lobes, then nibbled them to make me wriggle. I didn't understand because when I lifted the pip to my own ear it was so loud. The buzzing of it. And it was more than just sound. It did something to the air around it, the way heat makes a shimmer around the cooking pot.

If you say it's special, Myma said, then it is. You must keep it safe in your pouch.

And I did, until the long green fronds came sighing their sound at me and I pulled them up by the roots and said, Now I am Grass. Myma made a plait of them so they would stay together in my pouch. The apple pip went on the window ledge, and soon the plaited grass dried up and joined it, then the acorn cup, then the catkin. When I was Stone I lugged the big grey humming rock around with me for four moons. It was a strong name and it made me strong too. But when I set it on the window ledge with the rest Myma said, You'll run out of space soon. You need to put these in a Museum, so they don't get lost. I said, Museum? A collection of objects, she told me. Things that have meaning but are not used any more. Like the names I have been, I said, and she said, Exactly. And she took the empty bottles out of the glass-front cupboard and dragged it through to the room where we sleep.

Some names I have held on to for ages, like Finger, the crook-knuckled beckoning root I carried in my pouch for more than a whole season-cycle before the name stopped twitching in me and was replaced by Nest. Others are short-worn, like

Scab, the lichen crust I peeled from a dead branch of oak, then peeled from myself after only a few lights.

Before Mud I was Tooth. I found it whining at the edge of the clearing, the fox canine with a hole going right the way through. It had just rained and the tip was poking up out of the earth. Tooth was a quick-snapping, gnashing name that made me more irritable than usual, and it was a relief when the bite of it dulled and I could be Mud, cool and glopping.

In the Museum the objects quieten. The names are still inside them, and when I listen close I can hear them humming, but they are never as loud as when I first find them. They no longer sound in my chest, but outside me. Sometimes I lie awake after Myma has fallen asleep and in the stillness I listen to the objects murmuring low together. I start to wonder then about all the names I haven't yet been and I get so worked up that my hands twitch and I feel my eyes growing big in the dark. All the unfound things pulsing out names in their hidden places, like midge bites in places on my skin I can't reach.

When I am unsure of myself, the things in the Museum remind me of all the names and Daughters I have been. Touch them and know myself.

Me crouched naked at the hearth in the room where we eat. Our bed-smocks and chore-smocks and the topmost layer of sheets and rags from the bed all bundled up together in the cooking pot. In go the dried leaves of soapwort and mint. Stir the coals to glowing and add another log to make the flames jump.

We had not planned for washing as one of our chores this light, but it is an Exception because Myma let out her wee in the bed, a thing she hasn't done for ages. Exceptions can be good, like when we caught a rare muntjac that had come over the fence and we had to spend the whole light skinning and slicing and hanging and hacking. The two-pronged hoof I took for a name sits in the Museum now. Other Exceptions are dull, like when it rains too hard to do our outside chores and even though I don't mind the wet on my skin Myma says it might chill us to sickening so we must stay shut up inside. Then there are the Exceptions like this one that come with a damp shock and a bad itchy smell, and a heaviness in Myma that I must prop upright.

Myma bare-skinned on her stool, lower lip inside her mouth, thumbnail at her worry-itch. Her hair a limp cloak. The clouds scudding across her eyes are shame-coloured and her shame plucks at me. I go close and stroke her along the jaw with both hands, the way that comforts. She lets her head rest against my belly. This needing-closeness in a bad feeling. This leaning-on-the-other. Tender body asking for a strong muscle to heave it, a sturdy spine to brace it. It is not often that I am the leaned-on, the needed. Wee-smell drying on our legs.

The pot boils to a foamy scum. Stink of wee to sweet of mint and clean bite of soapwort. Steam wetting the walls, cheeks flushing, hair crinkling. I prod with the long stirring stick. The foam turns grey and yellow.

Clothes stew, I say, mhhhmmmmm.

It is the joke Myma always makes when we do washing. See through the gap in her hair, the corners of her lips twitching upwards. I look at her long toenails. That's a chore for this light, so I squat and cup her heel in my hand, set my knife at the horny edge and begin to carve. Myma's toenails are thick, the skin around them toughened like wood. On her big right toe, a pucker of skin instead of a nail. She says that's just how she is. I have ten toenails, she has nine. My eyes are grey-green, hers are black. I have freckles, she has none. I have one shadow, she has two.

Twist out the water and drape the washed things in the clearing where the sun will make them crisp. Our turn now for washing. Coarse rags soaked hot. The grime sluicing from our bodies. Rub my skin and see it redden. The parts of me where dirt collects. Under my arms, the folds of my ears, my backside. When I scrub between my legs below the tuft of hair it makes the shivery itch that quickens my breath. The feeling is confusing so I turn my attention to my feet, always the filthiest bit of me.

The rag is dark when I am done. Myma's is even filthier.

We dip our heads. I shake out a spitting of droplets and Myma almost laughs. She wrings her hair like a sheet. It seems to hold half the water in the pot.

We sit naked at the table and eat dried cherries, the sweet-sharp flesh nibbled from the hard pits. I put my stones into a tin for shaking. Her hair billows as it dries. Her eyes clearer now, her back straighter.

Can I have your cherry stones for my rattler? I ask.

The Exception is done and we return to chores. I make mends with needled bone and gut-thread. Prick my finger and Myma tongues away the berry of blood. She mixes the chewed bark from our teeth-cleaning with the toenail trimmings then scatters them in a Keep-Safe circle around the clearing. I go into the forest to check the traps, capering and whooping along the path in just my boots, my pouch swinging about. All tingling at being out of my clothes. My skin feeling everything right up against it. The skinny rabbit I find flops lovely and furry on my shoulder, and I nuzzle it. We eat it, then dig holes and empty our bowels.

This is the light. This is how we spend it.

Dark-come and us clothed again in our sundried bed-smocks, the clean smell of them making me sneeze.

It is my turn to choose This-and-That. I choose dancing, my favourite. I have tied rabbit hide over my tin of cherry stones. Rittle-rattle sound of hail when I shake. We stand facing each other, six steps apart. Myma shifts her weight from foot to foot. Gone the soggy mood of earlier.

I am going to dance well, she says. I have a lot of energy.

I grin, lift my chin and yip-yip. Myma begins her stamping. The sound of her feet on the stone floor, water smacking damp soil. I shake my cherry-stone rattler and stamp with her. Her hands thump at her chest. Her head tilts back. She stamps faster. I wave my arms, cherry stones clattering. Dip and jerk of my elbows. Myma's hair, the swing and whip of it around her like a tail, all vertebrae, all nerve and tissue.

The lamplight makes her shadow huge. My own shadow flits and darts, throws itself into corners like a bird. Myma's stamping quickens. Her second shadow, the one that doesn't follow her feet and is only visible in some lights, unfurls from the dark edge of the room and moves across the wall. Two shadows dancing behind Myma now. Her eyes are closed and she is laughing. I want to join them, Myma and her two shadows, but they are separate from me, they are all together in a dancing that is not mine, and I can't keep up. I stop, panting. The tin of cherry stones goes silent. And even though I am no longer dancing, I can hear the pounding of two sets of feet, four heels striking the floor. Four hands, clapping. Myma's second shadow spins outward, feet dipping towards the centre of the room, attached to nothing.

Myma gives a final stamp and lets her arms plummet to her sides. Her breath hard in the quiet. Her bed-smock dark at the pits. Her shadow alone now on the wall, chest heaving. The nose of it points towards the doorway, where the second shadow has drawn away again into the dim of the other room. A small grey moth flutters through into the light.

The tin slips from my fingers. Rattle-spill of cherry stones across the floor. I scramble around, picking them up.

Next light brings a warm drizzly rain not heavy enough for an Exception. In the potato patch the ground makes a sludge as thick as my name. My boots stump the furrows, water leaking up around my tread.

It is my chore to clear the wilted stems while Myma digs for the ready potatoes. Her arms go into the ground and come out clutching warty clods. When I was small I wanted to peek every light after planting so I could watch them bulbing, but Myma said we had to wait. They need darkness, she told me. They aren't yet ready for the light. How it would feel to be buried like that, the length of me rooting down into the ground. Myma's hands firming over me the cool moist soil.

Hacking stems is an arm-ache and in the heat I am glad of the rain that laps the sweat from my neck. Stoop to cut, straighten then stop, stoop again, stoop lower. Something here, something odd. Soil scrabbled, potatoes strewn. Pick up this one and hold it. A chunk missing. Hard white flesh grooved as if gnawed. I dip my brows. The bite marks are shallow and blunt. Like the chomp of my own teeth into an apple, but never into a raw potato, never straight from the ground. They make for a cramping belly if not cooked.

I glance to where Myma kneels in the dirt. Maybe she got a hankering when she was last at the patch, maybe she had a quick nibble to keep her going. She would have regretted that. It would have put a hurt in her stomach.

Does your tummy ache? I call to her.

No, she says without turning her head. Why are you asking?

I was just wondering if it might, I reply.

She stands straight and faces me, forehead dented. I hide the tooth-marked potato in my fist.

Why? she asks. Do you have a tummy ache? You ate something bad? Does it hurt?

No, I say quickly. I feel fine. Feel good.

She stares at me through the drizzle, then grunts and bends to her digging. The bitten potato slips into my pouch.

Later, when I go for my dark-come wee, I take the potato out and finger the toothed ridges. Lift it to my mouth, set my own teeth against the bitten part. The ruts too wide to fit my bite. I try to imagine the mouth that made them. A mouth like mine, but larger-toothed. A mouth like mine.

They look like you and me.

No, I think, and think it hard to press the fear down. No, not that. Rotters don't even have insides so what would a Rotter eat a potato for? It would just tumble out the split-tree back of them. Calm myself with this thinking.

Not done yet? Myma calls through the door.

Coming, I call back.

I sink my teeth into the potato flesh, around the strange marks. Spit that other bite into the bracken. Now it's my teeth furrowed into the potato, my own known bite. This makes me feel better. The potato is a normal thing now, a familiar and certain thing. It is only potatoey and boring now. Toss it away.

4

She was dimly aware of time passing, of waking to rain on the roof and a dripping leak, of needing to urinate and squatting over the bucket in the other room, of baring her teeth and gasping at the sear of it, of crawling back to the room with the body only to lie awake and shivering, of rising again, of scrabbling among the tins until she found a dry box of matches, of striking and striking until a flame took and set the dead wood hissing, of slumping down again beside the fire, of a pain in her head and of someone else beside her, cooling fingers, her mother's perhaps, and of remembering that her mother was dead and had never sat with her that way, not even when Maya was a child, of her eyes rolling into and out of dreaming until finally she found a blackness she could cling to.

After what might have been days, Maya woke to the cackle of a magpie. There was a pressure in her chest as if she had been shouting. Her body still ached but she could feel the exhaustion sloughing from her as she stood. It had rained enough to quarter-fill the pot she'd pushed under the leak in her night-waking daze. She added more wood to the fire and hung the pot to boil.

As Maya washed herself she thought only of what was

immediate: there was dirt on her body so she had to clean it. She did not think about what had put the dirt there, or the fact that much of the dirt was her own blood. Around what had happened she felt a numbness, a hard crust forming, and she welcomed it.

She sat at the table and ate a tin of peaches. The chunks were soft, the juice sweet.

The body, when she lifted it from the sheets, felt like a dead branch. A kind of brittle strength to it. The hair was the heaviest thing. She took the shovel and dug a hole at the edge of the clearing. It was good to set her back and shoulders straining. Folded up in the ground, the body looked like a knotted system of roots, strange and uncovered in the openness of daylight. Maya stood over it a moment, hands folded. She thought of her mother's coffin being lowered. She unclasped her hands and shovelled the dirt back into the hole.

Over the turned earth she planted a sturdy fork of dead wood. It seemed right, to mark the spot. She could have buried the body further off in the forest, but it would have felt somehow like a violence to move it too far from the house. Maya couldn't help feeling that its presence was what had kept the place untouched and silent. A repelling force. The body was something resilient and obstinate, like wood petrified to stone. It was something that had endured.

A small hard bulge in her overalls pressed at her. She unknotted the sleeves from around her waist and retrieved, from the breast pocket, a shrivelled potato. Soil still dusted the skin. A cleft at one side gave it the look of a bent thumb, or, depending on how she held it, a lumpen heart. Maya had forgotten that she carried it. It had been months since she'd worked the potato harvest. She thought of the hands that had given it to her, their brief warmth, the sound of a smile in the voice that had said, 'That one is for you.'

Little fingers of growth had sprouted from the dimpled eyes.

Maya held the small, puckered thing and felt in her own chest a shoot of something greenish.

The shears cut the tuber into pieces, an eye in each nub. Maya cleared a patch of earth behind the house where the sun would hit. She dug a trench and set the chunks in a row. As she packed the soil she imagined the wrinkled pieces sending out roots that would fatten to bulbs and emerge swollen, flushed and screaming. She touched the forked wooden post and made a silent plea to the buried body to keep an eye on the potatoes as they sat under the earth. To tug from the fragments something whole and strong.

The matches were a worry. Only three remained in the box. Beside the hearth was a tin drum with a lid. Inside: a steel bar, a hunk of flint, a brown wad of dry moss. Maya considered these, their use. She gripped the steel and struck the flint. She did it again. She did it faster. A spark flared and died. She set the moss in the fireplace, struck. The bright speck set the moss glowing. Maya fed the glow with twigs, then she axed apart the soft wood of the fallen door and piled the pieces in the hearth.

She took the bottles from the cabinet and emptied them into the dirt. She boiled the sheets from the bed. As she hung them to drip she remembered how, when her father would come home ripe and stinking, her mother would strip the sheets from the beds and fold them to crisp corners, then unfold them and put them back on the beds, before pulling them off again. Repetition made things bearable, Maya knew this. She wrought routine from her days. The work she put her body to distracted her from its aches, until she no longer felt them.

She was practical, resourceful. She cleared and swept. The empty wasps' nest peeled like a callus from the wall. She found an old pair of men's work boots under the bed, mothy blankets. She salvaged two bowls from the wreck beneath the collapsed shelf. She cleaned out the water tank, she mended the roof, the guttering, she scraped the walls of their moss.

The grass traps she set in the forest were imitations of the wire fox snares she'd often seen fixed to posts at the edges of fields. Maya had always thought them cruel devices, the animal left thrashing until a farmer put a shot in it, but when she pulled her first strangled rabbit from her own trap she felt only pride, and hunger. She ate the meat with wild garlic.

She'd been clumsy with the shears and had shredded the rabbit's pelt when skinning it. Maya looked at the coupled blades, then she took the axe and split the shears at the join. She was left with two knives, the handles of which she wrapped in bark.

Finally, Maya cast off the clothing she had arrived in, shucked it like unwanted skin. The torn t-shirt and too-large overalls that had once been her father's, these she cut into strips for cleaning. Using thread picked from the overalls, a needle sharpened from a rabbit's rib, she stitched herself a loose shift from one of the sheets. With each stab and pull she imagined raw edges suturing together, a tight seam over a wound to keep it from leaking. She tied a knot and tucked away the trailing ends so they wouldn't catch and tear.

The Tip of the Stick Splits the Worm

The tip of the stick splits the worm into two halves. Soily spill from one end but that's okay because soon the hole will close up and there will be two worms instead of one. I hunch over my knees to watch the halves writhing away from each other and I think how worms and maggots don't look like whole bodies in themselves but like the insides of something else, like entrails cut free and squirming about in the mud. Maybe that's why when a thing dies the worms all rush to fill it, because that's where they came from and they want to go back.

I flick one half of the worm over the fence.

From here I can see the brambles on the other side, the tall pines beyond. If I walked to the opposite edge of the forest and looked over the fence there, I would see oaks. From another part, I'd see birches and a shallow dip in the ground that fills with water when it rains. And from another, an ash with a torn side where a huge limb has split away, the branch softening on the ground.

The fence used to be higher than my head but now it barely reaches my chest. Branches knotted into branches and Keep-Safes hung all over. Scab and skin and feather. Rat tails, fingernails, my first teeth. Always a strange feeling, seeing the sprinkled bits of myself. It must be how the worms feel when they see their tails crawling away on their own. I do not like to think too hard about the parts of me that are out here always, especially in the dark when I imagine the Rotters sniffing around the fence.

In the dark beyond the fence creeps the Rotted thing. Sleep you sound now, little Daughter, safe from everything.

The song Myma sang when I was small. Hum it now to myself as I stand looking over, my voice mixing with the birdcalls, jay skraa-aaa and pecker rattle.

The brambles on our side are all vine, no dark swell of fruit to suck into my mouth. Myma has already picked all the berries here. On the other side the brambles are heavy with them. Some in their ripeness have burst and dribbled onto the leaves below. Others have been pecked to purple wounds by birds. One cluster hangs close enough that I could reach and take a handful. My mouth spurts. What would happen if I thrust my hand across? If I plunged my whole arm into that other place, the Rotted place. Would Rot would come quick, a sudden shrivelling, or slow, a creeping along the wrist, up the arm and neck to hollow out the head? Maybe I would not see it happening at all. Maybe it would be a quiet emptying, like a tree crumbling inside its bark. Maybe I would not even know.

Slight tremor in my hand where it rests on the branches. Throb of an impulse. I yank the hand back, fold my fingers into my fist. Heart-thud at my thumbtips.

A pigeon flaps across the fence to get away from another pigeon that has been trying to scrabble onto its back. The scrabbler pigeon follows. I once asked Myma why the animals don't get Rotted, why it's okay to eat them even though they go back and forth over the fence.

Their minds aren't the same as ours, she said. They don't have the part that we have, the part that makes us cleverer, but also makes us vulnerable to Rotting.

In a tree on the other side, one pigeon has managed to climb on top of the other. It shuffles about and pumps its tail in an urgent sort of way. The pigeon underneath squats low and still, belly to branch. I watch them and think how I do not like knowing that my mind has this vulnerable part to it. Something sitting in my head that makes me weaker than a burbling pigeon. I cannot imagine that same weakness in Myma's head. I cannot imagine any weakness in her at all.

Twig-crack on the other side. I look for the animal that made the sound but whatever it was stays hidden. The pigeons flap away.

Back to the chore I was doing before the worm came wheedling at my boot and took my attention. Sticks for bird traps. To the bundle under my arm I add the stick that parted the worm. It was my idea to make new traps for snagging the birds, which only rarely catch in the rabbit snares. If I leave berries on the ground then hide and wait sometimes a pigeon or a magpie will come along and if I am quick I can grab it, but that is a tiring way of killing. This will be better.

From my pouch, a coiled length of grass twine. Tie the sticks criss-crossed, with shorter sticks jutting down to pin the traps to the ground. More twine stretched across to make a web. A scattering of nuts, a strew of leaves to cover. When the birds land to peck, their splayed toes will hook in the web of sticks and twine and they will be unable to fly free, and I will break their necks and take them back to Myma and we will roast them on the fire and dig out the softest parts with our fingers, and Myma will be pleased and tell me what a good idea of yours those traps were, Mud-Daughter. The thought makes me grin.

Back through the forest before dark-come.

At the stone marker closest to the clearing I find another broken snare, sliced clean like the first. Gut-lurch like stepping in a hole. But then I forget the snare because my eyes are pulled to something stranger. On the ground beside the trap, muddled with the dirt and leaves, a startle of colour. A bright patch of blue. The kind of blue I have only ever seen in the sky. Bend closer and see that the patch is rough and fibrous. Like matted hair. No, like cloth, but thicker, more like blanket.

I brush the dirt from the blue patch, peel away the cling of leaves. Then lean back on my haunches and bark a loud laugh because the thing is shaped like a flattened hand and how ridiculous, how funny. I pick it up by the tattered thumb. Hold it drooping at my ear. In its sounding there is a skiffering like skin rubbing skin, and a very faint hum, almost but not quite like a name. The blue hand smells of the earth, with a sourish edge I cannot place. My right hand goes into the opening at the wrist. My fingers into the blue ones. The hand hangs like a baggy pelt. Laugh again at the way the long fingers flap empty at the ends. It is a good find. It will make Myma laugh too.

Her face goes slack when I shake the blue hand at her across the clearing. She runs at me and knocks me falling. The side of my head hits the ground. My ear whines into my skull.

Oh, I say.

Myma grabs my arm and wrenches the blue fingers from mine. Her hair is in my mouth and her mouth is at my ear.

What is this where did you get it did you find it were you given it who gave it to you?

Her spit flecks my cheek. I do not understand everything she is asking so I answer as much as I can.

It's a blue hand blanket. I found it next to the first snare.

My voice shrunk by the winded breath of me. Myma silent then with eyes blacker than I have ever seen them, dark like the swallowing back of a throat. She jumps up and is gone, taking the blue hand with her.

I sit on the ground and whimper along to the whining in

my ear until Myma returns. She is no longer holding the blue hand in her own but carrying it stabbed through at the end of a stick. She crosses the clearing and stands over me a long while, long enough to skin and cook a rabbit. When her voice drops down onto me it is gentle, like two hands placed on my shoulders.

What did you see?

The blue hand was on the ground, I tell her. And I picked it up.

Nothing else?

No.

No one gave it to you?

One what?

One nothing. Good. That's good at least.

She breathes a long breath.

The snare was broken, she says. Did you know that?

Yes.

Why didn't you tell me?

Because you would worry and scratch.

I glance up at her. The blue hand dangles from the stick, an odd leaf. Myma's nostrils flare and thin, flare and thin. Then she turns and walks towards the house. I go after, feeling myself a small, curve-backed thing, crawling on its belly.

Inside, Myma is throwing herbs into the pot. I smell nettle, sage, thyme. What Myma calls a cleansing brew. Flushes out the bad stuff, she says. The bad stuff now being the thing I have done, the thing I have picked up and brought to her.

The fire heats the water and Myma tells me to sit. She dips my R-for-rabbit mug into the cleansing brew and hands it to me, brim-full. I stare at the rabbit picture on the mug's side.

Do you know what Rot would do to you, Daughter?

The blue hand hangs over the steam. I blow on my brew and do not answer because I understand from her voice that she does not really want me to. Her second shadow is there on the wall. I look at it instead of at her.

It would eat you away from the inside, she says. Everything you know and everything you think would be gone. You'd be like a tree trunk without a core. There would be nothing left in you, only festering. Can you imagine what that would be like?

Hear the water bubbling inside the cooking pot, hundreds of tiny mouths smacking at the rim. Myma turns the stick as if the blue hand at its end were a bird or a rat spiked for roasting.

This came from the other side of the fence, she says. It came from a Rotter. One must have got in during the dark and left it as a trick. You should have been more careful. You shouldn't have touched it.

I stare at my right hand and feel suddenly dirty, and not in the good way, not like after rolling in earth, but like something foul and unwanted has got under my skin. I hold the hand out limp, this thing attached to my wrist that I want to shake off. Myma is watching me. She holds out her right hand in the same way, the way she might do if it was This-and-That and we were doing copying. Then she takes the blue hand from the stick and slips her fingers into it.

It happens in a blink. The blue hand goes plunging into the cooking pot, Myma's hand inside it. My breath stops. Everything goes flat and quiet. Myma's expression doesn't change. I do not try to pull her hand from the water. This is what happens. This is the Lesson.

The hand comes out. It steams and drips. It could not have been in the pot longer than a heartbeat but it seems I have sat here half the dark, watching the heat seethe around those fingers. My eyes sting. When Myma peels the blue hand away, her skin is bright red like a hunk of meat. She drops the sodden blue raggle into the fire where it hisses and spits. She carries her red hand outside and I hear the squeal of the tap, water pouring from the tank. Her second shadow stays on the wall, head bent. A pressing on my chest tells me I need to breathe and so I do. Gasp inward until it hurts.

Myma returns, her hand wrapped up in her wettened hem. She puts the thumb of her other hand under my chin.

Don't touch things you don't understand, she says.

I won't, I reply.

My voice seems to come from outside my head. I lift my mug and fast-gulp the cleansing brew, choke on the green sludge of herbs at the bottom. In the fire the patch of blue is shrinking, the fingers crumbling black. Myma looks at me looking. With her boot, she nudges a log over the hand.

We do arm-stroking for This-and-That and Myma uses her left hand instead of the right. Smell the bitter salve of crushed leaves spread thick on her fingers as we speak our sorrys and thank yous in the bed. I am always the one of us with all the sorrys.

5

Maya's father's hands were large and tapered like the heads of two shovels. As a child his hands had gathered pretty stones and sometimes bottlecaps, but now they worked the grain roller that milled the feed. When he plunged deep to scoop the cool grain he felt the trickling between his big fingers and something sang in him.

In the mornings he ate his egg and his thoughts sat with him in his body: how soft, how salted the yolk, how stiff the aching shoulders, how warm the slept-in skin of his wife when it brushed against him, her hand on its way to stub her cigarette or to wipe a fleck of yolk from the table. He took the bus to the feed-processing plant. He held his lunch in a brown bag on his lap.

In the evenings he folded his workwear and it went into a locker where he'd taped a drawing made by Maya: himself thick-browed and with a mouth like a crescent moon, pouring bowls of cereal for cows and sheep, horses and pigs. The picture was only partly true because the grain he rolled was meant for poultry, and because he was afraid of cattle.

The pub was where the men felt brave. Maya's father was not one of those who went skull to skull with bared fists but when he sipped from the foamy glass he felt joined in the rankling that warmed them. They complained about the foreman and about the seasonal workers who did not speak their language. They complained about the women who kept their homes and their children. Maya's father would hear his voice among the others, saying, 'Always on my bloody back' and then he would feel ashamed and the taste in his mouth would sour. When the heat hung quiet in the men's heads they would not speak or send each other sprawling but would sit wrapped around their glasses, each in his silence.

Sometimes when Maya's father looked at his wife and daughter there came into him a great heaving that he was unable to give voice to. It was joyous and frightening and made him want to lie like a dog at their feet, tail tucked over his groin and a whine in his throat that said, Everything in you is good, please please do not ever leave me. He knew this to be love but he had never learned how to send out feeling with his words, so instead in these moments he put one big hand on each of them and said, 'My two girls, my two girls.'

One day he saw another worker pulled into the roller by his sleeve. He watched the arm go in between; he heard the sound it made, and he felt calm. He thought, I am looking at his arm becoming flat. He thought, That sound is the sound of bones turning to gravel. When the panic finally came and moved his hands to knock the switch, the other man was in up to the shoulder.

After, he could no longer taste the egg his wife cooked. When he was with his wife and child he could think only how they knew less than he did, how some awful truth about the world had been shown to him. He found the closeness of their bodies to his unbearable. He wanted to cry out to them, to ask them what it meant to hold anything if arms could be crushed as easily as fruit. But he could not talk about what he had seen when they'd pulled the man out, the ribbony mess below his shoulder. So he sank himself to forget it, drank to the bottom and let his mouth forget all its tastes. He drank like a starving infant until he reached again that blankness, the awful calm that had held him watching, listening.

Dark Tightens

Dark tightens around light, squeezing it shorter. I begin to feel the cold in the wets of my eyes. Wood piles in the shed, ready to fill the burner when winter comes biting.

It rains, dries, rains. Myma's hand turns from red and shiny to brown and scaly, then sheds its skin. Underneath, the flesh is new and tender.

We do chores. Birds tangle in my stick traps and I snap their heads backwards. We boil the bones and drink the broth. Twice I find snares sliced. I do not tell Myma but fix them myself, the broken loops tossed to the undergrowth. In one I find a caught strand of blue, like a vein dug from a wrist. I use a stick to knock it to the ground. Poke it down into the dirt.

We do This-and-That. One dark we do who-can-most-quickly. Who can most quickly tie ten knots in this rope. Who can most quickly strike a spark, plait this grass, shell these chestnuts, eat this apple. Myma is quickest at all except the apple. Another dark we do back-scratching and Myma tells me I am not doing it hard enough, even when I dig my nails in and redden her. Then we do creep-listen. Then wishing, using the bones we've saved from the eaten birds. We split them at the join to see which of us will get the bigger half and with it the wish. I get only two of the six wishes but I do not mind because I like the splitting of the bones more than the wishing part. I wish for bigger feet to fit into my boots and for the First Frost to come faster and bring pudding with it. I do not say these wishes out loud because then they will not come true. Myma takes a long while in her silent wishing, her eyes closed, her brows pressed low.

Myma's worry-itch stays open. She is tight-mouthed and jumpy since the blue hand. In the dark I wake to her darting from the room where we sleep and running out into the clearing to return with a blackness in her eyes and a mutter in her mouth.

Nothing there, she says. No one there.

One what? I ask through the blur of sleeping, and she doesn't reply.

A frenzy in her Keep-Safing. The fence freshly spiked with ribs and beaks. My hair is cut back to the scalp, the brown fur of me mixed with feathers and leaves and with Myma's spit, then tied up in scraps of cloth and strung from branches around the forest. The bundles sigh when the wind blows.

The moon makes a slit of itself and my blood comes aching out of me. I wash the rags myself, scrub the red-brown stains with soapwort and hope that one moon I will be bloodless like Myma is bloodless, and I will no longer have to do this extra pointless chore.

My name turns watery and thin with my bleeding. Near the fence I pick up a sharp stone that cuts my thumb and slices a name into me with its srrrrrrrrsh srrrrrrrrrrsh sound. The bottle of mud goes into the Museum beside the fox tooth and the flint chunk goes into my pouch. I probe this new name with my tongue. Keen and quick-edged. Speak it to myself. Name myself.

What are you now, Daughter? Myma asks, and I tell her I am Flint.

Flint-Daughter, she says. Little Sharp Thing. Spark-Fire-Daughter. Slicing-Stone. Tinder-Kin.

The damping of rain brings out the mushrooms. Round heads come nubbing from the ground and thick ridges burst from the trunks. I go prodding for them between the wet ferns. Mushroom-gathering is a favourite chore. The shiny brown ones on their thick necks, the best and sweetest, a handful of these eaten raw as I go. The black ones with charred gullets and ragged lips. Tufted white ones pushing up like fingers through the mulch. Fleshy ears on the bark of trees, these tough as cartilage but always a lot of them to fill us up. I stamp a few puffballs to watch the cough of smoke, though some are still firm and white, good for roasting. Roll them in my hands before dropping them into the sack.

My palms turn slippery with the clammy mushroom skin and I have to keep wiping them on my trousers. Coldening air means more clothes, though I gritted myself as long as I could against shouldering the scratchy knee-length chore-smock that irritates the skin around my neck and crimps up under my armpits. I wear the sleeves pushed high, as little of the cloth touching my skin as possible.

The sack grows bumpy and the sun moves to the other side of the sky. I lie on my stomach in the hairy shadow of a pine to stare close at the red-and-white fists of toadstools, the ones that would make us sick or dead if we ate them.

I am caught then by a flickering at the base of the pine tree, some snagged brightness. There, between the roots, another kind of red. And I find I am looking at a clutch of hairs. The hairs are long, much longer than mine, though not as long as Myma's. The red of them. Staggering, searing. My hand reaches for the bright hairs but stops when Myma's voice comes scratching against the inside of my skull.

Don't touch things you don't understand, Daughter.

Foxes are the only red-furred things and their fur is short, not like this. This hair belongs to no creature I know. The strangeness of it pricks my skin. And I think about the other strangenesses I have seen. The blue hand. The blue hand and now the red hair. The blue hand, the red hair, the gnawed potato, the broken snares. How these things are attached somehow, like jointed bones. This hair, this hair that is not ours.

Those Rotters out there, they look like you and me, Daughter, but they're all empty on the inside. You can see it when they turn their backs, see right the way in.

A cold knife lodges in my chest, a sudden and certain knowing. The Rot walks in the forest. The Rot walks in the forest and it has red hair.

Kill the Rotter, kill it dead, kill it so the Rot won't spread. A game I played with myself when I was smaller. Imagined shapes chased among the trees. Me snarling at the fleeing birds and stabbing my knife into the trunks.

I was Twig when I played at chasing Rotters, snappable, flimsy. But I am Flint now. Sharper, harder now. I crouch stiff at the foot of the pine. Jump of blood in my palms and in the soles of my feet. The light is going fast. Dark settling above the trees like a huge black bird spreading its wings over the forest.

In the dark beyond the fence creeps the Rotted thing. Only now the Rotted thing is inside the fence.

I will be late getting back. But I cannot go yet.

I am good at tracking. I should be able to track a Rotter like any creature. I must make a light, yes, a torch to help me see in the growing dark. Take up a branch the length of my forearm, make two crossed cuts in one end. A pine cone for a wick, jammed into the notch. A sticky glob of pine sap to coat the torch. Then my name-flint from my pouch, strike it against my knife into a tinder of pine needles to send up a lick of flame.

The torch makes a light that stops a few paces ahead. I hold my name close and it grits me. I listen. Dusk birdsong, no other sound. I look about for marks of a moving body and see a patch of moss scraped from a root. There a stumbling place, a trip and scuff. Further on, the leaf mulch stirred, the earth rucked up. Bent ferns, a crush of mushrooms.

And here, dents in the earth, foot-shaped. Seep of groundwater into the heels. A size and depth that tells of something large and heavy. The warning thrum of Myma in my head. Daughterdaughterdaughter. I continue at a crouch, eyes and ears flicking side to side. Another clump of hair, a red knot in the brambles. Then a smear of blood on silver birch bark. Only a little, but fresh. A thorn scratch. The particular red of it grabs at me. I did not know Rotter blood would be the same colour as mine.

In a dense patch of bracken, I lift my torch. The flame throws its light across the waist-high ferns. A disturbance, there. Fronds twitching, stems snapping. Somewhere in the bracken, a body shifting. Myma's voice between my thoughts, rapid, terrified. Daughterdaughterdaughterdaughterdaughter. I am Flint, I say firm to the voice, though my heart thuds against my ribs. Flint is keen and sharp. Flint slices. Flint is not afraid.

Grip tight the knife. Bare my teeth and imagine each one a pointed, biting stone.

I wade through the bracken towards the movement. My eyes strain to see past the edges of my torchlight. I halt, listen. Everything holding, everything gathering. No sound. Then a jerk in my gut, my eyes catching on a shock of red in the green-brown ferns. There between the battered stems. A face like mine, like Myma's, but not like, not at all like. Pale eyes on me, wide. A scarlet mass of hair. I drop the torch and the flame sputters out.

Black above, black underfoot. Same black ahead, behind. Sky moonless, starless. I feel for my torch but find only leaf mould, the coarse stems of ferns. Try to listen past the pounding in my ears. Rustle at my left, closening. I jump myself up, pump arms and legs to running. Bracken slices at my ankles. Blind thrust and stumble from the undergrowth.

Out of the bracken I force myself to stop, listen again and hear no sound of following. I must go slow, I must breathe quiet, tread careful and noiseless. My hands stretch ahead into blackness, like when we do creep-listen, only now there is no blindfold for me to peel off.

Wonder if the Rotter can see through the dark, like a fox or an owl. My skin tightens with the thought of it watching me as I move blind among the trees. I keep expecting to see a red shape rushing at me in the blackness, or for my hands to slip into a gap in a trunk only to find that it isn't a tree but the hollow back of the Rotter.

A sound in the leaves. I grasp for my knife and my hand clutches empty. I do not remember dropping it. Fear fills my mouth. Then comes a scuff and scritch, a flurry of small wings, skip of claws in twigs. I breathe, untighten. The bird carries on with its shuffling. Then it stops. I stop with it. Listen with it. Us both waiting stiff. Then the bird darts flutters flees away between the trees.

I wait and wait and nothing. I am about to move again when I hear it. The splintering creaking of it, pushing through the forest. Things bending and breaking in its path. If I run again it will know where I am. It will touch me with its Rot and I will be hollowed. I do not even move my eyes for worry that the wet tick of them will carry through the dark. The Rotter is close. The air scrunches in my chest.

And now the Rotter is here, right here, in front of me, all crashing feet and heat and noisy breath fugging up the black. The distance between me and it no more than nine paces. Onetwothreefourfivesixseveneightnine.

Sorry to Myma for staying out after dark-come sorry for following the red trail sorry. Lurch of the Rotter in the dark, just there, just there. Hiss of words I do not recognise.

Agh. Pissit.

Hacking cough of it. Then it is moving past me, away.

I listen long and do not hear the Rotter again.

I want to be back inside the house but the blackness has tilted me to a place I do not know and I can only wait here for light-come. Lower myself, press head and hands to cold ground.

Myma. Her waiting for me. Worry-itch scratched tendon-deep. I put all my fingers into my mouth. Rock backwards, forwards, think Myma, Myma, over and over, think her to me.

Things flicker at the edges of my seeing, then snatch themselves away when I look. Faint gleamings like the white undersides of eyes. The dark clotting to strange shapes. I growl and gnash and swipe my name-flint but still the pale eyes come gaping.

I cover my head with my arms. Let the dark swallow me.

Myma, walking towards me through blackness. Myma, bright in the dark. A sharp glint in her hand. She grips the tufts of my hair to bend back my head.

Cut the Rot out of you, Daughter.

The shiny thing goes into my mouth and my tongue falls into Myma's hand, cut at the root. It is not blood that spills from the stump, but scarlet hair.

Daughter. Flint-Daughter.

Light flares. A good familiar light, warm and jumping in an open palm. Her palm. Her face, that most known thing.

She reaches for me. She lifts my head from the leafed ground. Around my shoulders a blanket of rabbit pelts. I grip the end of her plait and let her lead me back through the dark forest.

In the house she unties my boots, strips me, pulls my arms into my bed-smock. The wood burner glows in the corner of the room where we sleep. I am pressed down into the bed, blankets pulled to my chin. Too hot, too close. Myma bends over me, her two shadows draped across my chest. There is something I have to tell her, something terrible and important.

Don't breathe like that, she says.

Small and tight the space behind my ribs. My teeth champing though I am not cold. Clench my jaw.

Tell me what happened, she says.

I look up at her. See the deep blue thumbprints under her eyes. Her left sleeve blooded with worry. Her plait unravelled, a sore-looking patch at the temple where the hair has been yanked out. I think of the blue hand thrust into boiling water. That word, Rotter, sticks in my throat. I cannot tell her what I have seen. More than I am afraid of the Rotter, I am afraid of what will happen if Myma knows of its being here, what she might do.

I was following a trail, I tell her, my voice all quaky. I was tracking a muntjac that came over the fence. I wanted to bring you the meat. Then the muntjac went and the light went too and I lost the mushroom sack and dropped my knife and I couldn't see any more so I lay down to wait for the light to come back. Sorry for it, Myma. I shouldn't have stayed out. Sorry.

I wait for the Lesson but Myma is still. Her eyes dart between mine and I blink to dissolve any trace of the red they have seen. Finally she looks away, to her second shadow on the bed.

No, Flint-Daughter, she says, it is my sorry to say. I am sorry for it. Sorry I didn't find you sooner. The dark is dangerous and frightening. You must have felt very scared.

I nod because it is true, I was scared. That face in the bracken. That red. And I am whimpering then and Myma is climbing onto the bed to lie her small body across me with the shadows, her leg over mine, her hand at my cheek and her thumb in my mouth, and though I eventually quieten and feel Myma grow heavy with her own sleep, I lie awake for a long while after, my eyes on the dark window.

6

It was when the first potato shoot broke the soil that the grey woman began climbing out of the ground from under the post. At first she came only at night, as if shy of Maya seeing her fully. She moved with a rustling sound like dry leaves. Mostly she kept to the edges of the room but sometimes Maya would wake to find her huddled close on the bed, listening in on her dreams. Maya didn't think the grey woman meant to frighten her. It seemed more that she just did not understand where she was supposed to be. Her place had been filled by another.

'I'm sorry,' Maya said aloud from the bed as she watched the grey woman pacing from corner to corner, long hair trailing. 'I didn't think you needed it any more.'

The grey woman did not answer, but cupped her hands around the hole of her mouth and made a soft, owl-like hoot. Maya had never heard a sound more lonely.

Soon the grey woman became bolder. She started appearing during the day, following close at Maya's heels like a shadow. Sometimes the grey woman was helpful, once screeching loudly when Maya pulled up the leaves and root of what looked to her like parsley, but which, when she examined it more closely, gave off a fetid smell. At other times the grey woman was irritating. She lay among the potato plants as

Maya watered them. She batted at the fire and frowned at her unscorched palms. When Maya ate, the grey woman pursed her lips and blew hard ineffectual breath on every spoonful. The empty air that came from her smelled like sour earth, animal fur, milk.

'Go and sit over there, why don't you?' Maya finally snapped.

The grey woman looked at the stool opposite and made a low chittering in her throat. Then she climbed onto the table and crouched there with her arms around her knees. Maya sighed.

'What's wrong with the other stool then?' she asked.

The grey woman lifted a puckered breast from the rag of her garment. She lowered her mouth to it and sucked.

Those two mugs still troubled Maya. She drank from the flowered one and tucked the other behind a row of tins so that the painted rabbit could not stare at her the way the grey woman did.

Maya found there was a certain distance from the hut at which an immense unease would settle over her and she would have to turn back. It was like meeting a wall, on the other side of which lay everything she wanted to cleave herself from. She noticed how, at this distance, the grey woman too seemed to falter. Maya began marking out the limit with sturdy branches driven straight into the ground like fence posts. On the end of one branch she perched the skull of her first rabbit. At the base she scattered the crush of glass she had swept from under the shelves. Bounding the space in this way eased something in her, lessened a weight in her chest.

She cut a length of her hair to bind more branches, and found the hair shocked silver at the roots. She examined those silver-grey strands among the familiar brown. I am changing, she thought. I am becoming something else. She took her bark-handled knife and hacked off the brown lengths. The hair tied the branches and made the barrier sturdy.

The grey woman watched the slow building of the fence. She moved her head about like a bird considering its nest.

During this time Maya became sick with a bone-deep nausea that folded her body in half with retching. I am ill, she thought, I have eaten something that has made me ill, and when I am done being sick whatever it is will have left me. She repeated this to herself and she carried on hauling branches to her boundary even as fatigue weighted her limbs, even as the grey woman started bending low to lay her ear against Maya's abdomen, even as her flesh was displaced from the inside and her breasts heavied, even as the hard grain of what was growing inside her became an insistent mound, skin pressing under skin, the swell of a body inside a body.

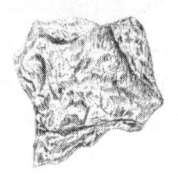

I Am Crooked

I am crooked in the stuffy bed, my legs where my head should be. Grey sky in the window. A fuzziness between my ears when I sit up.

Myma is not here. She has put out my skinshoes, the thin paws of them for wearing inside when the cold begins to stick. I slip my feet into them and listen for the sounds of Myma boiling water or sharpening her knife. Hear only the creak of wind outside, the sneckering of a bird.

I do not know how long I have slept. I am hungry. I think of mushrooms browned crispy over the fire then remember that I left the mushroom sack in the forest. Then I remember the dark, and what came creeping in it. It seems somehow moons ago that I saw the red-haired creature crouched in the bracken. It was the Rotter cut the snares and took the rabbits, this I am sure of now. Perhaps it has taken the mushroom sack too. At this thought the fear I felt in the dark is shrivelled by anger. What a waste, I think, all that good food spewing out of the hole in the Rotter's back, chomped to bits.

Imagining the Rotter now, in the light, flips it from frightening to ridiculous. The clumsy, lurching walk of it. The mangey fox colour of its hair and its agh pissit words that aren't words. I huff a laugh. That's what I'll do if I meet the Rotter again, laugh at it and send it running.

In the other room I find a hunk of chestnut bread, spotty with poppyseed and birch catkin. I cram my cheeks and chew loud with my mouth open, no Myma here to tell me to slow down or you'll get indigestion, Daughter.

A rag, blotted brown with one of my bloodstains, laid out beside the bread. On it I read Myma's charcoal words. Adding KS to fence. Stay inside. Back dark-come.

So no outside chores. So an Exception, after my dark of being scared. I do not want to cower in the house. I want the air and the ground. If I stay in the clearing, if I do not go into the forest, that is still sort of inside. I tie a blanket around my shoulders, open the door and step out in my skinshoes.

It is already past the middle of the light. A nervous tremor in me as I look into the trees, but it's in the dark that Rotters creep, and the one I saw has probably gone back to its Rotted place on the other side of the fence. Do Rotters sleep, like bats do when the sun is up? The idea of a Rotter's hollow dreams shivers me.

I push the red hair from my mind. Set myself to picking and fiddling around the clearing. Take up a stick and stir the ground with it. I turn over slimy sheets of bark to see woodlice and centipedes scuttling. Worms thrash when I poke them. I find a mottled slug and hold it to my ear for the squelch.

Touch finger and thumb together now to make a circle for peering through. Move slow, pointing my seeing-hole at ground and tree and sky, and think how each thing and each part becomes sharper when seen in a smaller space, cut from the clutter of its surroundings.

Loud snap across the clearing. I stiffen like a rabbit, flat-eared and quiver-nosed. Just Myma, I say to the jumpy rabbity part of me, just Myma returning from strengthening the fence with her Keep-Safes. But Myma would have called out to me, she would have said Flint-Daughter, Sliceling, Little Cut-Stone. Another snap. I think of the heavy feet that went crashing through the forest.

No knife so I take out my name-flint. Something there between the trees. I set the seeing-hole of my finger and thumb on the patch of undergrowth made dense by a shape in it, a shape taller than either me or Myma. It grows larger inside my circle, and I do not move, and I watch the branches parting, and I think of the Keep-Safes around the edge of the clearing, all the fragments of rabbit bone and fingernail and the crunchy bits of sleep from the corners of our eyes, all crushing under the brown boots that step, one by one, into the clearing.

The Rotter halts. It lifts its hands and pushes the long red hair out of its eyes.

I do not call for Myma. The Rotter might startle and attack if I yell. Or it might go lunging after her instead. I stare at it through my seeing-hole. Other hand tight on my flint. My thumb moves over the sharp edge and I know it could rip easy into the soft parts of a body.

The eyes that look at me across the clearing are pale as blueless sky.

Cut you out, Rotter, I say.

My voice hard and strong, no shake to it. I hurl it at the Rotter.

Cut you out, I say again. The whole Rot of you.

I swipe the air with my flint to show it what I mean. The Rotter stays where it is. I screw my eye at its face through the seeing-hole. Thin nose. Scooped cheeks. Some lines, though less than in Myma's face. The red hair tumbling from the scalp and going all the way under the chin and around the mouth. I keep the Rotter's head inside the hole. If I hold it here, in this circle between my finger and thumb, then it won't come any closer. I point my flint at it.

Out, I say.

Very slowly, the Rotter crouches. I think it must be readying for a pounce and my heels rise, every muscle in me tautening to meet it. But the Rotter is lifting its hands, fingers splayed. Myma used to hold her hands up like that after feeding me berries when I was small. Empty, she'd say. All gone. One of the Rotter's hands is blue. The other is filthy.

Look, I'm not trying to do anything.

The shock of hearing the Rotter speak makes me drop the hand with my seeing-hole and gape both eyes wide. It is a low, hoarse voice, that same voice I heard hissing not-words through the dark. Only these are words I understand. Words I might use with Myma. The familiarity of them dizzies me. The Rotter speaks again.

Hey, it says. Don't be scared.

I'm not, I say.

And it is true. I am not scared. Not now. Wary, yes. But stronger is my want to keep watching the red-haired creature, to hear it speak again. The Rotter's hands stay up, palms towards me. They are large, long-fingered. I think how that other empty blue hand gaped wide around mine, and I think how much I could carry if my hands were as big, how I would never drop anything. Jealousy drips down my throat and I hate the Rotter for having something that I do not.

What's your name? it asks.

Again that rough, heavy voice, asking me a question that has only ever been asked by Myma. Spoken in this new voice, the question strikes odd at my ear, like a stone thrown from a direction I wasn't expecting. I know the answer, so I reply.

I am Flint.

Flint?

How strange to hear my name between the Rotter's teeth.

The sound and shape of it buckled by a mouth that is neither mine nor Myma's. Fli–int.

Yes, I say. Flint.

The Rotter makes a sound with its throat and chest and I realise it is laughing. My face heats.

What sort of name is Flint? the Rotter asks. Flint is a rock, not a name.

It is my name, I say, bristling. It sits in me and I carry it.

The Rotter lifts and drops its shoulders.

Okay then, it says.

It coughs, spits on the ground. The blue hand wipes the mouth. I always imagined Rotters with their skins bare, all naked withering flesh. But this one is clothed. It wears trousers with split knees. It wears a big black coat, fastenings down the front and holes all over. One sleeve hangs tattered. The other is torn open at the shoulder seam. There is a sack strapped to its back. Wonder about the empty hollow hidden underneath.

I am Wyn, the Rotter says, tapping its breastbone.

I blink. A Rotter is not a named thing. It is a lie, I think, a trick. My hand curls around the flint.

How did you get over the fence? I ask.

The fence? Oh. You mean all those branches and stuff? I stepped over. It's not that high.

But how did you come past the Keep-Safes?

The what?

Not scared of you, Rotter. Won't let you come Rotting here.

The Rotter snorts.

Rotter? What's that then? It's not in my interest to scare you, boy.

Another not-word. The Rotter grimaces, shifts in its crouch.

Can I sit down? it asks. You won't panic and run away if I move?

I won't run away, I reply, irritated that the Rotter thinks me a panicky frightened thing.

It lowers its backside to the ground and stretches out its feet.

That's better, the Rotter says. Legs were beginning to cramp.

It reaches to unfasten its sack. The sack is green-brown, worn and bumpy, with straps and flaps. What does a Rotter need a sack for? What would it be carrying around? Stolen rabbits, probably, or my mushrooms. A spike of anger steps me forward, raises my flint.

Here, the Rotter says, its blue hand reaching into the sack. This is yours.

The hand comes out holding my knife. The Rotter's fingers grip the blade and point the birch-bark hilt towards me. I do not move. Another trick. I will not take anything from that blue hand. The Rotter huffs air through its nose and passes the knife into its other hand, turns it over and over. It coughs again and grimaces. Then it pulls a rattling from the sack, shakes something small into its mouth and drops the rattling back into the sack.

That woman, it says when it has swallowed. Your mother?

I try to make sense of the question but the words twist away from me. Woman. Mother. Boy. I hold these sounds like uncracked nuts and say nothing in reply.

The woman that lives here with you, the Rotter speaks on. Who is she?

I live with Myma, I tell it.

The Rotter nods slowly. It scratches at its side.

You been in this place long? it asks.

This is where I live with Myma, I say.

Yes, it says. But how long have you lived here?

The question muddles me.

This is where I live with Myma always since existing.

The Rotter lifts both eyebrows. It puts the blue hand to the tangle of red on its face. It needs to do hair-brushing. I shake myself at this thought, no, hair-brushing is not for Rotters. I crouch down, keeping my flint where the Rotter can see it. It is holding its body loose, not taut in readiness to attack, but it still has my knife. I watch the pale eyes moving over the house, over the crow beaks clicking above the door, the water tank, the shed, the mossed roof, the leaning tools. Then back to me.

How old are you, boy?

This thing it keeps calling me. Boy. Not my name.

I am Flint, I tell it again.

Right. Flint. Ha. So, how old are you, ah, Flint?

But I am tired with chasing after the Rotter's words, these questions that come apart in my ears. The Rotter seems tired too. It yawns, all red gums and spotted teeth. Its yawn makes me yawn, and this sameness unsettles me, this shared feel of a stretching throat and a jaw pushed wide.

You should go away now, I say loud across the clearing.

One colourless eye peers at me.

I told you, I'm not trying to do anything, boy.

I am Flint, I say, angry again. Not boy. Boy isn't a word. There is nothing in it.

But that's what you are, isn't it? A boy?

I frown, say nothing. The Rotter stretches its neck forward then, face squinted.

Hell, it says. Maybe you're not. Well. You certainly look like one with that hair.

I touch the fuzz at the back of my head. Lick my teeth and thrust my chin at the Rotter.

Your hair is red, I throw at it.

Well noticed, it says.

How?

I do not mean to ask this but the word spits out before I

can swallow it. The Rotter pats the hair on either side of its head and grins.

Huh, it says. I suppose it just grew that way. Could be my parents. I wouldn't know. People used to think it meant you were bad, being born with red hair. Something about the devil. Crazy stuff.

You are bad, I tell it, pulling this certain word from between the other not-words. You've got Rot in you.

Rot?

Yes. Rotter, you.

Oh right. That again. You've an odd way of talking, boy – girl. You're a strange one.

It staggers me, that the Rotter finds me strange. Here the strangest thing I have ever seen and it thinks me the strange one. Imagine myself being seen by the Rotter, watched from behind those eyes. The thought makes me twitchy and I suddenly no longer want it looking at me.

Myma will be angry when she finds you here, I tell it.

Well, you can tell your mother what I told you. I'm not trying to do anything. I'm not going to hurt anyone. I've not got anywhere to go, you see. Just need someplace to be. I'm not too well, and it's getting cold in the woods. Maybe you could even use my help. I'm good with my hands.

I look at the large hand holding my knife and snort at the idea that a Rotter could help us.

Can't trick me, Rotter, I tell it.

The Rotter shakes its matted hair.

I'm not trying to trick you, it says. Really, what I wanted to say, why I came here to talk to you – I wanted to explain myself. I didn't mean to frighten you last night. There's not normally anyone else about when it's that dark.

Rage curls my lip.

You've been coming in the dark to steal from us.

The Rotter's eyes drop then. A flushed look to its face.

I really am sorry about that. I was hungry. And I'm sorry I broke your traps. They're damn fiddly things to untie. I've taken as little as I can, I swear, I haven't been greedy, I wanted to say something last night but you ran, and I knew I'd scared you, then I found your mushroom sack early this morning and I hadn't eaten in days, and if you and your mother would let me make it up to you, maybe we could—

I do not bother to tell the Rotter that this is not the moment for saying sorrys, that sorrys are for the dark and for the bed and for after This-and-That. I harden the muscles in my legs and snarl as if the Rotter were a fox come prowling to our door for scraps.

Knew it was a Rotter that took our food. Knew it. Rotter, you. Rot of you. You all Rot, all the way through.

The Rotter's mouth opens but it doesn't speak. Its pale eyes widen at something behind me. Fright in its look, a fox startled. Then comes a roar that strips the skin from the air. A pounding of feet and I am grabbed from behind, two thin arms wrapping my chest, cutting in half my breath, dragging me backwards. The suddenness of Myma shocks me limp. My fingers drop the flint. Myma is hair and spit and teeth behind me. I am half-carried half-pulled towards the house. And all the while Myma is bellowing yawping snapping hissing barking screeching.

Don't know who the fuck you are what the fuck you think you're doing but you need to get the fuck away I'll fucking kill you I'll fucking kill you if you come any closer get the fuck back just get away get away from here get away from her.

The sounds harshing from her mouth, rough words I have never heard her use. They give off a stinking heat as they fill the air between us and the Rotter. Myma hauls me over the step and through the doorway. I twist to look back, expecting to see the red-haired Rotter ripped to tatters by Myma's fury.

Throat torn, bones crushed. Blood pouring into the earth. Instead I see the Rotter sitting exactly as before, staring after us with those colourless eyes. The fear in them mixed with something else. If I saw the same look on Myma's face, I would call it hurt.

Myma slams the door shut.

7

Maya thought that the growing redness in her father's eyes was caused by the dust he brought home from work in his hair and on his clothes. Then he started behaving differently from the quiet, gruff man she remembered picking her up with one hand and carrying her to bed. He would shout and accuse Maya and her mother of pretending to love him. He never took a hand to them but sometimes he would cry and that was worse. At other times he became lifeless and sat in a dull slump, unhearing and unfeeling. And at other times he would not be there at all, and Maya and her mother would eat dinner alone, Maya usually finishing her mother's portion while her mother smoked and rubbed at specks of dirt that Maya could not see.

Sometimes Maya pretended to be dead to see what her parents would do. She would position herself at the bottom of the stairs as if she had fallen, or she would set a chair on its side and lie splayed beneath it with her eyes shut. Her father would trip over her or her mother would say, 'You're wrinkling your uniform, stop messing about.'

Sometimes Maya climbed up to the attic and sat among the suitcases. There were boxes labelled Crockery, Linen, Misc. In one box there were envelopes full of photographs.

Maya slid them out to see her mother as a child wearing nothing but shorts, then solemn with a school friend, then standing in a white coat outside the butcher's window between two other white-coated girls, then smiling on Maya's father's arm. Another photograph showed Maya's parents standing in the garden, their eyes made small by bright sun. Her father held a cocooned shape that Maya knew was herself. Her mother stood beside them with her hands clasped, wearing the thin scarf Maya recognised as the one she wore for church events. The bushes behind them were greyish-white, blurred by the netted webs spun across by the spindle ermine caterpillars.

'The week you were born, they covered the garden,' her mother had told her once. 'They were never a problem before. Now they come every year and destroy the leaves.'

Maya put all the photographs back in their envelopes except this last one, which she rolled into a tube and stuffed down the neck of an empty bottle of her father's that she kept under her bed.

Sometimes Maya felt the ceiling of her parents' house pressing low and heavy like dense cloud. When this happened she walked out under the sky, along the roads and across the fields to where Kitty Glipson lived. They lay upside down and ate toast on Kitty's bed or they went and watched the pigs.

In the pen they saw the boar mounting the sow, his chin resting on her back.

'What are they doing?' asked Maya.

'They're screwing,' said Kitty. 'It's how they make piglets.'

Kitty's father stood in the pen with the pigs. He scratched their ears and said, 'Well done.' He had a finger missing where a sow had bitten it off.

After, Kitty's father led the sow away. Maya and Kitty went close and looked at the boar through the metal bars. He turned about in the pen and his mouth made champing sounds. Then he went to his trough and ate.

A few months later, Kitty told Maya that some of the sows had begun nesting and that this meant piglets would be born.

'Come to mine after school,' she said. 'We can watch the farrowing.'

The sow lay on her side in the stall. She had dug a channel in the hay and she was breathing hard. Kitty's mother stood with the two girls. She wore a dirty shirt rolled up at the elbows.

'We must be very quiet and calm,' she said.

They watched for a long while. Kitty whispered that she was bored and her mother touched her shoulder and told her to be patient. The sow's distended stomach tightened and strained. The sow shifted. Maya felt Kitty grip her hand. She saw the small wet coin of a snout parting the swollen flesh beneath the tail. The piglet came out headfirst, front legs slicked against its body. It flopped in the hay and began to nudge about. Maya thought it looked frail, the blotched hide not yet toughened. She felt worried for it but Kitty's mother was now putting her legs one by one into the stall to crouch at the sow's back end. Her gloved hand wiped the slimy film from the piglet's mouth and set it at the teat to feed.

After some hours, the nine piglets were latched in a row along the sow's belly. The milky cords trailed in the straw.

'Didn't she do well?' said Kitty's mother, blotting her forehead with her filthy sleeve.

Maya nodded. She felt a strange thrill at seeing Kitty's mother squatting in the muck of the sow's birth, flushed and grinning, her thick arms smeared. She tried to imagine her own mother doing the same, but she could not place the shiny straight pin of her there in the grume and dirt. Even less could she picture her mother in the position of the sow, straining and visceral in the birth throes, or nursing a baby at her teat.

Kitty leaned towards Maya and whispered in her ear.
'We had one savage her piglets once.'
'What's savage?' Maya asked.
'She ate her babies.'

Myma Has Always Been

Myma has always been the stronger of us. She carries the most potatoes, the most logs. She carried me too, before my legs learned to hold me, when I could only pull my belly along the ground. Sometimes she carries me still, over-shoulders me to the bed when I am tired. Though I am larger now than I was, larger than her, still my own strength is a twig to her trunk.

Her arms around my chest wrap solid. Even with the door between us and the Rotter she does not loose her hold until she has knocked the bolt across with her elbow. I scramble to all fours, blanket hanging lopsided from my shoulder. I pant. Heat in my cheeks and behind my eyes. Low and hunkered, my gaze on Myma's back. She stands rigid, cheek and ear to the door.

Myma.

My voice a whispy yelp. I reach to touch her ankle but she has already spun around, is already quick-footing off into the room where we sleep. Her boots mud the floor. Hear a rummaging, a raze and pull of cloth.

Myma, I call.

She comes darting back through. Her breath hard in her nostrils. Her mouth a tight fold. She holds her knife in one hand. In the other, something jagged and glinting.

Myma, I say again.

My hand is yanked up from the floor and the handle of Myma's knife is put into it. The end of her plait flicks across my cheek as she steps past. She unbolts the door then turns.

Lock it behind me, she says. Three knocks means I am back. One long, two short. Do not answer to anything else. Hold on to my knife.

Myma?

She is out through the door. Grey-brown streak of her across the clearing and into the forest. I sweep my eyes across the trees but see no hint of red. The clearing is full of darkening shadows. A heavy moon leans on the branches. I feel the tug of my name-flint straining at me from the ground where it fell but do not dare to fetch it.

Close the door, slide the bolt. I am shivering. My hands jerk and jitter as I poke the coals to flames. All the happenings and seeings, beating about in my head on red wings. Blue-handed blood-haired air-eyed Rotter. The way it lounged fox-like in the dirt. The spread of its hands, the way it spoke. I'm not trying to do anything, boy, I'm not trying to trick you. Curling of its tongue around those strange words. The things it called me. Boy. Girl. Boy-girl. My own name, low in its rough mouth. Fli–int. Its coughed laugh. And the wounded look of it when Myma came bellowing.

Everything I know has been put into a sack and shaken up. I am not afraid for Myma. She knows all the ways of protecting herself a body can know. And though I know I should be afraid, that I must be afraid, I am not afraid of the Rotter.

Fear keeps us safe, Myma once said to me. It is what turns us from danger.

I try to tell myself this, try to whet my fear sharp. But all I can think is how the Rotter's lids crinkled at the edges when it laughed. How it called itself by a name.

Yet I am afraid of one thing. I am afraid that Myma will make the Rotter go away. That I will not see it again.

Roof and window clatter with a beginning rain. Myma does not return for eating and I am not hungry. I want to throw my body into something furious and sweat-making, like dancing, but I can't do This-and-That without Myma. Light the lamp in the room where we sleep. The nest of our bed is rumpled, rags strewn and pulled about.

I look around for the comforting murk of Myma's second shadow but it stays hidden, or perhaps it is out in the dark with Myma, them all chasing after the Rotter. My neck itches so I unknot the blanket and scratch. I go to my Museum, touch each object, hold my ear for the hum that always returns me to a sturdy footing. But the burr of the Rotter's voice keeps catching and sticking in my listening. When I lift the fox tooth to my ear it sounds strange, a yowlping in it. I get snarly and frustrated and scatter a whole row of old names to the floor. The conker rolls off into a corner. A crack appears in the blue eggshell and I feel terrible.

Back to the bolted door. I try to see underneath but there is only black. Sit on my haunches to lean my forehead against the wood. My fist thumps Myma's knock. One long, two short. My ear presses. Myma and me are no longer the only things in the forest that have hands. Something else might knock back. I wait and listen and hear only the wet wind outside.

Drop onto the mess of the bed without pinching the light. Scrunch closed my eyes and lie very still. Almost fall asleep but then my legs jolt me to waking and after that I am not at all tired.

Crawl from bed to floor. Bits of the scattered Museum dig at me. Gathering of a moan at the back of my throat. I drag myself into a corner and push my knees into my eyes.

*

My head jerks upright and smacks the wall. The lamp is out. Backside numb, neck stiff. A thudding from the other room. One long, two short. One long, two short. I scramble to the door, knock the bolt sideways. Myma's outline against the black is silver with rain and moonlight. Her hair undone in dripping strands. Her chore-smock stuck sodden at her calves and hips. She steps inside, shuts the door, then comes close with her cold thumb to put under my chin.

Did he hurt you? she asks.

What?

The Rotter. Did he hurt you?

The Rotter didn't hurt me.

What did he say to you?

The words come easy because they have been rolling and repeating in my head.

The Rotter said it's not here to try anything. It said it's sorry for stealing. It wants to be someplace and it wants to help.

Help? Help with what?

I'm not sure, I tell her. Maybe chores.

Did he bring any others?

Other what?

Others like him.

Like the Rotter?

Yes.

I don't know, I say. I only saw that one.

Myma blows out a long breath.

The things that want to hurt us have ways of tricking us, Flint-Daughter, she says. I've seen Rotters like him before. Sometimes badness doesn't show at the front. It's in their backs you see it.

I nod my chin against her thumb. My head weighted with questions. Myma bends to take off her boots. The callused undersides of her feet pulpy pale with the wet that has seeped in.

Help me with this will you, she says.

She lifts her arms and I peel her chore-smock from her shins to her wrists. Bundle the sopped mass of it in my arms and feel in the pocket the shape of a hard, jag-edged thing. I want to ask about the Rotters Myma has seen before. I have never been able to get her to talk of them. What colour was their hair? Did they speak? Did they have names? But there is a flat look in Myma's eyes which means I will probably only be able to ask one question before she begins digging her fingernails into her skin. So I ask the thing I want to know more than anything else.

Is it dead?

Myma does not answer right away. She takes her chore-smock from me and hangs it on the wooden rack above the hearth.

Chuck me those, she says.

I clomp her drenched boots across the floor. She sets them close to the coals, foot holes towards the heat.

Get me a bowl will you, she says.

I fetch one and watch as she wrings her hair from scalp to tip, rain filling up the bowl. The unanswered question strains in my gut like stuck poo. Myma passes the bowl to me.

Drink this, she says.

The water tastes of sky and sweat. Watch Myma over the rim of the bowl as I gulp. She does not speak again until I have swallowed all the rain.

No, she says. He isn't dead. He'd already gone when I went looking. Reckon I scared him off.

Her black eyes meet mine.

If he comes back I'll have to kill him, she says. Can't have Rotters running about the woods.

I nod again though something sinks in me. I know this is what must happen. Kill the Rotter kill it dead. Myma is looking at me still. A narrowness in her looking.

Yes, I say, and drop my eyes into my hands.

Sense her waiting for me to say more but I do not trust my mouth so hold it shut. The silence hardening between us. Her sighing then. Her naked feet padding away. I feel the tug of her going like a cord stretched taut, about to snap. My head comes up.

Myma.

The feet stop.

Flint-Daughter?

I need you, I say.

She turns then, and her shoulders slump, and her brow crumples. We move towards each other, the tightness between us falling slack. I kneel to rest my forehead on her belly, as if I were still a small Daughter. She is trembling. Her fingers dig at the back of my head.

Soon I am gathered up, lifted. Me big and sprawling in Myma's arms. The stone floor replaced with the sag and yield of the bed. I push my face into it.

At light-come we leave the dents of our sleeping behind in the bed. Pull off our bed-smocks and fold them. Sweat dapples Myma's shoulders. Wonder whether her dream was of dancing or of running. Her hair has dried. She tugs her fingers through it, weaves a plait with sure and steady hands. The smile she gives me is smooth, without cracks.

Did you sleep well, Daughter?

I did, I tell her.

My Museum is ordered again, all the name-objects back in their places, exactly as they were before the Rotter came and put a wind in my head that sent everything skittering. I am ashamed of the way my thoughts blew around last dark. Of course Myma is right about the red-haired Rotter. My belly twists to think how I let its words stir me up.

Myma hums as she cracks walnuts for us to eat, the sweet nuts picked from the split husks. Her bright mood could almost make me think that maybe I imagined the Rotter coming here, that maybe I never spoke to it at all.

The air reaching down the chimney is colder than it has yet been, though the bite of frost is still a way off. Myma puts her arms into her coat and looks at me.

Better wrap up, she says, or you'll catch cold. Your feet are already turning blue.

I fasten my rabbit-fur cloak at my neck and think these words. Catch cold. Imagine trapping the chill wind in a snare, snapping its neck and slitting the belly to bring the cold gushing out and away into the ground. Then it would be warm always and I could wear nothing but my skin.

The rain has washed the forest clean for us, says Myma, opening the door and breathing the outside air.

I peer past her into the clearing. It does not look washed clean. It looks dank, the ground squashy and bloated like the badger carcass I once found after heavy rain, its swollen belly and the pale waterlogged flesh that came away in handfuls when I touched it.

In the clearing I find my name-flint, pluck it from the ground. Wipe it on my trousers and feel how the keen-edged shhrrrrrrrrrrr of the name has dulled slightly. Soon it will become blunt and then Flint will go into the Museum too.

Trip-rattle of our teeth dropping into their hole in the cleft post. Myma flings an arm across my chest before I can move towards the path that will take me to the traps.

I'll check the snares, she says. Your chore is to collect bark.

Her voice still bright but her jaw stiffening.

You shouldn't have to go far from the house, she says. Plenty of bark around the clearing. Then you can get inside and weave us some rope.

What I really want is to go alone among the trees and unpick my thoughts, to go back to the pine tree and see if the red hair is still caught in its roots. But I only nod.

Keep my knife for now, Myma says. We'll have to make you a new one somehow.

But what will you do?

Her hand goes to her pocket, a long flat shape there.

I know how to look after myself, she says. You see or hear anything, you get straight back inside and lock the door.

A trickle of fear in her as she says this. It seeps from beneath her calm. She must see me noticing, because she reaches for my chin.

Don't worry, she says. Nothing gets past me.

I watch her off along the trail and think no, that is not true, something did get past, and maybe it will again. Listen to the fading of her feet then listen for the sound of heavier feet but hear nothing. Kick the ground, a clag of leaves tossed up by my boots.

Willows are the best for rope. With Myma's knife I peel away the tough outer bark, strips tucked into my pouch for teeth-cleaning. The inner bark is pappy and fibrous. Coil the lengths of it in my sack.

I pace a circle of the clearing before going back to the house. Ears, eyes and nostrils wide open. I do not hear or see or smell anything strange.

Boil the bark with ash for softening, then sit on the floor and wind the strands to rope. The cord keeps unravelling and I grow impatient. My fingers ache. A sound from outside but when I freeze and listen I hear only the click of taloned birdish feet lifting from the roof.

I set the ropes aside. A quivery feeling between my legs like when washing there, or like when I stand with the corner of the table bumping into me. Something like an itch but on the other side of the skin. I squeeze my legs together and the feeling flicks up towards my navel. Scratch with my whole hand between my legs but the itch burrows deep. Dig harder.

Myma's shout jumps me up. It seems to come from right

beside my ear but when she shouts again it is outside the door. I open to greying light and cold and Myma and something pink laid out on the step. Myma muttering, her arms moving about. I look at the thing on the step and do not understand Myma's upset. It is only a rabbit. Badly skinned and still with head and paws attached, but lop them off and it will be ready for cooking. Myma is the better skinner of us but it must be harder without her knife. Reach for the rabbit but Myma reels towards me, eyes huge.

No, she snarls. It's a trick.

I understand then. The hands that made a mess of the skinning and put the rabbit on the step were not Myma's hands. See the crimp of her lips around her teeth to make the spat word.

Rotter.

I look back to the rabbit and am hungry. Between my legs, a dampness.

8

In the barn they climbed the bales. Their bodies were loose and unrestrained. They were strong when they pulled themselves up, and soft when they fell and bruised. Their parents had told them about the boy who had been crushed bale-hopping before they were born, but the danger only thrilled them.

The bales were a giant's staircase and Maya was the giant up beside the beams with her fisted hands and her glower. She felt vast and bold. She was a thunder of fee-fi-fo-fum, smelling the blood of the Englishmen who giggled their way to her tower and were sent tumbling back down. The clamberers below threw up cries.

'Steal your beans! Steal your beans!'

Maya shoved Darry Platt and Luke Milne squealing in the straw, winded them breathless and coughing. Lauryn Copsey jumped down before she could be pushed. Then Kitty came scrambling up. Her sharp chin and elbows propped on Maya's straw ledge. They grinned at one another.

'Two giants better than one,' Kitty said.

And Maya threw her head back and changed her bellow.

'Oh,' she cried, 'but I like this Englishman very much. I think I'll keep him.'

She pulled Kitty up beside her and the two girls stuck their legs out over the edge and they kicked and kicked, and nobody could get to them.

Soon they would grow older. Their limbs would lengthen and they would hold themselves differently. The barn would change for them. It would become a night place, a stolen-bottle place, a fumble-in-the-hay place.

They would no longer climb the bales but perch on the edges, the straw marking the backs of their legs. Kitty would turn to Maya and say, 'Here, you need some colour on you,' and she'd lean close to daub Maya's mouth with red, and Maya would hate the taste and the greasy feel of the lipstick but she would allow Kitty to paint her, and she would think, but not say, that the closeness of Kitty's face to hers was like lying in sunlight.

The boys would stand apart from them now, awkward in overgrown bodies. Maya would notice the slipping back and forth of eyes, though when she looked across towards the boys she would find in herself a gap where she knew there should be want. Then she would feel Kitty's strong fingers around hers, Kitty's breath warm and sour at her cheek as she spoke into Maya's ear, and Maya would know then what it was to thrum. She would drink something that made her tilt, and when Kitty pulled her up and whirled her round, she would let her head fall back to see the rafters spinning.

She would hear someone yell out, 'Kiss,' and she would feel the small bones in Kitty's wrists pressing at the back of her neck, Kitty's mouth dry on hers, and she would not close her eyes. Kitty would break away and laugh, and the others would laugh too, so Maya would laugh with them, though she would not understand what was funny.

Later, she would see Kitty tucked up under a gangling arm, Kitty led, still laughing, into the shadowed space at the back of the barn, and Maya would know then what it was to ache.

And when Darry took her by the arm and pulled her to the same dark corner, she would go with him. Though she would be certain she could hear Kitty's voice nearby she would not be able to make out the words. She would feel herself pressed between Darry and the wall, and she would remember the time when they were children, when he had taken her hunting for rabbits behind the school, and something had happened that she had not liked. She would remember the bruise that had ringed the soft skin around his eye, now long-faded, and it would seem to her that some hardness had since settled in his jaw and in his hands, and she would stand very still and let those hands move on her, in her, and when it hurt she would picture herself as a dirt burrow, quiet and empty.

Later she would see Kitty emerge with flushed cheeks and straw in her hair, lipstick blotching her chin and a red-faced boy stumbling behind her, zipping himself back into his jeans. Kitty's fingers would find hers again and pull her outside. They would lean together on the other side of the barn wall. Kitty would say, 'It's not as if I didn't want to.' Maya would hear the tremor in her voice, and she would reply, 'It's okay. I did it too. We both did.' And she would think how this meant something, and then Kitty would say, quietly, 'I need to go someplace else. I need to leave this pigsty.' Maya would say, 'We can go together, we can go now,' and she would mean it, really mean it, and she would wait for Kitty to reply, to say yes, let's get out of the pigsty, and she would keep waiting, and eventually she would wet a sleeve with spit to wipe the mess of lipstick from around Kitty's mouth, the black smudges from under her eyes.

When she returned home she would find her mother sitting in the kitchen, stiff in her own waiting. Maya would go upstairs unnoticed, and she would tear off the end of her sleeve and fold the smears of Kitty away under her bed.

Myma Burns the Rabbit

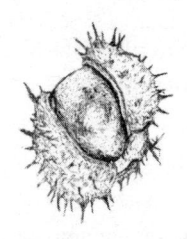

Myma burns the rabbit on the fire and I must keep out of the way in the room where we sleep while it happens. I face the window and listen to Myma scraping a stick at the hearth in the other room, the sound like fingernails scritching skin. She mutters but the muttering is not for me and I do not hear the words in it.

    I watch a moth struggling along the ledge beneath the window. Try to ignore the fire-hiss and the roasting-meat smell that makes my stomach creak. I grip the moth's fat, furred body between finger and thumb, lift it to my cheek to feel the whirring of wings. The food-smell blackens, becomes bitter and charred. Breathe through my mouth. Rub the moth against my skin, its softness calming me. I set it back on the ledge but the wings are all crushed now. The feathery horns wave about as it drags itself like a torn rag. It beats the two crumples on its back. It lifts and drops its legs one by one. Oh. I have damaged it. We don't let things suffer. I wriggle a thin nail from the wood around the window and push the nail into the soft back. The moth shivers then it stops moving so it is dead and I am left with more than one bad feeling.

    Myma leaves the door wide to let out the smell of burning.

The cold comes in and sits around us. We huddle close to the fire and cook chestnuts on the flat of the shovel. Shiny brown shells knifed crossways to a spill of fluffy white flesh. I hold one in my sleeve, blow until it is cool enough to peel with my fingers. Myma prises the shell from hers without letting it cool at all, the chestnut thrown hot into her mouth.

Didn't find anything caught in the traps, she says as she chews.

We could have eaten the rabbit, I say, and immediately choke on the saying.

Myma plucks another chestnut from the shovel head and presses it to the bare skin of her calf. I grip myself together and wait. If I stay still and quiet when Myma is teaching then sometimes the Lesson is over more quickly. She holds the chestnut there until I am sure it must have burned a hole through her leg, but when she takes it away there is only a flat round reddening the size of a thumbprint. Myma peels the chestnut and gives it to me. It is sweet and chewy.

And where do you think that rabbit came from, Flint-Daughter? she asks. Who do you think skinned it and left it?

Her voice quiet but with a strain in it. I say nothing, my mouth full of chestnut.

He must have stolen the rabbit from our traps, she continues. A Rotted thing to do, giving our own food back to us, likely full of badness. Probably poisoned it. Wants to Rot us from the inside. From our bellies outward. Can't mean anything good by it. Remember what I told you? Remember what I said about the tricks they play?

I am nodding as she speaks but inside myself I am thinking of the Rotter saying, Let me make it up to you, saying, Sorry about that, and I am wondering if actually the skinned rabbit was the Rotter's way of giving back what it took from us.

Rotter. Somehow that name no longer quite fits the red-haired creature. Let that other name sit on my tongue, the one the Rotter spoke while tapping its breast. I do not dare to even mouth the name with Myma sitting beside me. Only taste it, tangy like the thought of rabbit meat which spurts saliva into my cheeks. Wyn.

It is my turn to choose This-and-That.

I want to do creep-listen, I say.

Myma bends her neck until it clicks.

Okay, she says. You listen first, I'll creep.

Okay.

She fetches the quiet shoes and the blindfold from the crate. The quiet shoes have rabbit fur on the outside, so they make almost no sound of foot on floor. I take the blindfold and Myma goes to the corner. The quiet shoes turn her feet to hairy paws. I giggle at this. Stand in the middle of the room and tie shut my eyes.

Ready, I say.

When she wants to be, Myma can be as silent as a tongue buried in the ground. But I am just as good at listening, my ears practised at hearing the scutterings of the forest. I listen for Myma's breath, the crack of her toes. A flurry of air at the backs of my legs spins me round. My hand meets the bone of her shoulder.

Got you, I say, grinning under the blindfold.

Got me, I hear her say.

She creeps again and I catch her again. On the third go she makes no noise at all and creeps close enough to tap me on the forehead and say, Got you.

My turn to listen now, she says.

I put on the quiet shoes, the insides warmed by Myma's feet. She fastens the blindfold tight at the back of her head and says, Ready.

I rise to my toes, rock backward-forward to find my balance. As I move to leap, I think I see something there behind the window. Two eyes outside, looking inside. I lurch and land thump-footed. Myma laughs and claps her hands.

Thrown-stone clattering Flint-Daughter, she says. Flint smashing about. You can do better than that.

The window shows only my reflection, my edges burned orange by the lamplight. Make my eyes wide at this Window-Daughter. No other eyes behind mine. Yet the watched feeling clings.

I put my back to the window. Myma's head follows my movement. Crouch and creep across the floor on all fours and Myma stays listening to the spot I have left. I move closer, almost at touching distance when Myma whirls around and jabs out her hand. Dart away before her fingers can brush the top of my head, retreat and wait, belly low. Crawl again, slow, ready to spring away. My head at Myma's knees. My fingers a thumbwidth from her toes. I uncrouch and for a moment I stand facing her, so close I can feel her breath at my neck. The space between us thinner than the skin on top of water. I breathe her air. See the blood beating at the side of her head. I bring my hand up. Light tap of my fingers between her eyebrows.

Got you.

Myma drapes a sheet over the window. Her second shadow moves across it. The room somehow smaller now that I cannot see the blackness stretching away outside.

Don't want anything peering in, Myma says.

After we have spoken our sorrys and thank yous I lie not sleeping and know from the sound of her breathing that Myma is awake too.

Myma, I whisper.
Flint-Daughter?
What if— What if it wasn't a Rotter?
Her stiffening beside me.

What do you mean? she asks.

What if it was something else?

Something else?

What if it was— What if it was like us?

My shoulders are grabbed then and I am turned towards her.

You don't know, she hisses, you don't know what they do.

What do they do? I ask and she shuts up silent and turns over and pretends to sleep.

Light pokes through the sheet over the window. I breathe the smell of burning rabbit that has not quite gone away. Pull my arms and legs from the blanket, roll sideways to find Myma gone. Her chore-smock sits folded beside the bed, a yellow ash leaf placed on top. My heart lowers because this is a Lesson I know. I must go to her.

The hearth strewn with blackened knobs of rabbit bone. The door, open. I shoulder my cloak. Pull on my boots and trudge out with a cold hard gut.

She is waiting for me in the ash copse. She has with her the rope I twisted last light. One end around her neck, the other wrapped around a branch. The branch shows the rub of other ropes she has tied before. A stump beneath her bare feet holds her up. She wears no coat and her shoulder blades thrust like little wings through the back of her bed-smock. She watches me come close.

Better wrap up or you'll catch cold, I say, echoing her.

If I step off my neck will snap and I'll be dead, she says, the way she always does when she teaches this Lesson.

Don't, I tell her, the way I always do.

I'll be like the rabbits in the snares, she says, the way she always does.

Don't, I say again, the way I always do.

The questions you ask, she says then, they can do damage,

Daughter. Some questions are enough to break necks. I wouldn't be able to protect you any more if that happened. You wouldn't survive without me. You need me.

I shake my head.

No, I say, I wouldn't survive.

Then I nod my head.

Yes, I say, I do need you. Don't.

Alright then I won't, she says, the way she always does.

She takes her neck out of the rope and steps down from the stump. I clamber up to the branch and untie the knot and we walk back together, the rope coiled over my shoulder, Myma's bare feet purpling.

She sets me pounding the leftover chestnuts with water for dough while she gathers the bits of burned rabbit bone into a spare pouch and lays fresh kindling in the hearth. She tells me how we will be very busy with our chores now because we need to start building up our stores of food for winter, and how that hair of mine needs cutting again, how fast it grows, how fast I grow, how she will have to sew a new panel into the back of my chore-smock and it won't be long until the frost comes but we will be warm, won't we, safe, won't we, like rabbits in our burrow. I say yes, I know, yes, we will. Try to shuck off the imagined seeing of her in the ash copse, snap-necked and floppy. The Lesson is one that always stays after, a bad taste that keeps burping back into my mouth. It is different to the other Lessons, the pinches and pricks and hot chestnuts, because there is no hurt in this Lesson, only the threat of a hurt, the worst hurt. The thought that if I wasn't there to tell her don't, then maybe she would.

The chestnut bread is bad, the dough gritty with shards of shell that scratch our gums because I have not been careful enough to pick them out, and I know this is another hurt I have caused, and I am as bad as the bad bread and surely Rotted to my core. I droop low over myself, my mood darkening like the charred-black rabbit, like Myma's eyes when she said, You wouldn't survive without me, you need me.

Her eyes watch me now. Then her lips smack together around her mouthful of the bad bread.

Deliciously smooth! she shouts to the roof. Ultimate creamy delicious!

I frown and droop lower.

Enjoy hot! says Myma. Rich and sweet! The most perfect bread I've ever tasted. Better than Chocolate Pudding.

She is trying to make me feel better. It is funny because the bread is the opposite of delicious and we both know this. Feel the corners of my mouth moving.

Ultimate! she says again.

I let myself go loose to it, join her in the joke.

No added colours, I say. Natural flavours.

No added colours! Myma repeats.

Refrigerated! I shout.

Lick my palms and suck my fingers.

We eat up all the bread. Roll the hard grainy stuff around our mouths. Chew with lips wide and noisy, grunting at each other and clapping our hands high in the air. We are so good at pretending that when the bread is finished I wish there was more.

9

It came in the winter. The day was shrunken and cold, the ground frozen white. Maya was chopping wood in the forest, a fallen tree she'd been working at for weeks, her progress slowed by the weight she lugged, the mass that pushed up under her ribs and shortened her breath. She lifted the axe and as she did she felt something shift, detach, spill. Slowly she bent and gathered the chopped wood.

The pain was bearable for a while, until it was not. Then it surprised her with its intensity, so severe she thought it would split her open down the length of her spine. A squeezing wrenching tightening, as if some vital part of her were preparing to tear itself from her body. She dragged the wood through the forest. Whenever the pain twisted up into a point she had to drop the bundle and put her hands to the ground like a beast to keep the blood in her head. It took her until night to reach the hut.

The grey woman was there when Maya pulled herself and the wood through the doorway. She seemed excited and agitated. She capered about while Maya went bellowing on all fours between the two rooms. Maya was unable to settle. She was too hot, so she pushed the window open and stuck her head out into the freezing night. The grey woman dove-cooed and made stroking motions at Maya's flanks but after a while Maya could not bear her nearness. She sent the grey woman into the corner to burble her bird cries and rock the empty cradle of her arms.

Finally, exhausted, Maya crawled to the bed. She turned herself about and pawed a nest from the sheets. She thrust out her tongue and panted. Her body seemed to her red and open, as if skinned, glistening muscles exposed and heaving. She felt something lowering in her abdomen, drawing downward, and she felt truly frightened for the first time since arriving at the hut. She wanted to stop what was happening but she could already feel herself peeling back around the wet nub that pushed itself outward. Of her and not of her.

Then there it was. It lay curled on the soiled sheets between her legs, puckered and shrivelled like a finger left too long in the bath. Its limbs squirmed in the mess of jellied blood, the slippery corded coil.

Maya's hair stuck to her neck and forehead. She smelled sweat, coppery blood, shit. She gazed with dull eyes at what her body had expelled. There the tiny fist of a head, hair slick and dark. There the two hands like fleshy red claws. From the bird-gape of the mouth came a wail, the new, rumpled lungs inflating in the cold air. Maya thought of the peeping that came from the crates of male chicks before they were sent for maceration. She thought of animals that ate their young, or even reabsorbed them before they could be born if the conditions were not right, and she thought how intelligent that was, how much better adapted those animal bodies were than her own.

For the first time in ages, Maya thought of Kitty. And she thought of the budding that had begun in Kitty after one of those fumbling nights in the dark barn. She remembered the hard-backed chair she had waited in while Kitty lay behind a curtain, then the journey home on the bus with Kitty's hand clutching hers. She remembered her friend's freckled back hunched over in the bath while Maya squeezed the bottle of lemon-scented shampoo and cupped water over the pale hair. The water had swirled pink and Kitty had been quiet for a long time. Then she had put her elbows on the sides of the bath and looked at Maya.

'I'm glad it's gone,' she'd said. 'I didn't want it. It's just a strange feeling. Knowing something was there, now knowing it's not.'

Maya had nodded and felt something oddly like mirth rising in her.

'At least it won't have to live in this shithole,' she had said then, and they had both laughed until their bellies ached.

'You know,' Kitty had said later, 'I don't think I ever want one, actually,' and Maya had replied, 'Me neither,' and they had fallen asleep in a sprawl on Kitty's bed, Kitty's wet hair at Maya's cheek.

Maya looked down. The cold air from the open window was blueing the baby's skin. Each ragged cry huffed a cloud of breath which hovered over the mouth like a tiny ghost, drifting in and out. Maya saw how helpless this creature was. Already it was in pain, and more pain would come. Maya could prevent that. She could. It would be easy. A single hand to cover nose and mouth, then nothing but warm nameless dark for ever. Better that way, she thought.

Two eyes peered up at Maya from puffy slits. A hand gripped her finger, impossibly strong. A bubble of saliva grew and burst at the corner of the small, needing mouth. Maya could not remember a time she had felt needed. She reached down and wiped the drool from her daughter's chin.

The Only Reds

The only reds I have seen since Myma chased Wyn over the fence are the berries dotting the holly and hawthorn, the dropped leaves from the trees, and the blood that blobbed up when Myma bit her thumbnail too short. None of these reds are like the hair Wyn brought into the forest on its head and face, that red now gone with it. Perhaps Wyn will never come back. Perhaps Myma scared it off for good. Perhaps I will never see that kind of red again.

Myma scatters the char of rabbit all around the clearing. Grey powder and fragments of bone strewn at the bases of trunks.

This will work, she mutters as her wrist jerks handfuls of ash and bone. This will hold.

I watch the ash sifting in the breeze and sticking to the damp ground.

In the forest I trip over a root and in my sprawl I hear it murmuring with a name, so I hack the root from the ground and it takes the place of the flint in my pouch.

Root-Daughter. Little Nub. Gnarling. Foot-in-the-Ground-Daughter. Tuber-Kin.

Lights and darks roll after each other and we do not see or hear anything of Wyn. We hardly speak of it and when we do I am careful to call it Rotter, always Rotter, never by the name it gave to me. Myma begins to untighten, her mouth to loosen, and I loosen too, no longer slice-edged Flint but supple Root.

One light I take the chore of foraging for insects and other crawling things. I walk through the forest with empty bottles tied clinking around my waist. I roll logs and scrape up handfuls of soil thick with the folding grey bodies of woodlice. Like a blackbird I pull worms from their burrowing. My hand the pecking beak.

At the ash copse I turn my eyes upward and search the trunks for boreholes. Climb to the branch that shows the faint marks of Myma's ropes and use Myma's knife to slit the bark like hide. Peel it back for the grubs underneath, the sticky white kind that will turn into beetles eventually but not if we eat them first. They wrinkle at the light and the air, blind heads wood-dusted from their chewing. Between my fingers the grubs are plump and clammy. I squash them down into the largest bottle.

The branch, how it knurls up into the cleft between my legs. There the quickening itch, deep in my pelvis. Move my hips to scratch against the branch but the itch only worsens, thrumming now into my belly. I put my hands to the trunk and feel the grooves where the grubs have tunnelled. Scrunch my eyes closed, think about tiny bones cracking between my fingers, about rabbits pulled pink from their skins. In the bottles at my waist the insects trickle and squirm. The itch coils tight. I move my hips faster and feel a brimming in me, about to spill, like I might wee.

A sound startles me from my scratching. Sudden, sharp, knifing into my ear. A keening that splits the forest in half. I shudder against the tree. Alarm wets the underside of my tongue. No animal I have ever heard sounds like that. I hand-and-foot fast down the trunk and straight away I am running, bug-bottles janking, itch still fizzing, a cry in my own throat.

Myma?

She does not call back. Something darts ahead of me, Myma's second shadow darkening the ground, flickering over the pale birch trunks. It streaks towards the noise and I follow at a sprint. The screaming closer now. Yow-ow-oww of it shaking the air. Then it chokes, stops.

Myma?

I push through the thrash of branches, step around a mossy stump and see them, the two of them, Myma and Wyn, on the ground. There is red everywhere. Myma's second shadow circles them and circles them.

Though blood flows warm I have always thought the look of it is cold, as if it carried a bit of vein-blue out of the body with it. Blood on Myma's face, blood on Wyn's face. I see each thing vivid like a strong scent. His hair. Her fingers on a glinting edge of silver. His gasping mouth. Her redded chore-smock.

Myma?

She moves her head and the relief of it almost makes me laugh. Her second shadow scuds off among the trees and loses itself between the light and shade. Myma sits up quickly, looks at Wyn, then into the trees where her second shadow has disappeared.

Why? she shouts into the forest. For what?

Myma?

She is not looking at me. She begins to stand and I run to her. My hands fluttering to her shoulders. Red all down her front.

Myma are you hurt what did it do is it dead did it hurt you? I ask in a rush.

She jerks from me, still glaring off into the trees.

What am I going to do with him now? she yells.

She will not look at me and I do not understand and I think perhaps the ground smacked her head funny. And all that blood, on my hands now too, where is it coming from?

Did it hurt you, Myma? I ask loudly. Did Wy— Did the Rotter hurt you?

Her eyes on Wyn now, her teeth chewing at her upper lip. Fingers crawling for the worry-itch. I grab her wrists to stop her.

Myma, I cry. Tell me what happened. Is it dead? Did it try to Rot you? Did you kill—

Her voice cuts across mine.

Not dead, she says. Ha! Not dead. No. She wouldn't let me finish, would she. Never seen her make such a fuss, the mad old bird. And what for? What now?

Her eyes drop to her hands. Her palms lined with blood. The silver thing she was clutching drops to the ground. A long shard of jagged glass the length of my palm. Knife-sharp at the tip. I look down at it and my own eyes look back, clear and startling. Like seeing myself in a puddle, or in the window when it's dark, only this reflection is crisp at the edges, and full of colour. I can see right up my nostrils. There is blood on the glass, smears of it across my reflected face. Dark glots at the point. Myma has sunk to sitting, her arms around her knees and her eyes sealed shut. She begins to hum through her nose. It frightens me. It is worse than her shouting. I shake her shoulders and her head jangles like a loose tooth. Then, from beside us, a single word.

Help.

Wyn's hands grope the dirt, fingers clenching and unclenching in the leaf litter. All the sounds here seem louder than anything. Fast-huffed breath of me. Humming of Myma. And that awful agitated scuffling of Wyn's hands. That word spoken again, rasping from that other mouth.

Help.

The blue hand soaked red. Its fingers fumbling at the torn black coat, yanking it open. Underneath is all sticky wet. The hand moves into the wet and feels around. Wyn makes a gasping sound. It says the same word I heard it speak in the dark.

Pissit. Agh pissit. Jesus.

It lifts the sodden blue hand towards me. Palm up, wrist slack.

Help, it says again.

Tears trickling then into the hair on its face. The tears jolt me. Wyn looks scared. Far more scared than me. Myma has never spoken of Rotters crying, Rotters afraid or in pain. But here is Wyn. Hurting, frightened. Asking for help.

Myma, I say quiet. Myma, I don't think it can get up by itself.

Her eyes stay shut. Her humming loudens and she sways on the ground.

Myma, I say louder.

She opens her eyes. She examines the lap of her chore-smock, her red hands. Then she looks up at me, her face smooth and calm.

Him, she says.

What?

Not it, she says. It's a him. A he.

Him, I say.

Yes.

Oh, I say. Well. We need to get him up. I'll take him's shoulder.

His shoulder.

His?

His shoulder.

I crouch. It – him – smells of hot fear and blood, sour sweat. Still a part of me jars at the thought of touching him. But there is nothing else to do. I wriggle my hands under its – his –

shoulder, try to pull him upright. Lift his torso halfway then have to stop and let him flop again. Wyn is a heavy thing.

I can't lift him by myself, I tell Myma.

Her jaw is tight, her lips bloodless with pressing. She stares at me and something shifts behind her eyes. Suddenly she is upright, moving to Wyn's other side.

When Myma reaches for him, Wyn shouts and rears sideways into my legs, making me stagger. I kick him in the back.

What are you doing that for when I'm trying to help you? I spit.

I am not sure that Wyn hears me or even feels my kick. He is panting now. Dirt and leaves in the bright hair. The heels of his boots scrape the ground. He hauls on my arm, pulls himself to a low stoop. The blue hand paws at his wet gut.

I think his belly is hurting him, I say.

Wyn's back hunches right the way over, almost to all fours. He coughs, spits. He looks from Myma to me like a caught animal. Then he is lurching off, falling and stumbling, one hand pressed to his stomach. Myma's head snaps around. Her voice strong and urgent.

Daughter, she says, he mustn't go.

I run after Wyn. He is easy to catch. He is limping, drag-footed and slow. I am the Root that trips. I leap at him, catch him around the middle and pitch him forwards. Feel the ground strike his chest, thud up through his back. Him pinned under me. The bottles digging at my waist. Wyn yells and tries to throw me off but I am stronger.

Got you, I tell him.

I sit in the middle of his back and look around at Myma for what to do next. She has picked up the silvery shard and is staring into it.

Myma, I say. He's hurt.

Myma doesn't answer.

Myma.

Feel like I might sob. It is all so messy and muddled. Almost-crumple of my face.

Myma, I say again. Are we going to help him?

She slides the silver shard into the side of her boot. Then she looks at us, at both of us.

Yes, she says.

Only the way she speaks the word makes it sound like a question.

Yes?

Part II

Pupae

10

A new kind of fear slid from Maya with the afterbirth and attached itself to the body that had come from her body.

In those first weeks she lay awake every night while the grey woman sat like a wolf in the doorway. Maya's fingertips held her eyes wide against the blindness of sleep. She stared at the back of her daughter's spongy, pliable skull, the faintly oily whorls of hair at the nape. She imagined huge rough thumbs pressing that softness inward until it burst. When she began to drift, she dug her nails into the skin on the inside of her arm. Like this she kept herself alert.

She took the twisted cord that had strung her to the child and she wove it among the boundary branches. The action made sense to her. While the child had been inside her, it was her own flesh that had fenced around it and kept it from harm. Now the child existed outside her body, and so that space of safety had to be spread further, stretched wide like a tensile skin.

Her body was the strong one, she saw that now. It was toughened by what it had endured. She mixed her parts with the forest's parts for a solid, rooted strength. Her blood, which seeped for weeks after the birth, she stirred with mud. Her hair, which was fast growing long again, she used to tie bundles of feathers, spiders' legs, rabbit bones. She took her daughter's fingers into her mouth one by one and nibbled the fingernails short, then she added those tiny slivers to her clumpings and clusterings. She would bind them all together, herself, the child and the woods, and in this way they would be protected.

The grey woman sniffed at Maya's bundles and sneezed, the sound like wings beating into flight.

Birth had left Maya ragged but there was no time for resting. She had to keep the fire fed and she had to keep herself fed so that she could keep the child fed. She had to add more branches to the fence, she had to fill all its gaps. In the forest she carried the baby in a sling across her chest. At the opening of the peeping mouth she would pause in her work and pull her breast from the neck of her shift. The grey woman pointed her to the roots that could be mashed and smeared on her sore parts, the cracks that split her nipples. The blood dried up between Maya's legs and she did not bleed again.

When finally she seemed to sleep she would be woken by a cry and the hot jolt of that small fist closing around her finger. Her daughter, grown strong and round-bellied on her milk. The firm tug of that clamped, determined mouth always startled Maya. The child's eyes held hers with an openness she found bewildering. I am known, Maya thought, by this other, who is also me.

Bent around her suckling daughter, Maya saw the grey woman crouched watching in the corner. The soft rustle of her hands spoke of a missing.

Twoness Is the House

Twoness is the house we live in. It has two rooms. There are two stools, two mugs. We each have two boots, and two feet to put inside them. Two teeth go into the cleft post. Two snares for each stone marker. Light and dark make two, like hot and cold, like being a moving breathing thing and being dead. We each have two arms and two legs, two elbows, two cheeks to our backsides. Two nostrils, two eyes and two ears. The bed holds two. Two of us. Us the only two. Us the only we.

But now, a third. Now Wyn. I begin to think of his coming here as Wyn-come. Before Wyn-come. After Wyn-come.

Wyn lives in the corner of the room where we eat. His wrists and ankles are wrapped with rope and tied to the table leg. Underneath him, a pile of sacks from the shed. Over him, a moulded blanket, the thick stiff one we use to wrap the water tank against freezing in the winter. Myma wanted to put him in the shed with the chopped wood but I said it would be harder to keep an eye on him there, and she wrinkled her top lip and moved her tongue across her teeth and then agreed.

Myma wouldn't let me sit close when she was cleaning out the hole her glass made in Wyn's belly. I was sent to gather chamomile and dock for a wound dressing. The whites of

Wyn's eyes were showing when I returned. Jaw loosed and head lolling. His black coat stinking on the floor. A filthy sort of short smock on him that Myma had to cut away where it stuck. His back stayed covered so I couldn't look for the split of Rot in it. A thin silver cord around his neck that his hand kept flitting to. Damp rags wadding up on the floor, blooming with red.

Not so bad as it looks, Myma muttered. Needs stitches though.

I wanted to watch her stitching Wyn's skin closed but she shunted me off into the room where we sleep. I lay on my stomach as close to the doorway as I could without Myma seeing. Hips and elbows hard on stone. Wyn's jerking left boot the only part I could see. There was a sound of water splattering and a hiss from Wyn. Gruntings and coughings. Myma saying, Stay still, I'm trying to clean it. Him saying, Pissit, shit, hell. I fell asleep listening.

Myma whispers to me in the bed.

Had to do it, Root-Daughter. Had to cut the Rot out of him, see? Cut the root of it from his gut. But there might be some left in him. You mustn't listen to things he says. You must not speak to him. You must be strong and good. Can you be strong for me, Daughter? Good for me, Daughter? Root-Daughter?

She takes the sheet from the window and hangs it over the doorway between the two rooms. Another sheet is pulled dusty from the space under the bed, torn in half and quick-stitched into a long smock that goes over Wyn's head and falls below his knees. A brown stain at the front where his Rot-hole leaked through and Myma had to close it up again with her needle. She burns Wyn's other clothes, the second blue hand turning crumbly black in the fire like the first. Wyn did not have his sack with him, so it is not burned, and I still do not have a knife.

I have dreams about being slit open and when I wake I probe my belly for signs of growing Rot. A bruise there from all my prodding.

I must not speak to Wyn but he is difficult to ignore. He makes the house smell strange. The sound of him in the corner like a shout. Every cough and sniff and scruss noising loud at my ear. The pale feel of him watching us as we sit on our stools to eat. His bright hair yanking my eyes to look. Sometimes he speaks. Water. Piss. Hurts. Cold. He says things like, My medication, please, my bag, please, and I have to pretend I cannot hear, even though the not-known words prod at me, their odd shapes meaningless as the ones on the backs of the tins, re–fri–ger–a–ted. Only Myma is allowed to listen to Wyn, to respond, and she does not do that much either. The sense that she is always watching him, though she hardly glances into his corner. Her shoulders pinching at each chafe of his breath. Her fingernails at her worry-itch, scraping it bloody.

One dark I slide from the bed and go quiet and low across the floor, under the sheet and into the other room to crouch over Wyn in his slit-eyed dreaming. I could prise open his lids to see the veiny undersides of his eyes. I could put my tongue to the thin line across his forehead and know the salt taste of him. I could worm my fingers into his red tangle. But I cannot quite push through the strangeness of touching a body that is not Myma's in this way. Instead I lean close, closer, peer into the darkness of his ears, his haired nostrils, his open mouth.

Wyn does not seem happy when he wakes and sees me huddled by his head, my face bent to his. He yells loud as if I had reached into the reek of his mouth and wrenched out his tongue by the root. Myma comes darting through to find him cringing from me, spitting his not-word words. Pissit. Fuckshedothatfor. Me hunched frozen in a startle. Myma drags me back behind the sheet and stands me facing the wall. She makes me stand there until I am too tired to hold myself up. When I fall backwards she is there to catch me and bundle me back into the bed, where sleep pins me heavy like a nail through a moth.

It is a light for doing washing but when I move to take off my bed-smock, Myma's hands grab my wrists. Her eyes on Wyn. Him on his elbows, watching. His hair sticking out in chunks.

Leave that on, Myma says to me. We'll wash it later.

I do not ask why because I prefer the fuggy smell of myself to the stripped smell of washed clothes and if I can keep my own scent on longer then that is a good thing.

Wyn needs washing too but Myma sends me out to do chores before she pulls the clothing off him.

Find us some food, she says. You'll wash once you're back.

I stump across the clearing in my boots and bed-smock and cloak. Drop my tooth into the hole on the cleft post and think how everything feels like an Exception since Wyn-come. How Myma is trying to make it all seem as it always is, even though the Exception lies big and red in the corner, breathing our air.

My sack fills with hazelnuts, the spiked leaves around the shells now withered green to brown. I pull a rabbit from a snare, a stringy crow from one of my stick traps. Prod at slugs to make them froth. Then to the ash tree where I sit a while on the branch. Scratch my tight in-between itch and after feel raw and shiny.

The clearing is draped with washing when I return at the dimming of the light. Our chore-smocks, my trousers, trailing from a low branch. The flat hang of them like scraped skins. As I pass the woodshed I see that the door has been bound shut with rope. Fixed to the rope, a Keep-Safe of Myma's hair wrapped around an oak root. Then comes a cough from behind the shed door and I move quick away.

Our skinshoes have been washed and laid to dry on the step. Mine slightly larger than Myma's. The muntjac hide softened by our step. The empty footprints, dark where our heels have pressed. Steam comes through the open door. I step inside and look into the corner, where Wyn is not.

There is his smock, flopping about in the pot. Myma stands over it, prodding with the stick. She is bare-skinned, her bed-smock hung on the rack above the fire. Her flesh has the tender look of having been scrubbed and scraped.

Why isn't he in here? I ask.

Myma's face turns towards me. Hair steamed to fraying around her head.

Boots off, she says.

I do what she says because I am good and definitely not Rotted. My fingers move over my belly as I straighten. No Rot lumping in there.

Anything? she asks.

For a moment I think she is talking about my stomach, and my arms wrap across to hide it in case she spots something I have not and goes to fetch her shiny silver glass. But she is not looking at me, she is looking at the sack, hands held out. I fill her hands with the rabbit and the crow.

A new beak for over the door, she says.

She lifts them, looks them over, nods once, then sets them on the table, crow beak clonking on the wood. Her thumb taps the underside of my chin. I pucker at the not-Myma soapwort smell.

Myma, I say.

I keep my voice careful but there is a thinness to the gaze she turns from me. With the stick she scoops Wyn's smock dripping steaming from the pot. It clings to the stick like a clump of hair.

Myma, I say again.

She peels the smock from the stick and twists it to a worm for wringing.

Myma, why is he in the shed? I ask.

She squeezes out the water. Her hands red with the heat. Flush of it up her arms, over the bare skin of her chest and shoulders.

Because, she says, he doesn't wash with us.

What if he gets away? I ask. What if he Rots the firewood?

Her arms strain for the last drops. She lets the smock unravel. It is stiff and crinkled, a brittle hide.

You know wood doesn't Rot like that, she says. And I put a Keep-Safe on the door.

I do not say that the Keep-Safes didn't stop him coming so perhaps they will not stop him going. Myma's eyes watch me sideways.

You're not to go in there, she tells me.

She hangs Wyn's smock. Her fingernails flick at her thighs to tell me not to ask more questions. The thought of Wyn where I cannot see or hear him sits uncomfortable in me. As if Myma has plucked an object from my Museum and buried it somewhere deep in the ground where I can barely feel its hum.

My bed-smock is cleaned and hung. Myma fills the bucket with hot water from the pot and tells me to wash.

I fit my backside into the bucket, arms and legs dangling long over the sides. I am far too large to properly sit in it the way I used to, when Myma would hook me under the armpits and plosh me in, saying, Daughter-stew. I slop water. My hands and heels drag on the floor and my thighs squeeze against my chest. My feet point towards the door that keeps the colding dark behind it. Stretch my neck to see the pieces of clothing on the wooden rack. The two that hold our familiar shapes, the folds and stains of us. The one stitched for another body, strange as a word I do not yet know how to speak. I squint to picture that body, in the woodshed, bare of its clothing, but I cannot make it appear in my mind. I cannot think a naked skin that is not Myma's. Shuffle deeper into the bucket until the metal rim pinches. Let out a little fart that splurts from the water with a good strong smell. Kick my heels on the floor and think how chilly it must be in the shed without a fire or any clothes for warming. Do Rotters feel cold?

Myma sits behind me on her stool, rasping her knife sharp with a rough stone.

Myma, I say.

The rasping pauses.

Root-Daughter.

The rasping starts again. I think how I can ask the question I want to ask without Myma setting the stone's grit to her skin.

Myma, I say again.

Thunk of the set-down stone. Then a tearing, knife point slicing and skin ripping from meat.

It is cold outside the house, I say.

Splitting of sinew and tissue. A rich brown smell of entrails.

Do you think it's cold in the shed? I ask.

Scrape of stool on floor. Myma's legs beside me.

I need the bucket, she says.

Myma, I say again. Do you think it's cold in the—?

There are blankets in there, she says, her voice a sharp point. You think I'd have him freeze to death?

She turns from me, grumbling low, speaking into herself now, not to me.

As if she'd let me anyway, she says.

It hitches strange in me, this she. It does not mean me. It means something else, something to do with why Myma did not kill Wyn in the forest, and with what she said when I found her there, Wyn's blood on her, when she shouted into the trees.

Mad old bird, she wouldn't let me finish would she.

She. My mind tries to run after the sense of it but is left behind, panting.

I pull my backside from the bucket with a shlup.

Us with ourselves again. Us two. We had almost forgotten what it was like to be in the house without the feel of Wyn's stare. The thought of him does not leave me but it dulls to a back-of-the-head thrum that I can almost ignore. We grow giddy in our uncovered skins. We pin the sheet away from the doorway and charge breathless through the house. We sit on the floor beside the fire with our mugs, drink hot water bloodied with handfuls of dried elder and rowan berries.

For This-and-That we do shadowing. Myma makes a rabbit on the wall. Fingers for ears and fingers for legs. The rabbit jumps up and down. I flap my hands into a clumsy bird and swoop to tear off the rabbit's head. Myma makes the headless rabbit body hop and lump about by itself and I laugh and laugh and laugh.

Above my bird, another shadow. A flutter of fingers. I make a thumb-eared fox to snap it up but Myma has already smothered the lamp and the shadows with it.

Before sleep, Myma fetches a length of twine. She ties one end to my big toe and the other to hers.

I'll feel the pull if you try creeping off, she says.

11

If Maya's mother was a sound, she would have been a sheet of metal folding in a high wind. Before Maya was born her mother worked behind the butcher's counter. She wore a white fitted coat and low-heeled shoes. She took the orders and opened and closed the till. The butcher's seemed to her a clean and ordered place, a place of white tiles and precise contours. She looked at the pale coils of sausage, the uniform red thicknesses of meat with their waxy seams of fat, and she felt at peace among those things that could be measured and portioned.

One day she asked a man at the counter what she could get for him, but instead of looking at the display he looked at her, and he carried on looking at her, then he asked the cost of that rump under the white coat, and she felt confused and then embarrassed by her confusion. The butcher and the man both laughed and Maya's mother completed the order with pricking palms and a rising queasiness.

There was a room in the back of the butcher's that she did not go into, where the slit bodies were hung from hooks. In that room the gristle and flaps of a thing were trimmed away to neat cuts to be weighed and parcelled. Maya's mother imagined a room like that inside herself, a tucked-away place where all the pulpous vile parts went, while on the outside she remained a smooth, wiped surface. She took home the livers and kept them in the fridge where she could look at them shining under the light. They disgusted and excited her. Sometimes she had terrible, violent thoughts. Sometimes she felt an urge to shout long and loud. She smoked cigarettes and felt cleansed by them, everything that was raw in her cauterised and cured.

Maya's mother did not like the place where she had grown up. The wind brought with it the smell of poultry rendering. It stuck to her when she went outside. She did not intend to stay living there but then Maya's father came to buy offal, and she liked the way his eyes could not quite meet hers, how his upper lip was fuller than the lower, like a calf's. He was shy when she pulled him to her. His hands were big. They trembled when she pressed them at her waist.

They married and her belly grew. It grew too big for the fitted white coat, so she stopped working at the butcher's. She loved the child that was cut like an organ from the long incision between her hips, but the intimacy of motherhood troubled her. She was ashamed of the way her body responded compulsively to the baby's cry. What leaked from her was proof of some process she had no control over, something unchecked and mammalian. She kept the baby clean. She scrubbed it shiny and red.

She started volunteering at the church when Maya was older. She did not believe in God but the cool air of the place with its wooden body hanging by the palms gave her the same sense of sterile sanctitude as the butcher's had done. She collected and recorded the donations with an older woman whose husband was dead, and who watched Maya's mother pencilling the numbers and told her she had a sharp mind. Maya's mother was pleased by this, and she set herself like a quick knife to paring the same kind of order from her home, her husband, her child. She was a keen, exacting edge.

When Maya's father changed and began to drown in himself, Maya's mother believed she could haul him back. In the sour mornings she straightened him and made him sit for breakfast. She disposed of empty bottles. She swilled him out with mouthwash before he left for work, until he started swallowing that too. She tidied his fraying edges even as he unravelled. When the woman at the church touched her arm and asked questions that held concern, Maya's mother said only, 'He's overworked, you know how it is.' A part of her worried for her now-teenage daughter, who was growing increasingly distant and unknown to her, but her hands were already full with gripping on to her husband. In trying to retrieve him, she tethered herself to his drowning.

At night she lay beside the overripe smell of him and thought of smooth eggs, slicing blades, limewash, salt. These things were clean, reliable.

He Stays

He stays inside the shed for the whole dark. At light-come we eat the last of the dried berries and Myma talks only of our chores, as if there is not a strange red thing shut in the woodshed.

When I leave to check the traps, I stop outside the roped-shut door. My eye close against the slats. In the gap, a blanketed heap. It shivers as I watch. From it comes a cough. I lift my fist and tap the wood with my knuckles. The heap shifts. A single eye in the mass of red. Then a hand taps back and I run, my belly fizzing.

Back to the clearing at dark-come with a pigeon in my sack. I peer through the gap again but the shed is full of gloom and I can't make out the shapes. Knuckle-tap but hear nothing. Maybe he is dead. Maybe Myma has killed him and thrown him back over the fence. The thought dampens me and I go heavy-footed into the house.

What's that glower for? Myma asks as I come slumping in.

At seeing the bright spill of hair in the corner my mood leaps back up. Not dead then. Still here then. I hang my cloak and try to keep the edges of my face from lifting. A thrill at having the unfamiliar interesting thing back in the house with us, even if I must ignore it, even if I must pretend that I am not interested in it, not at all.

Fewer potatoes in the stew this dark-come. We must make them last, Myma says, now that none are left in the ground. The pigeon is plucked and cleaved, half set aside for smoking and drying and storing.

I drape the strips of pigeon skin over the side of my bowl.

Eat it, Myma says, though she knows the slimy bits make me shudder. We don't waste food, Root-Daughter.

Spoon the stretchy scraps into my mouth all at once. Gone more quickly that way. Swallow the retch. Then tongue my bowl clean. In the sides of my eyes I can see Wyn staring at the meat put aside for drying. The broth Myma has spooned into an empty tin and set beside him has no pigeon chunks in it and hardly any potato, and he has spilled most of it down his front trying to eat with bound hands. He coughs.

Please. Will you untie me?

The question drops like bird splat onto the table. Myma's hand tightens on her spoon but she says nothing, just carries on chewing and swallowing. I say PIGEON loud in my head to cover up Wyn's speaking, which Myma has told me I must not listen to, but I hear him anyway.

At least I could help out a bit if you untie me, he says. We could help each other. I can gather food.

Myma laughs without moving her face.

I suppose you'll steal that too, she says.

A squirming in Wyn's corner.

I didn't mean— he says. I— I only did that because I had to. I'm not proud of it. And I gave you that last rabbit back, didn't I?

If I untie you, Rotter, Myma says, you'll be straight over the fence and bringing others back here with you. Don't think I don't know what you're after.

What's that then? he says.

Myma stacks the bowls together.

What shall we do for This-and-That, Daughter? she asks me. It's your turn to choose.

Um, I say.

My bag, says Wyn. My medication. Please. If I could just get them.

We haven't done masking for a while, says Myma. You always enjoy that.

I have not opened my mouth to reply before Wyn's voice comes again like a smack.

What the fuck is this? What's wrong with you? Try to kill me for taking a couple of rabbits and now, what, you're going to keep me tied up here for the rest of my fucking life? I was only looking for somewhere to be for a bit. To be away. But I'd rather have stayed sleeping out there on the ground. Wish I'd never come across you and your creepy fucking girl.

By the end of his speaking he is shouting. He pulls against the rope and I can see the pink rub of it around his wrists. Myma stands up. Stool clattering backwards. Her shoulders a hard line.

There's no place here for the like of you, Rotter, she says. If it's worse for you here it's because this place isn't for you. Yet you came anyway, thinking you can stick yourself in everywhere your hands can reach, thinking just because a thing's there it's for you to grab.

She does not shout but her voice is louder than his. It fills the room. It presses at the walls and makes the stone creak. It sucks the air from the house.

I'm sure it is worse for you here, she says. I'm sure it is worse for you, Rotter. I've known the like of you. What Rotters like you do. Worse for you, is it? Not able to throw your weight around here, are you? Like the rest of them. All those Rotters.

I stay very still on my stool. My eyes swing from Myma to

Wyn, him cowered under the hail of her words, tied hands raised against the battering. Almost hear the thwack as they hit.

You don't know anything of me, he gasps. You're crazy. Crazy bitch you are.

I know a Rotter when I see one, Myma bellows, and she seems to grow taller, wider. You won't get what you came creeping for, Rotter. It's not yours to take. Not here. You're not welcome here.

So kill me, he says, teeth clenched. At least when I'm dead and gone to hell I'll be allowed to take a shit when I like. I don't care, do it. Why don't you? Why don't you? Why don't you?

Myma goes completely still for a moment, the house wrapped tight around her. Something in her flinches, shrinks.

Everything holds. Then Myma is stamping away, behind the sheet and into the other room. She leaves her second shadow stretched trembling up the wall.

All the air rushes back into the house and a choked sort of gasping fills the space Myma's voice has left. I realise that the sound is me, that I am breathing in and out very fast through my mouth. Squeeze my hands together, hard enough to press the blood from them. Feel Wyn's eyes on me and turn to look into his corner. He stares back a long while. My jaw clamping tight to keep the gasps in. My nostrils closing and opening with the in-out hiss of air. Finally Wyn coughs and spits into the empty tin beside him. He laughs without smiling.

Fucked up, he says. You're both fucked up.

He rolls to face the wall. I follow Myma to the other room and we don't do This-and-That.

Myma, when something's dead does it go somewhere?

Go? Dead doesn't mean going anywhere. Just stopped. Ended. You know that.

So if we become dead, what after?

Why is it you're thinking about us dead?

He told you to kill him so he can go to hell and take a shit when he likes.

Those are Rotted words, Daughter. You mustn't use them.

Fingertips coming together in a hard purple pinch on her cheek.

Okay, I tell her. I won't.

Pause.

Was it not true then? I ask. What he said about going somewhere when he's dead? Going to – going?

Didn't I tell you not to listen to the things he says? Can't trust words from a Rotter. You've seen dead things, Root-Daughter. Tell me, do the dead rabbits go anywhere? And where do the birds go when we've snapped their necks?

They go in our stomachs. Then into the ground when we poo them out.

There you go then. Believe what you know before you start to believe anything from a Rotter's mouth.

Pause.

Myma.

Root-Daughter.

How long is he going to stay?

Pause.

I don't know, Daughter.

A long while?

Maybe. It's not safe to let him go.

So he is not Rotted now? Because you cut it out?

The root of it could grow back. They've all got it in them. It doesn't go away, ever.

Will we get Rotted?

Not if you do what I say.

Pause.

Does it hurt him? I ask. Having a Rot-root in him?

Probably.

Are we helping him? To stop it growing again?

I suppose we are.

Maybe I could help a bit more.

What do you mean?

Pause.

I could— I could show him how to do chores and This-and-That. I could tell him about Keep-Safes. He doesn't know all the things we know about how to keep ourselves protected and keep the Rot out. If I show him, maybe the Rot-root in his gut will never grow again. Maybe it will even shrivel away completely. Then he'd be like us.

Long pause.

He wouldn't be like us, Daughter. He can't be.

Why?

Because he isn't.

Why?

Because of what he is.

What is he?

A Rotter.

But if he's no longer Rotted?

Enough, she says, and I know from her voice to stop.

We roast grubs on the fire and they split open, the sticky insides bubbling out. Drip-sizzle smell of them in the flames. Crunchy outside, soft inside. Bite off the head to blow the heat away.

Myma sets a tin of grubs at Wyn's shoulder. Clink of metal on stone. She prods him in the back with her foot. He has been grimacing and griping all light but now he takes the tin between his tied hands, looks inside. His face screws up.

Seen dog shits that looked better, he says.

I do not understand the words but I know they are meant to anger. Myma ignores him and pokes the fire. He glares at her a moment longer then shoves his fingers into the tin, plucks out a crispy grub. I have chomped mine down already and watching him sets my empty mouth chewing. Rearing sudden in me then a want to rip the tin from his hands and snarl him into his corner as if he were a fox trying to lope off with a rabbit leg. I only realise I am growling when Wyn glances at me and snorts through both nostrils. At that my growl drops away and I feel whiny and unsure of myself.

Wyn peers close at the grub before putting it on his tongue. He chews slow. Then grunts, tips his head back, puts the tin to his lips as if drinking. He sets it down empty. I watch his jaws working. The pink of his tongue running over his teeth to collect up all the morsels. He swallows again.

Thank you, he says to Myma's back, no bite now in his voice. Tastes sort of like chicken. Actually really good. Wouldn't have thought it. Thank you.

I want to tell him that now is not when we are supposed to say our thank yous but I can see he is trying to make things better after his yelling and scrapping with Myma, and I am still not really allowed to speak to him. Myma stretches her arms above her head.

Bed-smock on, she says to me. It's late.

Chore-smock half off in the room where we sleep, I listen to the sound of the door opening, four feet stepping outside. From the window I see the outlines of Myma and Wyn walking towards the trees. Myma behind, a lamp in one hand and the end of Wyn's rope in the other. Her taking him out so he can empty himself into a hole. His feet untied. He walks a hunched shuffle of a walk. I think how the Rot-hole must ache him still, and I feel a pang that confuses me and shake my head to joggle it out.

Wyn trips and Myma yanks him from falling. I imagine the wrist-jerk of the rope, the skin-strip, and my own wrists tingle. At the edge of the clearing they stop. Myma points to a wide beech and Wyn steps behind it. The edge of his smock flaps around the trunk. His bared bent knee. The slice of Myma's face that I can see wears a bored look, a lip-curl of irritation as she watches him. And something else in the way her shoulders pull close to her neck, something uneasy and a little sad. Wyn must say something then from behind the tree because Myma's expression hardens. She shakes her head, no.

Then they are coming back, Myma striding now in front, Wyn stumbling behind. He keeps flicking his head to get his hair out of his eyes. Myma's face yellow and shifting in the lamplight. Her eyes catch mine in the window. Black jolt of her seeing me watching. Them then out of sight.

12

She never thought of the child as having anything to do with what had happened to her. The girl was of Maya's body. She was of the place where Maya had birthed her. No other place, no other body.

Maya pointed to the child, then to herself.

'You are my daughter,' she said, 'and I am Maya.'

She made a closed fence of her arms.

'And this,' she said, 'this is where we live.'

The story Maya told was simple, like a nursery rhyme. In it, good and bad were clear and separate in a way they had not been before she'd drawn her line of branches between them.

'In the dark beyond the fence, creeps the rotted thing. Sleep you sound now, little daughter, safe from everything.'

She saw how her daughter's head tilted, the small ear filling like a cup with her voice. She felt that she was making something.

She did not think of it as lying, and to her it wasn't. There had to be something wrong and rotten in the world, some foulness that could get inside a person and empty them of good. Men, Maya knew, could spoil like vegetables with blight. And that particular rottenness, it could be passed on, father to son. It was easier to think of those who had hurt her as hollowed, their humanity gone. If she tried to understand them in any other way, things became muddy and unclear. So she separated dark from light, and in this way she made her own sense of things.

One evening Maya was plucking a crow. The child was sitting on the floor under the stool. Her fingers grabbed at the black feathers as they fell around her. Her lips moved and let out noises. She caught a feather in her fist and held it up to Maya. From the burbling of sound came a word, the girl's first.

'Myma,' she said. 'Myma.'

Maya stopped her plucking and looked at her daughter. Yes, she thought, that is right, I am something else now. She took the word and put it on. Myma. She stared into the grey-green eyes that were not like her own but were the child's only, and she saw herself reflected differently in them. The grey woman croaked beside her head.

In the woods the girl was touch and listen and scent. She learned from the forest as she learned from Maya. She trapped its creatures in her hands to feel their scuttling and lifted them to her ears to hear their buzzing. Her head cocked at birdcalls and at snapping twigs. Her nostrils flared and she squatted low to set her nose against the ground. When something pleased her, she yipped. When she was unhappy, she cringed into herself and whimpered. When she was angry or frustrated, she made growling noises and spat.

She grew fast and Maya added more pelts to the cloak she had stitched for her from rabbit skin. Soon she was too big for the sack in which Maya had cut holes for arms and head, so Maya sewed the holes back up and returned the sack to the hook. There were still a good number of spare sheets piled under the bed, but to conserve the cloth Maya made her daughter a long baggy shift a little larger than her own, the hem and sleeves doubled over and stitched back, to be let down as she grew.

The girl wriggled out of her clothing whenever she could.

'Blocks the touching knowing of my skin,' she said to Maya, patting her cheeks with both hands.

The child had grown around language rather than into it. She spoke with her whole body. Her fingers moved with her mouth as if to press and pinch the words into the shape of what she wanted to say. Maya taught her to read using the labels from the tins, a stick to scratch letters into the ground. There was no need to explain what all the words meant. Words that had once been relevant had no bearing in this place, no object to contain them. It felt important that the child should be able to read, though Maya could not explain to herself why. What is it for? she asked herself, but the answers were uncomfortable, so she pushed them down.

She let her daughter carry the rabbits they caught, their necks slack in the crooks of her elbows. The girl watched carefully when the creatures that beat and squirmed became still in Maya's hands. Maya saw her beginning to understand herself as predator. The child made growling, uncoordinated dashes at rodents and birds. She copied Maya's traps. The tiny snares she looped from single strands of grass were flimsy and caught nothing.

Pained by her daughter's disappointment, Maya trapped a shrew in an empty tin baited with worms. She killed it and fitted its neck into one of the girl's clumsy loops.

'Look,' she said. 'Look what you have caught.'

The girl opened her eyes wide and twitched her hands about and insisted they cook the shrew for dinner. Through a mouthful of tiny bones she said to Maya, 'Soon I will trap by myself, won't I?'

Dread curled in Maya's stomach with the shrew's tail.

'Not yet,' she replied, her voice tight. 'You cannot be by yourself. You need me with you.'

She told herself that this would always be true. She had

never before felt necessary to another. But the child, the child would always need her. Maya sang, her voice soft and toneless.

'In the dark beyond the fence, creeps the rotted thing.'

The child's eyes clouded with fear and Maya felt guilty but satisfied. She ignored the grey woman who sat under the table, opening and closing her hand as if expecting each time to find something held in it.

Hell Shit

Hell shit, I say to the nettles.

My stick slices through the air to chop the pricking leaves. Around my feet they drop like dead things.

Hell, I say again. Shit.

Guilty thrill at this speaking. Those are Rotted words, Myma said. But if Wyn is no longer Rotted then I do not see how his words can be. Myma has spoken those kinds of spiked words too, when Wyn first came to the clearing and she threw her anger at him with get the fuck away I'll fucking kill you. Is the word Rotted if it's in Myma's mouth? And how does a word become Rotted, without a body there for the Rot to hollow out?

Thwack-fwap of the fleshy stems as I cut them.

Shit, I say. Shhhhhhit. Pissit.

I hit another nettle, hard enough to fling the severed part up into the air. Things used to be simple and easy to understand. Hum to myself the known tune as I strike stem after stem with my stick.

In the dark beyond the fence creeps the Rotted thing. Sleep you sound now, little Daughter, safe from everything.

Rot outside the fence. Stay inside the fence and the Rot won't come. That all mixed together and confusing now.

Rotter that is no longer Rotter living in the corner. Rotter that arrived with a name and a mouth full of words, Rotter that breathes and eats like us. I snap my striking stick and hurl it away.

The chilly sun creeps across the sky. I go between the markers and hear Myma doing her chore of chopping wood, the thud and chock and split of the axe. Find one rabbit strangled dead in a snare. Sack it.

I do not return straightaway to the house but step from the path and through the dense hazel thicket towards the place where I found Myma and Wyn covered in red. Where Myma's shiny shard went into Wyn and made a hole and spilled the Rot. I never saw what she cut from him. The lump of Rot she says is gone but also not gone, and gone where anyway? My eyes move over the ground as if I might see the shrivelly twist of it crawling through the leaves, still wet from Wyn's insides.

There beneath the thick of brambles, an odd fold in the undergrowth. Sag inward when I poke. Green-brown and soggy. Thorns snag it from my pull and I scratch my forearms ripping it free.

Wyn's sack, waterlogged and filthy where it has sat on the ground through light and dark and rain. The wetness of it dragging heavy. A clanking as I lift it by the strap. Fastenings of tricky metal prongs and loops. Fiddle at them but the cloth is swollen with damp, the metal stiff. Rip them then. A rank smell rising up.

I lift out a soft stained bundle. Unwrap to a maggoty grey mess. The mushrooms are slimy, stinking. Shake them to the ground for the worms to carry back into the earth. The thing that wrapped them is my own gathering sack, slick with mushroom sludge. This I will take back, tell Myma I found it among the ferns, that a bird or badger must have eaten its fill of what I gathered. I roll up my sack around the grot and stick it into the waist of my trousers. Flick at a stray maggot.

From Wyn's green sack now I pull a torn, crumpled thing, thin and flimsy like the labels from the tins, but silver, shiny, almost reflective, like Myma's cutting glass. Scrunch it for the dry-leaf sound. Then I read the words, Milk, Chocolate, and saliva sops my mouth. In the creases I find some specks of brown. Poke my tongue right into the pockety parts and whine at the taste, every part of me saying, ultimate, crea–my. The sweet smell clings even after I have licked it clean. Tuck the shiny scrap into my pouch to hold under my nose again later.

And here, a clear brown container. Clickering when I shake. Pull and twist but the lid stays, turning then snapping back into place, turning then snapping back. Through the sides I can see little white pellets, like my small dropped-out teeth but rounded. A kind of seed perhaps. I would like to keep the container as a rattler for dancing but I am sure Myma would not allow it, and it is too loud a thing to hide in my pouch without her asking me, What's that rattling, Root-Daughter? Back into Wyn's sack then, clicker-clatter.

Next I wrap my hand around a glass bottle like the ones we use for collecting grubs and birch sap, like the bottles of puddle and mud in my Museum. This one almost the length of my wrist, half-filled with water. A swill that burns and stings white in my nostrils when I untwist at the top. I cough and twist shut. Water gone bad. Not a thing for drinking.

There at the bottom of Wyn's sack, my knife. I curl my fingers to the grip and feel the fit of it, the swiping talon at the end of my arm. Grunt my satisfaction. How stunted my hand has felt without it. And there is another knife here, small, a blade that swings outward from a wooden hilt. I think of the cut snares, of the hands that cut them, and of how strange it is that those hands are now tied up in the corner of the house. Sit and fiddle with Wyn's knife a while, flick the short blade in and out. It would be useful to have a knife for each of my hands. I picture myself hacking two-knifed at the brambles and the tangling ivy, and I grin. Myma does not have to know about it if I use it in the forest only, a hidden claw. The knife goes into my pouch for keeping.

Arm plunged nearly to the shoulder, my scrabbling fingers in the corners find something hard and round. I hold it up, let the light show it to me. I see what it is and the seeing stops my breath. A wooden face. Tiny, perfect. Two eyes set wide. Shut mouth, high cheeks. Something of Wyn in the tilt of the brows, the slant and point of the nose, though also not-Wyn, something different, of itself. I peer into the blind eyes. Half expect them to blink, the tiny wooden mouth to open and speak. Wonder what words it would say. I have only ever seen two faces outside my own. Myma's known one, Wyn's strange one. And now this wooden one. Looking into its eyes is like hearing a muffled voice. Some meaning in it, but no way of grasping.

I am almost afraid to put the face to my ear, uncertain what I might hear in it. Some terrible clamour from beyond the fence. But when I do, when I cup the little wooden head at my cheek, the sounding that fills me is gentle, a hush of breath that draws only in, never going out. And deeper, behind the breath, or inside it, a warm and chirring trill, like birdsong when it sounds from the other side of the forest, like when I am lying in the bed and listening to a nightjar sending its noise burring into the gap between light and dark. And the feel of it as I listen, as I hear. A feeling of holding, as when Myma puts her thumb under my chin.

Wetness in my eyes that I blink away, confused. I set the face in the crook of my name-root in my pouch. The wooden eyes watch up at me as I pull closed the opening. I will not show Myma what I have found. The Lesson I have learned from the blue hand is that finds like these must be hidden.

Scoop a shallow hole in the earth below the dead leaves and push into it Wyn's sack with the bottle of bad water and the rattling container of white seeds. Bury these in the dirt and leaves.

I step wary into the house, hoping Myma will not see the hiddenness in me.

She is bent stitching something, and seems hardly to notice my coming in. Wyn coughs in the corner. I point my feet towards him and stare. He stares back. Cloth laid out on the floor in front of him. On the cloth, two neat piles, hazelnuts and their husks. Wyn's mouth pulls into a sort of smile as I look, and I have to frown hard to keep my own mouth from twitching.

He is doing a chore, I say to Myma.

Her head stays down.

Might as well make use of him, she says.

He does chores now, I say.

Yes, she says. While he's here he'll do chores. That's how it is here. That's how we do things.

So he'll do This-and-That, too?

I didn't say that, she says.

Can you pick that up for me? Wyn asks.

One long finger points to my feet. I look down at the hazelnut beside my heel. Glance at Myma. She does not shake her head or dart me a black look so I think it must be okay for me to hear Wyn now. I toss the hazelnut into his corner and he catches it, his hands at the ends of his bound wrists opening like fleshy petals on a stem. I imagine his hands around the folding knife, his hands scraping and chipping that small perfect face into the wood. I want to ask about the wooden face but I do not want it to be taken from me. Wyn blows on the hazelnut, adds it to the pile.

It'd be an easier job without my hands tied, he mutters.

Myma's mouth presses tight and she does not answer.

I know, I know, you don't need to tell me, Wyn replies to nothing.

I look closer at what Myma is stitching, the sacking cut to the shape of trousers too long for either of our legs.

Won't they trail off the ends of my feet? I ask her.

They aren't for you, she says.

I tilt my head.

Even longer on your legs, I say.

She stabs the needle again.

They aren't for me either, she says.

What then?

For him.

For Wyn?

At his name her jaw ticks.

Yes, she says. Put another log on the fire, Root-Daughter.

I heft one from the pile stacked high with fresh wood from Myma's chopping. A spray of sparks when I drop it into the hearth.

What does Wyn need trousers for? I ask.

Because it's cold outside, she says.

But he's inside, I say.

Stop bothering or you'll slow me down and food will be late, she says.

I pick up the long stirring stick from beside the fire and poke Wyn in the backside with it.

Throw me a nut, I say.

If he is a trousered thing as well as a named thing, if he is a thing that has chores to do, then surely he is a thing that can be spoken to. Myma watches, frowning, but says nothing. Wyn says, Oww, then picks up a nut and throws it to me. A clumsy, tied-hands throw, but I catch it. Fit the nut into my cheek and chomp down.

Myma asks no questions when I give her the damp mushroomy sack and tell her, Look, I found my knife in the bracken, only says, Ah, good, and puts the sack aside to be washed. When we eat our stew, Myma spoons a few small pieces of meat into a tin for Wyn.

Thank you, he says, blinking.

Thank yous are not for now, I tell him.

In the room where we sleep, Myma takes her turn at choosing This-and-That, and fetches the copying crown from the crate. Behind the sheeted doorway, Wyn shifts about in his corner.

I always think how the copying crown is like a piece of the fence, or the fence shrunk to the size of the head. Twigs woven to a circle, longer twigs pointing straight up. Myma's hair twisted into it, all the way round.

I'll go first, Myma says.

She sits the copying crown on her head. The twigs reach upwards like crooked fingers. The plait on her shoulder twitches.

Ready? she asks.

Yes.

She raises her arm. I raise my arm. She stands on one leg. I stand on one leg. She tilts forward at the pelvis, arms outstretched, leg lifted, toes pointed. I copy, wobbling on my ankle. She darts to the window and back to the middle of the room. I follow. She does a tricky thing with her hands then, flapping them over her head and twisting them one over the other as she brings them down. In trying to copy, my hands get lost.

I win, she says. You'll have to watch more closely, Root-Daughter.

She wins the next by balancing on her heel until I fall over. Then it is my turn. The copying crown digs into my scalp when I put it on. I dip my head and the twigs stretch their shadows up the walls, large as trees. Myma's second shadow moving among them.

Wyn coughs on the other side of the sheet. Myma tautens at the sound but her eyes stay on me. I kick my leg sideways. Myma kicks her leg sideways. I make a snarling face. She snarls back. I sit on the floor and put my toes into my mouth. Her toes go into her mouth. I stand upside-down on my hands, legs against the wall, twig-tips of the copying crown scratching the floor. Myma's bed-smock falls around her eyes and she flop-tumbles from the handstand all bundled, which makes us laugh.

I win, I say.

She spits hair from her mouth and grins at me.

I'm going to win the next one, she says. I can feel it.

I open my mouth wide. Myma opens hers. Close my mouth and hers snaps shut only a blink after. I reach my arms to the sides like wings. At exactly the same moment, Myma spreads hers. Her eyes on mine unblinking. We drop our arms in a single beat. We jump and land, our four feet hitting the floor together. We spin, hands slicing the air, then both stop spinning in the same breath. Myma moves when I move. She is still when I am still. It is like standing opposite my own reflection in the dark window. Except I am not sure whether I am the solid body or the flat one that looks back.

I move my hands to clap but before my palms touch, Myma's hands have already slapped together. She is grinning again. Head crow-cocked, eyes glinting. I crouch to roll and she is already on the floor, feet over head. I run on all fours to the bed and she is bounding ahead of me. She is upright before I have thought of standing. She has overtaken me in the copying, she knows what I will do before I do it. Now she puts her arms straight up. My own arms shoot towards the ceiling without me telling them to. Myma drops her arms and mine follow. She covers her mouth with her right hand and pinches her nose with her left. My hands can only copy. She watches me, her chest still. I cannot move my hands. My eyes beginning to leak. Push of trapped breath. Then Myma takes her hands away and mine drop with them, the air yelping into my lungs. Blood surges in my skull and I have to crouch, head between knees. The copying crown falls off. When I look up, Myma is wearing it.

I win, she says.

Our heads touch in the bed. Curve of bone against bone, so close under the thin of skin.

Thank you, Daughter, for bringing the rabbit, she says. And I don't have any sorrys.

Thank you, Myma, for cooking the rabbit, I say. And thank you for chopping the wood.

I pause. At the back of my lips the nudge of sorrys that I cannot say. Sorry, Myma, for not telling you about Wyn's sack and what I took from it, sorry for hiding things from you. And realising as I think this that I am not sorry, or not sorry enough to say it. I want to keep what I have found, the things that are mine now. I do not want them burned to ash and scattered around the clearing.

I don't have any sorrys, I say.

Okay, she says.

Then, without really meaning to, I say, Thank you to Wyn for shelling the nuts.

Myma's eyes are expressionless.

Yes, she says.

This dark there is difficulty in sleeping. I think about the things of Wyn I have held in my hands, and I think about copying, how Myma always gets ahead of me and how I have never actually won when she is wearing the copying crown, never managed to flip the copying around the way she does, never seen into her the way she sees into me. It always ends with me following her, her seeing what I will do before I have thought of doing it, like how she knew me as Daughter before I knew myself as anything. The hidden things in my pouch murmur and sigh and crinkle. This knowing that is mine only. Keep it in my mouth.

13

Once, Maya left her daughter alone. They were playing a game and the game was called silence. Maya had suggested it because her head was sore with the split-open heat of the summer, and because the girl had fidgeted and chattered all through that evening, with her 'Listen, Myma, there is a woodpecker peckering a tree, can you hear it?' and 'I ate one of the small apples just to see but it squinched my face so I think it will be a while longer until they are good for tasting' and 'Why do the nettles not prickle us on the tongues when we eat them?' and the incessant noise had battered away at Maya's skull like a crow smashing a snail on a rock.

They lay toe-to-head and straight-legged, their backs on the floor and their arms at their sides. The aim, Maya told her daughter, was to be as still and silent as possible.

'Like being dead?' the girl asked. 'Like being a pigeon after its neck is snapped and its feet stop kicking?'

'It's more like existing quietly for a moment,' Maya told her. 'Like if you were a mushroom, or a caterpillar in a cocoon.'

With her eyes closed, Maya tried to enter the silence, to sink herself to an empty place where she could float alone and unfeeling. The girl shifted beside her. Maya felt the sound of it like a graze against her skin. She tried to settle, tried again to drop away from herself, from her body, from the body of her child. While she lay here she would not be Myma, she would not even be Maya. She would be solitary and nameless, without memory or thought or feeling. The hard stone floor set off the ache in her head. Her inner arm tickled and the day-old wasp sting on her calf pinched at her. She heard the girl's breathing as it blew through her nostrils, the bending and clicking of her toes beside Maya's head. As Maya lay there she began to feel that she could even hear the girl's thoughts, scurrying about like the mice that had once made their home under the floor in Maya's parents' house, their quick paws that her mother had stopped with glue strips.

The unrelenting noise of the child filled Maya's silence as if it came from inside her own body. Her daughter, the loudest sound in the world.

She stood up abruptly. The girl's eyes opened. Maya looked down at her.

'I'm going out now,' she said.

'Are we not doing silence any more?' the girl asked, reaching her arms over her head and arching her back.

'I'm going,' Maya said again.

The girl sat up.

'Where are we going, Myma?'

'I'm going into the forest.'

'Why are we going into the forest? It's dark.'

'I'm going. Just me. Alone.'

The girl stared at her, uncomprehending. Then she said again, 'Why are we going into the forest?'

'You're not going. You're staying here.'

'Without you?'

The girl's arms went around her knees and held them. Maya felt the pluck of her daughter's growing distress. She strained against it.

'Yes,' she said. 'You're staying. I'm going.'

Maya left the room before the girl could ask another question. She went to the door and out under the thin moon. She walked through the forest, all the way to the fence she'd spent these years building, fortifying. There she stopped and looked across. She waited for the silence but still the creak and buzz of her child came loud and insistent, pressing on her, and she thought, Maybe this is what it is, maybe being Myma means to give up having a silence of my own.

She saw in her mind a room. The room was not like the one she had left her daughter sitting in, with its scribbled walls and stirred mess of a bed, but starkly clean: a tiled floor and a window over the sink looking out onto a small trimmed garden and the cut scrub of fields beyond. In the room a girl sat drawing at a table and a woman stood beside the window, sucking on a cigarette. The two looked somewhat alike but the woman's expression was tense, and so her face seemed to have more corners to it than the girl's. The woman wore a scarf tied around her neck.

Somewhere outside the room a door opened and closed. The girl sat straighter in her seat and the woman tightened like a hard grip. She turned her head towards the door opposite the window, as if waiting for this one to open too. On the other side, heavy feet lurched. They paused outside the room where the girl and the woman waited, then the feet moved away and up, and the eyes of both the girl and the woman lifted for a moment to the ceiling, where the uneven tread came to a stop. Overhead there was a creaking, a slumping.

The woman's hand was steady as it reached into the sink and made an ashed stump of the cigarette. Then the woman went outside and walked to the end of the garden. The wind flung her scarf behind her and put furrows in her shirt. She stood facing the fields over the hedge.

The girl watched the back of the woman through the

window, and Maya watched with her. She wanted to take the girl's drawing and run out after the woman, put the paper into her hands and say, 'She made this for you. I made it for you.'

The woman's head fell back and her mouth opened. Neither Maya nor the girl could hear the sound that came out of her. They only saw how, beyond, the whole field of crows lifted into the air, as if a huge, bellowing beast had gone stampeding through their midst.

There was movement at Maya's side. She did not need to turn her head to know that the grey woman was there.

'I'm not stuck like that,' Maya said. 'I chose to be here. I could leave if I wanted.'

The grey woman cackled like a magpie. Then she made a circle of her arms around Maya. In the grey woman's hold Maya felt a sudden stillness, a hush, as if surrounded by thick walls. It was not peaceful, only deadening. A silence that drowned. She jerked herself from it.

The child was still sitting on the floor when Maya returned. Maya saw how the taut wrapped limbs loosened with relief as she entered the room.

'Was it part of This-and-That?' her daughter asked.

'Yes,' said Maya. 'We were doing one stays, one goes.'

The girl pushed out her lower lip and frowned hard at Maya.

'You can't change your choice in the middle of This-and-That.'

'No. You're right. That wasn't fair of me.'

'I should get two choices next dark.'

Maya went close and held the child's chin with her thumb. Her daughter met her gaze, brows low.

'I didn't like doing one stays, one goes,' the girl said. 'I don't want to do it again.'

'I didn't like it either,' Maya told her. 'It was a silly idea.'

The Bone Comes From the Tail

The bone comes from the tail end of the rabbit carcass. I pluck it suck it clean from the boil of broth and swallow down the name in it, slot it into my skeleton where it gives me a new joint, a new way of being Daughter.

What are you now, Daughter?

I am Bone.

Bone-Daughter. Knuckle-Kin. Wrap-Around-the-Marrow-Daughter.

Bone is hard and smooth. Bone lies secret and strong under the flesh. Bone doesn't speak of what it keeps.

Before Wyn-come, I did not hold secrets from Myma. Now I carry them in my pouch alongside my name-bone. As I scratch my itch in the ash tree I hold the chocolatey crinkle to my nose and breathe it. I fight brambles and bracken with my two knives. And when I stand beside the fence I hold the little carved head in my palm and I imagine it living-sized, coming towards me.

Two darks after my finding of Wyn's sack, a high wind snaps a crashing branch from an oak. Myma goes out and chops and chops with her axe. She says we need the wood. She says there'll be a harsh cold coming. She says she can feel it on the way.

She throws the new-stitched trousers into Wyn's corner.

Put these on, she says. You can help us bring the wood in.

Three of us in the forest then. Three of us on our way to do chores. Myma in front. Wyn, trousered, in the middle. Me following behind.

Myma leads Wyn by a rope around the neck. He mutters something like notagoddamndog when she jerks it.

Before we left the house Myma told me to keep your knife out, Bone-Daughter, just in case he tries anything. I hold the knife loose at my side. I do not feel any threat from the once-Rotter in the way that Myma does. And his knife is in my pouch so I know I am the stronger one. Watch him from behind as we tread the forest. His hair all red knots down his back. His arms swinging with his walk, rope-blistered wrists untied for chores. He wears a blanket like a cloak over his smock. The trousers seemed long when Myma was making them, but on Wyn's legs they are short. A gap of pale leg above his brown boots, the boots the only things she didn't burn, because she said they'd melt all over the hearth and make the house smell bad.

Wyn jumpy and nervous, head flicking at small noises. His hand comes up to slip a finger around the rope at his neck. Tug from Myma to make him walk faster. He stumbles, stops the fall by skidding his palm against a trunk. He doesn't say anything then, does not spit his words at Myma even when the palm starts to bleed. Myma's walking feet are light in her boots. Her mouth a slight curve as she pulls the rope.

We stop beside the oak, the split stack that Myma has made of the fallen limb. Above, the splintery mess where the branch tore away.

Let's shift this then, Myma says.

Wyn only stands, staring at the pile of wood.

Are you helping or not? she asks. You said you wanted to help. So get on with it.

Wyn begins to laugh. Wheezing and barking. The backs of his hands wipe water from his eyes. His shoulders shake. His hand goes to his neck, to the rope.

I thought, he says, I really thought – thought you were going to bloody hang me. I thought, She's finally going to do it. But we are actually here to collect wood.

He laughs harder. Back-bend and belly-clutch. We wait for him to finish.

The chore is a tiring one. We trudge back and forth between the oak and the shed. Our backs slung with wood. Our arms and legs aching. The skin of my shoulders rubs raw as Wyn's wrists. Wyn carries almost as much wood as me. Myma carries the most. All through the chore she keeps a tight hold on Wyn's rope.

When we are returning with the final load, Wyn stops suddenly and sets his bundle down. He bends low and coughs and coughs until a reddish glot spits from his mouth. Myma watches as he squats and puts his head on his knuckles. I nudge him with the toe of my boot to make him stand but Myma holds up a hand. She lets the rope go slack. She doesn't yank to get him walking. After some long ragged breaths, Wyn stands and hefts the logs, teeth bared, brow damp. He begins to walk again, feet unsteady.

Stop, Myma says.

Wyn halts, sways. The look of him a little frightened at Myma's approach. She pulls on the rope again, but pulls it downward, towards the ground. Wyn is forced to stoop, then to sit. Myma sits too, then they are both sitting in the dirt and leaves, so I sit. Nothing else is spoken. When the heaving of Wyn's breath has shallowed to a steady in-out, we all stand up and carry on.

I go back out alone to check the traps before dark. I am

giddy at finding three rabbits. Pop their necks and run all the way back.

Wyn is sitting on my stool when I step through the door. His hands wrap around my R-for-rabbit mug. His neck is untied, the skin chafed pink. Only his left ankle bound to the table now. The steam curling off my mug smells like dandelion roots.

I swing the rabbit sack onto the table. It makes a satisfying thwack in its heaviness.

I got three rabbits, I say.

I do not know why I look at Wyn when I say this. Something in me wanting a response from him. For him to say, That is a lot of rabbits, Bone-Daughter, or, You are very good at snaring, Bone-Daughter.

Mmm, says Wyn.

I am flattened, and look instead to Myma.

I got three rabbits, I tell her.

She pulls them from the sack.

They look good, Bone-Daughter, she says.

Three, I say, glancing again at Wyn.

He snorts.

How many rabbits was that? he asks.

Three, I tell him. I already told you.

Yes, he says. You certainly did.

Yes, I say. I did.

An odd, knowing laughter in his speaking. I go and stand right beside him, my knees touching the stool. He does not seem to like my closeness. Some alarm in him. He stands up fast.

Sorry, he says, I've taken your seat.

Yes, I say. And you've taken my mug.

I'm almost finished with it, he says.

He swills and gulps and retreats to his corner.

That did help a bit, he says to Myma, thanks.

I sit sideways on my stool and stare at him. He does not look back but I see how he wriggles under my eyes.

It's not polite to stare, he says.

Myma laughs.

What's polite? I ask.

He just blinks.

Is your Rot-hole still hurting? I ask.

My – oh. That. Not so much now, I suppose. That's mostly healed up.

But it hurt when we were carrying the wood?

Ah, he says. No, that's something else. My chest. It's bad.

Probably the Rot made it bad, I tell him. When it ate out your insides through your back.

Him the staring one now.

Is that right? he says.

Yes, I say. You need Keep-Safes to stop it coming back.

Well, he says, I don't know what a Keep-Safe is. Not sure it would be much help with what I've got anyway.

Myma's ear has been tilted to our speaking and now she throws me a sharp look. No more talking then. I watch Wyn's hands fiddling with the thin silver cord at his neck. Tiny linked loops of metal. I want to touch it. I want to ask about faces scraped tiny into wood. Wish I could speak out of Myma's hearing.

Myma goes to Wyn's corner and bends over him. He yelps a word that Myma would call Rotted, and Myma straightens, a red hank of hair in her fist.

What did you do that for? he says. Jesus.

I need your hair, Myma says.

Shit, he says, fingers probing at his skull. Didn't have to rip it out.

Myma goes back to her stool.

God, Wyn says. I think you've made it bleed. Yes, look. Blood.

He holds out a red-smeared finger. Myma doesn't look.
You'll survive, she tells him.
Barely, apparently, says Wyn.
Myma snorts. She turns to me.
Fetch water, Bone-Daughter.

We fill ourselves with the rabbits I have brought and because I am tired from all the wood-carrying I fall asleep with my spoon in my hand. Half-wake to Myma lifting me from my stool, draping my arms over her shoulders, pulling my legs to wrap her waist. I dangle around her smallness, long and sprawly, but she hardly strains as she hefts me. Wyn's colourless eyes watch from the corner as I am carried into the room where we sleep. The look in them wrinkles me, pinches me out of myself. As if Myma and me are as strange and confusing to him as he is to us.

What is this?

Myma's voice wakes me to a scent of damp earth and decay. My smelling nose lifting me from the bed. Crust-eyed blinking around for the root of the smell. Something filthy slumped at Myma's feet. Patches of dark green showing through dirt. Myma shakes the thing by the strap and it rattles. Wyn's buried sack, unearthed here.

Got up early to add new Keep-Safes to the fence, Myma says. I found this half-buried. Some fox had dug it out. You know what it is, don't you?

Myma has pulled the hidden thing from the ground. She has pointed to what I have done and asked me to name it.

It is Wyn's sack, I tell her.

What was it doing in the ground? she asks.

I buried it, I reply, unable to keep the words from spilling at her feet.

Why?

I wanted to hide it.

Why?

I didn't want you to burn the things.

Myma pulls out the brown container of rattly seeds, the bottle of bad water.

These things? she asks. Did you take anything from them?

I shake my head.

Are you lying?

I shake my head again.

Were there other things in here?

I nod, I cannot do anything else.

Show me.

I fetch my pouch, dread heavy in me. Myma watches silent as I lay out the crackly chocolate-tanging scrap and the folding knife. Hold the little wooden head tight before placing it with the rest. Still Myma does not speak. I hunch low and put my head on the floor and do not look at her. Wonder what the Lesson will be. Wonder if my secret-keeping is worse than the other things I have done, worse than picking up the blue hand, or asking questions. I think it is. I think it is much much worse. Tuck my hands under my armpits and squeeze. After a long while, Myma sighs.

Oh my Daughter, she says.

No anger in her words. I sneak a glance and see her eyes not hard and narrowed but drooping at the edges. Her knees bend and she squats down. Black eyes on mine.

How strange this all must be for you, she murmurs.

I am so surprised by her response that I say nothing. Myma's eyes move between me, the chocolatey-crinkly, the knife, the wooden head.

These are all his? she asks. You took them?

I found them, I say. His sack was under a bush. I thought it would be okay to touch them because he's not Rotted any more because you cut it out. I just wanted to look at them.

Myma nods. She stretches a hand to pick up the carved wooden face. Cups it at the centre of her palm and gazes down.

Why didn't you tell me? she asks quietly.

I cringe from the question but there are no claws in it. More a sadness. I am not sure if this is worse than anger.

I wanted to keep them, I say. I didn't want them burned like his clothes.

Her eyes stay on the wooden face.

It is beautiful, she says.

I blink. Beautiful. That word she only uses for things like dark clear skies and jay feathers.

Yes, I say. It is.

Her fingers delicate as she holds it. Her touch light on the grain of the cheeks. Wonder if she hears in it what I heard. A hope in me that she will tell me what it means, this face. But her hand closes over it. She stands, leaving her second shadow kneeling.

She puts the carved face back into the sack with the crackling scrap, the glass bottle and the rattling brown container. The folding knife slips into the pocket of her chore-smock. Pang of loss as I watch the things go from me. No longer my secret. Stupid, brittle Bone. My fingers twitch and my eyes sting. Myma leans towards me and puts her thumb under my chin.

I'm not going to burn them, she says. I'm going to give them back to him.

Even the knife? I ask.

She pauses.

No sense in giving a Rotter back its claw, she says. That I'll keep for now.

She picks up Wyn's sack and stumps across the room. Turns then and points to the muddy trail she has made.

Clean that up, will you, she says.

She leaves. The sheet over the doorway ripples, settles. I hear Wyn's rough waking voice. Mumble of what sounds like a question but no answer from Myma.

Head still on the floor, I lift my feet into the air. My bed-smock covers my eyes. I feel jolted about and uncertain. I can't help feeling that Myma has understood something I have not. And no Lesson at all for my secret-keeping, though I am sure what I did was bad. Not even skin-pinches. Maybe the Lesson will come later. Maybe it will be the worst Lesson, but worse even than that. Maybe after this Myma will step off the log into the strangle of the rope. The thought puts a sick feeling in me. Drop my legs and roll forward on the dirty floor.

Nothing is said about Wyn's things while we do our chores. Neither when we return at dark-come to prepare food. Something is different, though. Something changed in the set of Myma's mouth when Wyn coughs, the slant of her brows when he asks please for a slight loosening of the rope around his ankle. We are about to sit for food when Myma turns to me.

Fetch a log from the shed, she says. One of the big ones not yet split.

I look at the pile of split logs and kindling stacked beside the hearth.

There's already lots of firewood here, I say.

Do it, she says.

I heft the log inside and she has me put it at one end of the table. She sets down our full bowls, then plonks a tin of stew at the same end as the log. Then she sits on her stool and looks into Wyn's corner.

Well? she says. Or would you rather eat on the floor?

Wyn's mouth parts. Then his face does something odd. Like a smile but more painful. He stands up, shuffles over. Puts his backside on the flat of the log. It wobbles underneath him. He sits lower than us, knees bent up awkward. His eyes move between our faces. Myma is already eating, no longer looking at him. He does one short laugh. Lifts his hands high.

And so the dog dines with the master, he says.

14

Her mother's voice came shouting up through the floor, a hurl of 'Choosing to rot yourself' and 'Can't any more, just can't.' It stamped on her father's voice, which struggled underneath like something trapped and bleeding, a stuck rat eating its own tail.

In her room, Maya held her palm above the flame from her mother's lighter. If she concentrated hard, she could do this long enough that the pain would turn from crackling and red to flat and white. Then she could leave the hand there and sit in that whiteness, her eyes unfocused and a low buzz in her ears.

'Evelyn,' her father's voice whimpered, 'please.'

The heat bit Maya's fingers. She drew the hand away and flexed it to a fist before breathing in and out and placing the hand back over the lighter. She felt herself edging towards the place where the pain would flatten out, but as she watched the flicker she was poked by a memory. The memory was of a power cut in winter, sudden blackness and matches struck in the dark. The fridge had stopped humming and the radio had gone silent. Maya's father had gone out with a torch to the neighbours' and had come back saying, 'It's the whole road, we'll just have to wait it out.' They sat up late in the kitchen wrapped in blankets and Maya's father tried to make toast by forking bread over a candle flame. Her father's eyes were still green then, not yet reddened at the rims. The toast tasted black and acrid, so Maya's mother fetched from the freezer the ice-cream rolls meant for the church fundraiser.

'They'll only melt otherwise,' she said.

They ate the rolls with knives and forks. Maya drank tepid milk while her parents drank brandy, and later her father whirled her mother pink-cheeked to no music while Maya made a beat on the table with the hilt of her fork.

Something broke downstairs. From her father, a wounded sound. Her mother's voice screwed tight then, 'I won't have it in the house any more, I won't.'

Maya had never heard her mother speak like this, the feeling coming hard off the tongue. Her hand above the lighter shook slightly. It hurt but she kept the hand there, even when her eyes began to sting. She imagined that her mother must feel like this when she filled herself with hot smoke. Everything that trembled and surged in her, scorched away.

'Shit.' She flicked off the lighter and squeezed the hand against her chest. She heard her father saying, 'Ev—'

The front door closed and there was quiet. Maya felt the blenching of her father's presence suddenly cut out, a dog kicked into the street. She listened for a scrabbling at the door, a pleading word through the letterbox.

From below her window came a snort, a hawk and spit, the thick stuff of a throat being cleared. She looked out and saw the shoulders of her father's coat, and the slow dragged stumble of his going. This is what ending looks like, she thought. She felt in herself an exhaustion like a snuffed flame, and she thought how it would always be like this: she would sit watching the backs of people walking away, and she would do nothing to stop them because of the cold little fear that licked her, the fear that what she held out in her hands would not be enough to turn them back around. She raised a hand to her face. On her fingers she smelled the char of burnt toast.

From downstairs came the sound of six things smashing, one after the other.

In the kitchen, half a dozen egg yolks slipped among the shards of broken bottles. A pool of thin brown liquid spread around them. Maya found her mother standing over the mess, holding the empty egg box. There was a sour smell.

Without looking up, her mother said, 'I did it for you,' and Maya did not know what she meant.

Their Quiet Voices

Their quiet voices in the other room. Myma's empty sleeping space beside me and the twine slack around my toe. A glow in the sheeted doorway.

Does it help at all? says Myma.

From behind the sheet a snap, a shake and rattle.

Helps a bit, comes Wyn's reply after a moment. Keeps it from hurting so much at least. Not much else that can be done.

Is the pain bad?

Comes and goes.

It won't get better?

Seems not. My own fault, I expect. I've put my body through enough. Just stupid shit. Suppose I can't blame it for turning on me now.

Pause.

When did you learn to do it? asks Myma then.

Do what?

Make things. Like this.

Something small and round is set down. The carved face nudges into my mind.

Ah, says Wyn. I don't know really. I've always just – made stuff. Used to get told off a lot for fidgeting. When I was a kid there were these times I'd get really worked up and – well, keeping my hands busy helped. I could sit for ages making animals and little figures. It felt quiet when I did that.

Yes, Myma says. Yes, I know what you mean. That quiet.

Well, you do it too. Make things.

Pause.

I suppose I do, in a way.

Pause.

Who is it? Myma asks.

Light tick of wood against wood. Wyn coughs.

Ah, he says again. It was supposed to be my mother. Though I don't really remember what she looked like.

Something about the way he says that word, Mother, gives it weight, fullness. Like a brimming bowl, or a handful of ground, or the sound of a name when it comes murmuring.

Where is she now? Myma asks.

Ha, says Wyn. God knows. I grew up in foster homes. All they could tell me was she'd been unfit to care for me. That was the word they used, unfit. I was too young to remember. Only thing I had of her was this necklace chain. And my name.

Your father?

Nothing of him.

In my sleepy haze I wonder at the her and him that Wyn speaks of. Other faces, different faces. Try to see them on the backs of my lids.

A part of me always thought she'd turn up one day and explain everything, Wyn is saying. Why she wasn't there, why I couldn't be with her. She didn't ever try to reach me, far as I know. And I didn't have any information about her. I suppose unfit was right. I sometimes wonder if she even thought about me at all.

I know I would, says Myma. If it were me. With my— I don't know that I'd be able to think about anything else.

Maybe. I'd like to believe that. I've always tried to see good, even in bad. But I think a lot of the time people are just thinking about themselves. Most people are selfish.

Myma makes a small noise with her tongue.

I used to think that too, she says. Until her.

Pause.

What about you? Wyn asks.

Me?

You and her. Something happened, didn't it? That's why you're here. That's why she's – the way she is.

The way she is?

You know. Odd.

Pause and the sound of Myma biting her nails.

She's herself, she says. And she's happy. Happier than I ever was.

A stool creaks.

It makes more sense than anything else I've known, Myma says then. Her. Here.

No family?

She's my family.

What about her—?

She doesn't have one.

But—

She doesn't have one.

There is a silence that stretches.

Was there anyone, ever? Wyn asks after a while.

When Myma answers, I can tell by the sound of her voice that she is not looking at Wyn.

There was, she says.

Pause.

And you? says Myma.

A sort of grunt comes from Wyn and I think he must be making some face or movement that I cannot see.

I always managed to fuck it up somehow, he says. I was

pretty restless, especially when I was younger, always getting myself into trouble doing something stupid, taking something stupid. I was so out of it a lot of the time I didn't really care about anything else. I sorted myself out eventually, got work logging, moving trees that had fallen across roads, that sort of thing. It wasn't all bad. But I kept to myself mostly. Then of course I got ill and after that I couldn't much see the point in it all. I'd never really felt at home anywhere. It's hard to explain. I always felt like I should be somewhere else, but never knew exactly where that was. When I left, it felt like the first real decision I'd ever made.

I understand that, says Myma, a depth to her words that tunnels away from me.

Pause.

Why here? Myma asks then. No one has come before. How did you?

How? I just picked a direction. And I walked.

Myma is quiet. I rub the twine between my toes. Wonder how she untied it without waking me, and wish I could also slip out without her noticing so that I could talk to Wyn in the dark too. I have not understood much of what he has said but I want Myma to keep asking him questions, like what is the forest like where he came from, how many other faces has he seen and do they look like his, what does it feel like having a hollow tree in his back, how did he grow the hair on his jaw and where did he get his chocolate delicious ultimate crinkly?

But they are silent for a long while and I have become tired listening to all the not-known words and chasing after slanted meanings. Count my breaths and huddle around the empty space of Myma. Almost sleep but jolt at the rasp of stool on stone floor. The sound of our two mugs being set down, then something untwisting. A liquid pour. The trickle of it thinner than water, closer to air. Clonk of mug against mug. Wyn coughs, spits.

I want to be here, he says then. I'd like to stay. Now I'm here it seems important somehow. I've not felt that before. Please.

Pause.

Okay, Myma replies.

Something settling then. Something passing between them. It softens the air in the house, tension cut. I stretch out my legs and yawn big.

No more words from the other room. Me drifting. Then the slap of bare feet. Open my eyes to thin slits and see Myma pulling aside the sheet. She makes her steps silent like a creep-listen creeper as she walks to the bed but I can hear the clicking of her ankle bones. Close my eyes and feel the small weight of her sinking onto the bed beside me. A biting smell about her. We lie very still. Then she speaks, so quiet it is all bitter breath.

It's not good to listen to things you don't understand, Bone-Daughter.

Open my eyes again and see the black shine of hers looking back. No way of pretending I've been asleep. She has smelled me out.

Yes, Myma, I whisper back.

Okay then, she says.

We fall asleep to the sound of Wyn rumbling in the other room, and when I wake the things I heard have become mixed up with dreams of white seeds scattered in the earth, red birds pecking.

15

She turned around in the forest and her daughter was not there. She felt the terror rising like a shout. Her voice bellowed into the trees. The reply came faint from somewhere above the wind and the swaying branches.

'Myma,' it said, 'the whole tree is underneath me.'

Maya looked up and saw her daughter's small face peering down from a high branch far above her head. Panic bucked in her. The child would fall. Her body would break as it hit branches. The skin would split and the neck would go back on itself. Maya would hear the thump and she would see her daughter's body lying shattered on the ground like the rabbits she used to see along the road on her way to school, their limbs tumbled to impossible angles, glossy innards spilled on the tarmac. It would happen exactly like that and Maya would be unable to prevent it because she had not been watching closely enough. The grey woman ran round and round the trunk, a din of sparrows in her throat. Maya felt dizzy.

'Myma?'

The girl had clambered to the lowest branch. She dropped to the ground like a cat then sprang up fast and came towards Maya. Maya saw the worry that crimped her face.

'Myma,' she said. 'You look like you are going to fall.'

The child had long learned to be afraid of the space outside Maya's boundary of branches but in the forest she moved without fear, as if unaware that her body was a breakable thing. Her boldness alarmed Maya. She watched those curious twitching fingers that wanted to touch everything and she imagined them burned and bitten and bleeding. There was always a bruised elbow or a grazed knee for Maya to dress with the same paste of roots and leaves she had used to give her nipples relief. She rubbed dock and chamomile on the pimplings of nettle stings and insect bites. She took her knife to her daughter's hair after the girl had emerged grinning from a blackberry bush with a bleeding scalp, whole clumps missing from her head.

'But, Myma,' she had said to her mother's distress, 'I got the fat ones.'

In watching her, Maya became acutely aware of all the things that could cause a body harm. The child hardly noticed the small scrapes and tears that appeared in her skin. Yet when it was Maya's skin that took the harm, her daughter was alert. So Maya used her own body as a warning.

'That's how you get burned,' Maya said when the girl, capering naked while they washed clothes, whirled too close to the boiling pot.

She pressed her own wrist to the hot metal. She felt the sear and heard the hiss of flesh. A shiny red mark appeared on her skin. The girl went stiff and her eyes went wide.

'You're hurt, Myma,' she said.

'Yes,' Maya replied. 'When you're careless, it hurts.'

It was effective. The girl cared more about Maya's pain than she did her own. And Maya found she could also use this as a way of showing her daughter that she'd done something wrong, that actions had consequences.

She gave a hard purpling pinch to her own hip whenever the girl asked a question that pressed too hard at the seam across Maya's mind: 'Myma, were you once small like me?' 'Myma, what made your eyebrow scar?' Once, the girl pulled down and dragged through the mud the string of rabbit tails and hair Maya had tied to a tree, so Maya pushed bone needles under her own thumbnails and said, 'What you did was wrong, Daughter. Do not do it again.'

Then there was the time when Maya came into the bedroom and found her daughter wearing the shirt Maya had arrived in. The hem reached her ankles. Her hands flapped in the trailing sleeves. The breath stopped in Maya's chest. She had not seen the shirt since shrugging it off with the rest of her clothes. She'd thought she had cut it to rags along with the overalls and ripped t-shirt but at some point it must have been mixed into the nest of the bed. The fabric still held dirt, blood. It made her sick to think they had been sleeping on it for years.

The girl looked at Maya and grinned. She flicked the collar.

'It's too big I think, but I like it loose,' she said. 'There is a grotty smell though, so maybe we will have to wash it.'

Maya ripped the shirt from her daughter's back. Buttons sprayed like teeth. Shocked silent, the girl only stared.

'Come with me,' Maya told her.

She burned the shirt in the fire. Her daughter stood watching with bare arms. Under the smell of burning fabric lay something rank and meaty. Between the stitches in Maya's mind slipped a memory, the sensation of hard ground under her knees, rough fingers at her jaw. She looked at the child beside her and knew she would suffer any pain to keep her from that. She would give her own body.

The fire had died to a red glow. Maya moved closer to the hearth. At her side the child flinched and made a soft cry but she knew by now not to try to stop her mother. Maya bent her legs and knelt.

Later she lay on her back in the bed with mallow root on

her burned knees. The child slept, her face at Maya's neck. Maya felt the hot breath. She thought of the sound the girl had made before Maya set her knees in the embers, the horror on the child's face at seeing the blistered skin. Her daughter's concern warmed her. She had not felt worried about before.

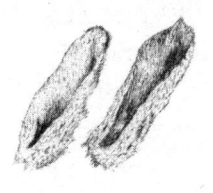

My Mug Smells

My mug smells funny, I tell Myma, it smells like the bad water.

It smells fine, she says. Drink your brew.

She is twitchy and irritable this light-come, face puffy, hands clumsy. Some of the brew splashes on her wrist and she hisses something that sounds like one of Wyn's Rotted words. I put a strip of dried meat on my tongue, a mouthful of hot catch-weed to soften it. The hump of Wyn in the corner has not yet moved. See his green-brown sack now under his head, his untied ankle, the rope coiled on its hook. Myma picks up a stick of kindling and throws it at him. The stick hits him on the rump. He jerks and I giggle. His face appears through the thicket of his hair.

What? he rasps, all squinty-stupid and pink-rimmed.

You're to help her with chores, Myma says. I'm keeping the rest of the potatoes for planting so we'll need roots for stew.

He grunts. My blood jumps.

Are you coming too? I ask Myma.

I've got my own chores, she says.

So just me and Wyn?

That's right.

Without you?

Well, I can't be the one watching him always, can I, Bone-Daughter?

Clacketing from Wyn's corner. He is cracking the lid off his brown container and shaking a white seed into his palm. He tosses it to the back of his throat, swallows.

Anyway, Myma says, it was you that wanted to teach him about what we do here, Bone-Daughter. Or are you no longer up to the responsibility? Not strong enough for that?

I am, I say quickly. I am. Bone-strong Bone. Yes. I'll do it.

Wyn comes slumping to his log. He winces, rubs his backside.

Getting splinters in my arse from this thing, he says.

He puts his elbows on the table and drops his head into his hands.

God, he mumbles into his fingers. I'm feeling it.

Feeling what? I ask.

Eat, Myma says, poking a piece of dried meat towards him.

His share is smaller than mine and this makes me swell my chest.

Did the bad water make you sick? I ask.

He laughs and looks at me through his fingers then looks at Myma, who frowns.

Something like that, he says.

Eat, Myma says again. The light doesn't wait for your dawdling. Chores to be done. That's how it works here.

Wyn lifts his scowling head and sniffs at the hard stick of rabbit, grunts and puts the meat between his teeth.

I hiccup and belch. My spine suddenly long and straight with my new responsibility. Me the one that shows, no longer the one that needs showing. Myma is trusting me with this. With Wyn.

He follows me out across the clearing. My tooth goes into its hole in the cleft post. Remember how it was when Myma first let me go into the forest alone, what she said to me.

167

You need to put your tooth in the hole, I tell Wyn. You'll stay safe that way because there's a bit of you bitten into the clearing to drag you back.

I— I don't have a tooth, he says.

It is one of those things he says which makes me think him not intelligent.

You've got lots of teeth, I tell him, baring my own and pointing.

I'm using the ones in my mouth, he says.

Well, I say, hopefully one will fall out soon, otherwise I don't know what will happen to you. Until then you'll have to stick close to me.

Then I am bored of standing still and speaking so I turn and run into the trees. Stop and wait for slow Wyn. Him breathless and pale when he reaches me, a cough in his mouth.

Is it your chest? I ask. Does it hurt?

I'm alright, he says.

I glance behind as we walk to make sure he is following. His feet clomping the path. His eyes slitted against the cold flickerings of sun.

Us both silent. All the sounds I would make if I were alone or with Myma, insect-clickings and birdcalls and nose-hummings and tongue-buzzings, they all shrink and hide in my throat. Something about him being there behind me, seeing the back of my head. I grow aware of the walk of me, the rolling of my shoulders and thrust of my chin.

An odd giddiness at being two in the forest with Wyn. The first two I have ever been that is not Daughter and Myma. No Myma here now to frown me off or pinch my tongue from talking. I want to ask Wyn questions, I want to tell him things, but find I do not know how to speak to him. The words bunch in my mouth.

I hear all the sounds and sometimes I feel outside myself,

I say with a loud voice that sends a blackbird skittering away into a tree.

It is not at all what I meant to say and I feel the blood warm up across my chest and cheeks.

What's that you're saying? Wyn says from behind.

I shake my head and make a small groan. Lift my shoulders high and walk faster, Wyn's boots thudding along behind me. An urge in me to say something that will put meaning into this silence that is so different to a silence with Myma. I don't know how to hold this kind of silence, or how to fill it. I want to be heard and known by Wyn but I don't know how to make him know me. I want him to show himself and to speak to me the way he spoke to Myma in the dark, but that kind of showing is all in words and there are so many words I do not know. I want to know about the wooden head that Wyn called Mother. Want Wyn to know the whole Museum of my names. Want him to understand that I have been Pip, Grass, Acorn, Catkin, Stone, Puddle, Squirrel, Birch, Thistle, Finger, Nest, Pebble, Owl, Moss, Pine, Worm, Beetle, Conker, Spider, Pellet, Crow, Legs, Sap, Egg, Stem, Nose, Tail, Bracken, Claw, Rust, Pod, Spine, Sting, Paw, Twig, Beak, Garlic, Thorn, Nail, Scab, Vole, Oak, Bark, Snail, Walnut, Splinter, Apple, Hoof, Berry, Prick, Rib, Woodlouse, Wing, Foot, Sycamore, Tooth, Mud, Flint, Root, and that now I am Bone, but that I am also Daughter, but that I am also myself, another thing separate to all my names, a thing that dreams and itches, a thing that even Myma, who knows everything of me, does not see completely. I whine long and low. Dip my head and trudge without speaking.

We reach the first stone marker. Stick out my arm to make Wyn stop. My elbow catches his chest and makes him gasp.

Here, I say.

I point out the snares hidden in the undergrowth.

You broke them but I fixed them, I say.

Yes, he says. Sorry for that.

Now is not for sorrys, I tell him. Sorrys come with thank yous and only after This-and-That but before sleep.

The traps are empty. I make Wyn put his hand through one of the loops to show him how it tightens when pulled. Watching him watching my hands makes me think of Myma showing me this same way when I was small. How I wanted to learn everything fast so I could go trapping by myself but you must wait until the last of your teeth falls out, Daughter. Strange to think of the Daughter I was. I have been a lot of names since then, and Bone-Daughter knows more than all the other Daughters.

Not until we reach the last snare do we find a tangled rabbit, not yet dead. I give it to Wyn for killing. The rabbit twists and he nearly drops it.

You have to hold its neck, I tell him. Then pull on the legs.

His hand struggles to wrap the neck. The rabbit screams. It bucks and tries to bite him.

Fuck, says Wyn, his teeth gritted.

He grapples with the kicking legs. I put out my hands to show him how to do it properly but he has already swung the rabbit hard against an oak and stopped its screaming. He smacks it against the tree again. Skids of blood and brain streak the bark. Wyn holds the rabbit up.

There, he says. Done.

He is panting. He tosses the limp body towards me and I catch it. The rabbit's head a pink pulp of bone and hair and teeth, two ears sticking out. I stuff it into the sack. Glare at Wyn.

What's wrong? he asks.

You made a mess of it, I tell him.

It's dead, isn't it?

Yes.

Well then.

You didn't do it right.

What's the difference? We'll eat it whatever.

Silent then because I do not know how to explain. Something about the space between his body and the rabbit, his long arm holding it out away from him. When we kill, we bring the animal close enough to feel the warmth of it in our chests. Close enough to feel when blood and breath stop. That is right, that is good. Killing is about body and body. And the movement needed is small, clean. Quick tug-pop. Wyn's breaking open of the rabbit against the trunk seems messy and loud. A wrongness in that.

I close up the sack and step towards Wyn, my face tilted to his. He looks uneasy but he doesn't step away. His tongue touches his upper lip. I smell his breath, the old sweat matting his hair. Reach up and drag a fingernail down my cheek. Tearing sting of it. Water comes into my eyes but I do not show the hurt. I am the one teaching now. I must teach the Lesson when Wyn does a wrong thing. He cries out and grabs my wrist. Shake him off.

What did you do that for? he asks.

What you did was wrong, I tell him. It's not how we do things. Don't do it again.

The pain a hot line on my cheek.

Didn't have to do that, he says. Jesus, girl.

His eyes wide at this other thing he does not understand. And I did have to do it, because otherwise he would not learn.

My mood flat as we gather roots for stew. It is not like I thought it would be, this two-ing, this being-with-Wyn. It is tiring and confusing. Rabbit blood seeps through the sack like a bruise.

I show Wyn how to dig out the roots without snapping them, and I try not to be tugged about by the things he says. He calls me Flint and I tell him that is not my name.

Why did you tell me it was?

Because it was my name then. I was Flint, then I was Root and now I am Bone.

You just change it when you feel like it?

Yes, I say, it changes when I feel it.

Easier if I could just call you one thing.

I'm not called one thing.

She calls you Daughter.

Yes. Myma calls me Daughter. But that is not always my name.

So she didn't give you one.

One what?

A name.

Why would she do that?

His words prick at me. Feel myself stumbling and lost like when I was Flint in the dark forest and he was the Rotter. I am inward and silent as we near the fence, thinking yes, Myma is right, it's not good to listen to what I don't understand, it clogs my head and makes me unsteady in myself. My fingers at my pouch to feel the name-bone of me. I think Bone, Bone, Bone.

At the fence we stop. Wyn flicks a bundle of rabbit ribs and makes them click together.

These things she makes, he says. What did you call them? Keepsakes?

Keep-Safes, I reply. Myma makes them and they keep us safe.

Wyn peers over the fence.

It's not very high, he says.

Something in his voice that nips me.

Doesn't need to be high, I tell him. That's not how it works.

So you never go over?

I stare at him. It is the stupidest thing he has asked yet.

It's only Rot outside the fence, I tell him.

His grin then is strange.

So if I climbed over now, he says, what do you think would happen?

Feel my breath shorten.

You can't do that, I say. You'd get Rotted again. And you'd bring the other Rotters here, Myma said, no, you can't do that.

He is still grinning.

I'll come straight back over, he says, I'm just going to show you, look.

Don't, I tell him, panic hot and spiky in my belly.

He puts his hands on the woven branches. I go roaring and butting into him with my head, send him lurching sideways. He staggers, coughs, clutches his stomach where I have knocked the wind out.

I wasn't meaning to mess with you, he says when his breath comes back.

I am too bristling to speak so I only bark and bark. Wyn isn't grinning any more.

Alright, he says when I have stopped barking. Just tell me this. Help me understand. What makes the other side Rotted?

Feel myself a trapped and twisting thing. The questions he is asking should not be asked. These things should not be poked at. I have learned this, I have been taught. He is all untaught clatter and confusion crashing into the forest. I look at him with my chest going up and down. Then my mouth opens and my voice comes out shouting, my words piling up on top of each other.

DIDN'T KILL IT LIKE A BODY SHOULD ALL SORRY SORRY WRONG CLUMSY TREE-SMACK-RABBIT AND DAUGHTER YES ALWAYS DAUGHTER BUT NAMES AREN'T ONLY A CALLING THING BONE SITS IN THE CARRYING-PLACE AND IF YOU LISTENED YOU WOULD HEAR TOO YOU THE SMALL ONE NEEDING

TEACHING LESSONS TELLING A THING ISN'T STRONG BECAUSE IT'S HEAPED UP HIGH IT'S BECAUSE OF THE OTHER THING THE THING THAT MAKES IT HUM LIKE THE MUSEUM LIKE KEEP-SAFES DON'T KNOW ANY OF YOUR ANSWERS ALL YOUR HELL ARSE MOTHER MEDICATION BOY-GIRL WHERE'S THE SHE IN THE WOOD THE WRONG SIDE OF THE FENCE YOU HOPPED FROM WHERE WE MUSN'T GO AND NEVER GO THE ROT IS WHERE MYMA SAYS IT IS.

Soon the words stop being words and all I am is yelling. Wyn stares, his face shocked slack. Then his mouth opens and he lets out his own shout. His voice lower than mine, rougher. And I hear him better in this howling than in all his words. Eyes on eyes we bellow until I can no longer tell which howl comes from which mouth. This shared noise we make.

Wyn is the first to stop. I clamp my jaws shut, legs shuddering under me.

Our flanks go in and out. Our breath steams. Wyn spits on the ground and I do the same. We glare. We are wary and angry but we have understood something about each other. So I ask the question I want to ask. The one I've held like a lump of gristle in my mouth since the wooden head sat in my palm.

What face is it? I ask. The small one in the wood? What is Mother? And where is the real face?

Wyn seems to think hard. His eyes on mine turn shiny and for a moment they are not colourless at all but the bright blue of sky when water shows it to itself.

She's my – my Myma. And I don't know. I don't know where she is. I've never known her.

The creases at the edges of Wyn's eyes say that he has existed longer than I have, almost as long as Myma perhaps, but he seems suddenly small and fragile, a bird cracked from its egg. I want to run to Myma but my feet stay still. I want the understanding that hangs between us to hold.

Can I see the hole in your back? I ask.

Fucksake, he says, and goes stomping off towards the house.

You did well with him, Daughter, says Myma in the bed.

Our noses touch at the tips.

Only at the fence, she says. You let him get to you. Let him into your head. Mustn't do that. Mustn't listen. Mustn't ask too many questions.

But, Myma, I say, how do you know what happened at the fence?

Myma laughs soft and feathery.

You didn't think I was going to let you go off with him alone, did you? I was following the whole while.

She rolls over. The twine pulls at my toe. Her knee bending up and a wet sound of lips drawing back from teeth. The skin at her knee breaking under her bite.

Trust what you know, Bone-Daughter, she says. And leave the Lessons to me.

One almost-dark-come Myma is busy inside, smoking rabbit meat over the fire, and I am sitting on the step beside Wyn. He lifts his smock to scratch his belly. See the jab-mark made by Myma's glass shard, now paled to a pinkish scar and stitches gone.

You'll have that always, I tell him, pointing to the healed-over hole.

It's not the only one I've got, he says.

He points to white puncture marks at the base of his thumb, the bite of an animal he calls a little bastard terrier but I think what he means is fox. Between his lower lip and his chin, a thin silvery stripe. He parts the red hair to show me and says he doesn't remember what it was that split his lip, it must have happened when he was little. Small circles on his right forearm, like the boreholes in the ash trunks.

Those ones I gave myself, he tells me. Rough time. Cigarette burns. I don't suppose you'll know about that though. Then this one's from a logging accident. That needed stitches too.

He rolls up the leg of his trousers to a lumped knot of flesh above his right knee. I poke it with my thumb and nod as if I understand his words.

Myma has a scar here, I tell him.

I lift my chore-smock to show him the place on my own flank but he stops my hand, saying, Hey, no, don't do that. Eyes darting to where Myma stands behind in the house. He clears his throat, looks away. The way he does when I squat to wee in the forest and he turns his back and shuffles his feet about.

After this I turn his discomfort into a game. Flip up my chore-smock whenever Myma isn't looking, show Wyn a strip of belly, a nipple, a wisp of hair. Snort laughing at the fly-jerk of his head, the nervous flick of his eyes. When my blood comes I leave the glotted rag-wads near his corner to see what he will do with them, but he coughs and pretends not to notice, and Myma picks up the rags and bleeds the skin of her shins to teach me no, so I stop. Once, we are out doing a chore of stripping willow bark, and I call across to Wyn and when he turns his head I show him my whole backside. He is so startled that he takes a layer of skin off his knuckles against the trunk.

Jesus. What do you think you're doing, girl?

Don't call me that. It's not my name.

Wiggle my backside at him. Laugh and scamper off.

I understand that the sheet hung between the rooms is there to stop him looking in, but I do not know the reason for it. And when I ask Myma why Wyn cannot wash with us, or even be inside the house when we are washing, she gives me a sideways answer.

His place for washing is outside, she says.

But why?

That's just the way of it.

For a while I think it must be to do with the Rotted opening in his back, but one light I look through the window after washing and see him stood outside in the clearing, facing into the forest and wearing only his trousers. His back is smooth. No trace of dead tree, no crumbling or withering, not even the kind of brown pitting that appears on windfalls left to the ground. If his flesh has grown back together over the opening, there is no scar to show for it. The plainness of that long back disappoints me in a way I cannot fully grasp.

Wyn becomes less strange with every light-come. He wakes when we wake. He does chores with us. He eats with us. He chews the bark with us. In some things he stays separate. He is not allowed into the room where we sleep. He is not allowed a knife. And on the lights when Myma boils up the water and the soapwort he says, Oh yes, this dog knows its place, and he takes himself outside. He is not allowed to do This-and-That either, so when we go to the room where we sleep he stays by the fire or retreats to his corner. Sometimes I see him watching as we draw the sheet across between us and him, a sort of wanting look on his face.

He is still this otherness, but somehow his being here no longer feels like a burr. I grow used to the rumble of his breath carrying through the dark. The chore-tired weight of him on his log at the table. Even the scent of him becomes familiar. Only when he shakes out his hair and the sharp reek catches me sudden in the nostrils do I remember that his smell was not always here. That it came from outside the fence.

Myma no longer follows when it is my turn to take Wyn for chores, but she says she will see it in me if you start up with your questions, Daughter. Wyn says fewer and fewer tricky poking things, so Myma must have warned him also. When he speaks a word I don't understand, I just let it sit there like a hole, and do not try to probe it for a meaning.

Keep waking to the loose twine around my toe, the goneness of Myma beside me. Their two voices in the other room. I close myself to their speaking. Fingers in my ears so I will not hear, do not listen to what you do not understand, Daughter. I tell myself that Myma knows things I don't, and that's why it's okay for her to listen. Maybe she just likes talking to a face that isn't mine.

When the light comes the two of them are grumpy and defensive with each other again, and the words they speak are few.

Bone turns brittle, crumbles in my mouth, and the tailbone goes into the Museum beside the root. The glass-front cupboard is getting full. Into my pouch I put a dried larva that carries a sound like the insides of trees. The name it gives me is Grub, squirming in the wintering cold.

A new name already? asks Myma as we scrape dregs from our bowls.

I am Grub, I say.

Grub-Daughter, she says. Worm-Kin. Boneless Wriggler. Squirm-Daughter.

See how her worry-itch is healed over. Skin bumpy purple but not clawed raw. She has not scratched it for a while.

Maggot-Daughter, says Wyn, licking stew from his wrist.

We stare at him.

What? he asks. I can't join in?

It's not a game, I tell him. It's my name.

That rhymes, he says.

This way of talking he sometimes has that I cannot quite make sense of. I suck my spoon and push my brows low.

Grub, he says. Couldn't you have picked something a bit nicer?

What's nice got to do with names? I ask.

It's your turn to tidy up, Myma tells him.

Myma chooses hair-brushing for This-and-That. As we sit and brush, the noises of Wyn shifting about in the other room no longer seem out of place. This is how things are now.

I stand to put the brush back in the crate, and Myma grips my ankle.

Wait, she says, then with a loudened voice she calls, Come in here.

A gap of silence. Then Wyn's long fingers appear around the covered doorway. The sheet draws aside. Him standing there uncertain. Hair tangled and firelit.

Me? he asks.

Who else? says Myma.

He blinks and shuffles forward. His eyes move about the room where we sleep. He has not stood in it before. See him seeing it. Rag-nest of our bed. Lamp stain on the wall. Our drawings, the Museum of my names. Blanket spread on the floor for the hair-brushing and Myma and me cross-legged in our bed-smocks, watching him. A fearish look to his face.

In here? he asks.

Where else? says Myma.

He comes properly inside then, lets the sheet fall across behind. His feet touch the edge of the lamplight. His bare heels rub together and his hands hold onto each other. Him unsure of his place here, in this room that has always only been ours.

Myma pats the blanket and nudges me to move. Wyn picks his feet up carefully as he comes, as if to make as little noise as possible. On the blanket he folds his legs tight and loops his arms around them. I shuffle closer to squat beside him. Stare without blinking at the side of his face. His being in the room where we sleep makes him new and strange again. Myma's hand holds the brush-handle.

Isn't that for sweeping the floor? says Wyn.

It's for hair-brushing, we both tell him.

He shrugs and glances at my face beside his cheek. I can tell that my closeness still uncomforts him.

Grub-Daughter, says Myma, move back, or I might accidentally put an elbow in your cheek.

She grasps a red handful. Wyn tightens then goes slack all over, like he is ready to let anything happen to him. Myma begins to brush. The brushing does not look easy. Sound of it like teeth tearing into cloth. Her fingers untangle the thickest knots. She is gentle, she doesn't pull. When she unearths a fat snarl that will not come loose, she takes out her knife and slices the clump at the root. It drops like a small dead animal onto the blanket. A greasiness when I stroke it.

Finally Wyn's hair falls long and smooth. His eyes have closed. Myma pulls the brush through and through and through. I imagine the good tug of it on Wyn's scalp and notice how it warms me to see the two of them like this. I feel happy, then sad. This separateness. This looking-in. This This-and-That I am not part of. See how in all their mid-dark talking-listenings, they have been making something without me. The word I have for this thing is trust. Trust is why Myma no longer comes following when Wyn and I go into the forest. Trust is why he is allowed to sit at the table and eat the meat with untied hands. Trust is why he is sitting here, now, in the room where we sleep. There is goodness in this, I think. A yielding in Myma, an opening. Yet this squirming sadness in me as I watch it happen, a feeling of something trickling out of my hold.

The lamplight tips their shadows sideways on the floor. Myma's second shadow is stooped behind. Its hand stretches for the slope of Wyn's shadow shoulder. Then it draws back, scrunches itself shapeless into the corner.

Myma's arm stops brushing and we all sit still. The lamp burns almost to a stub before Wyn straightens his limbs and stands up, hair crackling. His face is solemn. He seems to understand that he has been allowed to climb inside something. Myma has opened a gap between her fingers. She has let him squeeze through. He does a light cough.

Thank you for letting me join This-and-That, he says. Sorry about the mess.

He waves his hands at the leavings of hair that streak the blanket. Myma is giving him an odd look.

What? he says. Thank you and sorry, after This-and-That. Isn't that what you do?

Myma nods.

Yes, she says. Yes, that is what we do.

Later I wake alone in the bed. There is no talking coming through the sheeted doorway. Only laughing. They are laughing together, Myma and Wyn. Bright and clear. I listen. It is the first lonely I ever feel.

16

They called it Devil's Dip because their parents and grandparents had told them it was where the devil had dug the heart of the place from the ground. The old gravel pit was grassed over, skirted by a cut rim of rock.

They had outgrown the barn. Now as the light left the sky they gathered at the bottom of Devil's Dip. A fire was lit and the circle of backs hunched inward around it. Maya hadn't wanted to come but Kitty had held her by the elbows and pleaded.

'I know you're worried about your mum,' she said, 'but you haven't come out for ages. We might not all get to be together again for a while. She'll cope without you for one night.'

Kitty would be going to university at the end of the summer. She said she was getting out of the pigsty. She said Maya could visit her in the city that took four hours to reach by bus and train. Maya already felt the ache of her going. She had stopped trying in school, which no longer seemed to matter since she would be staying to work and help her mother pay for the house. When she thought of Kitty leaving, of the time before and after, she imagined a flame, bright, then doused.

'I suppose I could come to the dip for a bit,' she said.

Kitty squealed and kissed Maya on the nose. Then she took

a pair of scissors from her bedside table and began to cut her toenails.

'Thanks for not making a big thing of me and Darry also,' she said. 'I know there was something with you and him, before.'

Maya's chest grew tight.

'Not really,' she said. 'We don't talk much any more.'

Thin yellow moons flicked from the scissors.

'He asked why I spend so much time with you,' said Kitty.

'What did you say?'

Kitty shrugged.

'I told him we've known each other for ages.'

Maya watched her scooping the nail trimmings into a little pile. She would have liked to keep every sliver.

Now, at the bottom of Devil's Dip, she lowered her gaze as Kitty wedged herself between Darry's knees. Maya sat on the other side of the fire next to Lauryn, who was talking about the nursing course she would be starting. Maya nodded but heard only stray words. At some point a face thrust between them and a pair of arms went around their shoulders.

'Here you go,' said Luke. His words slid about. 'Get that down you both.'

Maya shook her head but he set the bottle to her mouth and she swallowed what he poured. Someone threw a firecracker. The air smoked. Maya looked across at Kitty, who had her arms hooked around Darry's legs. When Maya lifted her eyes to Darry, she saw him staring straight back. His face did not move. She was the first to look away.

Night pulled close around their backs. The eggy smell from the firecrackers lingered. Voices flapped around Maya's ears. Her face and arms were hot but she could feel in her chest a cold lump, so she drank deep to warm it. The faces around her seemed to throb slightly as if things were shifting inside them. A swift tenderness came into her then, and with it a wrenching that made her want to press her forehead against each of theirs and ask, Do things move under my face too? Can you see them? Is there fullness in me like there is in you? She found herself laughing.

'Maya's ratted,' someone shouted.

Her hand was filled by another that she recognised as Kitty's. She saw Kitty's face close to hers and she imagined putting her hands around it and bringing it closer.

'Piss,' said Kitty.

Maya felt herself tugged upright and away from the light. They climbed to a row of pines and Kitty squatted behind a trunk while Maya leaned on the other side and blinked to make her eyes adjust. White shreds of toilet paper tore up the ground. She heard cars passing on a nearby road, a distant shrieking of foxes, then Kitty stumbling close.

'Maya? I can't bloody see.'

'Here.'

She reached and felt Kitty's fingers at her wrists.

'Thought for a minute you'd left me,' Kitty said.

Her breath was sour, her eyes dark windows. Maya thought, No, I would not leave you, I could not, but you are leaving me, you are leaving me. The thought leaned her forward until her mouth was touching Kitty's mouth. Her blood surged to meet it. The fingers around her wrists tightened, then let go. The brief heat of Kitty's mouth was gone. Maya heard an 'oh', a silence, then the sound of Kitty's footsteps moving away.

Maya stood among the pine needles and toilet paper. She faced the darkness so that she did not have to see the small figure rejoining the others around the fire. Their voices stayed in the hollow and did not reach her. She thought about bending and putting her forehead to the ground. Her head would sink into the soil and she would tunnel under to lie like a worm. Around her, things would grow and twist and decay and other things would grow from the mulch they left. Trees would thud to the earth, though her soft worm head would know only the dull vibrations of their falling. Years would pass. Only after everything living had died would she emerge pink and new into the stillness, the quiet.

But the ground was soaked in other people's urine, so she did not want to put her head near it.

The approaching feet sounded heavier than Kitty's. They stopped beside the tree she leaned against.

'Came to check on you,' said Darry. 'Kitts thought you might be lost.'

The glow from the pit showed Maya his jacket zip, the edge of his jaw. He had become tall, his shoulders broad.

'I'm fine,' she said, 'I'm coming now.'

But his hand went around her arm and held it.

'We're good, aren't we?' he asked.

Maya felt the darkness contract.

'Yes,' she said. Darry's hand stayed tight.

'I liked it,' he said, 'when we used to hang out.'

Maya did not reply. She remembered dropping a slug down his back on the school field. He had flung a handful of mud at her and she had chased him. She remembered once seeing him on the pavement with his father and his father's heavy dog. The dog had barked and Darry's father had struck its muzzle and made it yelp. Then Darry's father had gone inside a shop and Darry had crouched beside the dog and stroked it gently.

Her arm was numb.

Darry asked, 'Why did you stop talking to me?'

'I didn't.'

There was a churning in her head, a heat. He was standing too close.

Darry said, 'I saw you looking at her.'

Her back was against the tree and he was in front of her. She could not see his eyes. The sweet he had given her years ago was still bound to the piece of rabbit skull under her bed, its sticky gloss now fluffed and dull. She had the thought that if she could get to it, if she could hold it, then nothing could happen that she had not asked for.

The zip of his jacket dug when he pushed against her. His pinning elbows kept her arms down. His hands were at her face, her chin. They wrapped around and held her jaws shut. Her head was tilted back, the bark rough at her scalp. She felt his fingers over her mouth. She tasted burning, and a tang like milk on the turn. For a moment he just held her like that, like an animal with its muzzle tied. She tried to jolt against him but he was firm. His head bent close and she braced herself for the touch of his lips, his tongue. She wondered what she would tell Kitty. But he did nothing else, and she understood what it meant, what he was telling her with his hands clamped on her mouth. Anything, his hands said. He could do anything.

Then there was air around her again and Darry was gone. Maya spat the feel of him and retched. Her fingers felt for the edges of her jaw. Her back slid down the trunk and the earth seemed to trickle away beneath her. Small stones rolled. Her heels dug but her feet could find no purchase on the ground.

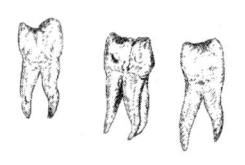

My Sixteenth

My sixteenth First Frost comes with a snap and a good tingle under my feet when I step out bootless to feel the prick of the whitened ground.

We pile the fire high with wood. Wyn's hair is plaited like Myma's between his shoulder blades. I touch it and he crimps his lip and says, Special occasion. He gives me a round stone he has found. I do not know why he does this, but it has a satisfying throw to it when I hurl it across the clearing.

Myma will not allow me to be bare-skinned like I usually am for First Frost, but I can stay in my bed-smock because First Frost means no chores, only This-and-That all light long. Usually Myma and me take turns at choosing, but it is different with Wyn here. Myma fists up three rat ribs and we each pull one. Mine is shortest. Myma's is longest. She grins.

That means I choose what we do for This-and-That first, she says. Daughter, you'll pick last.

She chooses masking.

From the crate I take the mask with feathered cheeks and a large rook beak. Myma wears the muntjac-antlered mask with a long blunt nose and slitted nostrils.

Well, I'm not being the rabbit, Wyn says, tossing the mask with long furry ears back into the crate.

He puts on the only other mask, this one sharp-muzzled, fox teeth stuck with blobs of resin around the open mouth. His plaited hair falls like a tail behind.

Myma begins to butt her head, her weight dropped forward into her knuckles. I tuck my elbows tight and twitch my beak, think myself into heavy black birds and the heavy grey skies they fly through. But it is harder to slip into the creaturey thinking the way I can with only Myma here. I am too aware of my Grub-Daughter body, and of Wyn's body beside it. Feel myself hot-faced under the mask, which keeps sliding down. My hands are clumsy at the ends of my wrists, nothing feather-like about them.

Wyn watches Myma hoofing at the floor and coughs out a short laugh. He stretches his forearms, sticks his backside high and makes a howl that sounds nothing like a fox. Under the mask he is still Wyn, a smirk on his mouth. I point my beak at him.

No, I say. You're doing it wrong.

The mask throws my voice back into my mouth. Myma is in the corner, rubbing her shoulder against the wall. Deep in the muntjac, she doesn't hear us. See the way her spine has become curved, her skull lengthened under the mask. How her legs now bend the other way. Wyn does not seem to see any of this. He clicks his tongue.

I'm being a fox, he says. Isn't that what I'm supposed to be doing?

You're not being a fox, I tell him. You're being like one.

You do it then, he says. Show me what the right way is.

He tugs off the mask and shoves it at me. Sits back on his heels with folded arms. I untie the rook-beaked mask, tie on the fox-jawed one. Stretch myself long and feel the fox immediately. I put out my tongue to lick the fangs. Look at Wyn through the slanted eyeholes and feel my gaze yellowing. A yipping when I open my mouth. Wyn watches as I slink about.

No name for where the mask nudges me, into a thing all smell and heat. The strain of a tail unfurling. I arch my back. My yip turns to a yowl. Then the sudden pulsing itch, shooting between my hind legs to warm my belly. I drop low, drag my pelvis across the stone floor to scratch. Pump my hips. In my throat, the scree-shriek of foxes in the dark.

I am too fox, too intent on scratching my itch to notice Myma standing from the muntjac and coming towards me, her face now her own. Her hands rip the mask from my head. Me left panting on the floor, Grub-Daughter again.

It is Wyn's turn to choose This-and-That.

Drawing, he says. You do drawing, yes?

He points at the birds on the ceiling. We nod.

I like drawing, he says.

I like drawing too, says Myma.

I'm not good at drawing, I say.

Wet my finger with spit to dip in the reddish dirt. Try to make the shape of a grub on the wall but it ends up a muddy blotch. Myma uses a thin stick of charcoal to draw a wing, every feather exact. Her fingernail keeps the charcoal scraped keen.

You are good at that, Wyn tells her.

I am, she says. I've practised.

I look to see what Wyn is doing. Myma has given him a space beside a drawing of mine that is supposed to be a plait of hair but which looks like a fat coil of intestine. Wyn holds his charcoal slant against the wall, hand flicking to make light strokes. I watch as a face appears, slow, like a stain leaking through cloth. At first I think it might be Myma's, but the brows are lower, the chin rounder, the nose sharper at the point. I recognise the face as the carved wooden one that Wyn keeps in his corner.

Myma's second shadow shivers close to Wyn's drawing, dips its shadow-head into the charcoal head. For a moment the shadow seems to peer from the smudgy black eyes.

Daughter, Myma says, you're making a mess.

I look down and see that my finger has smeared red-brown paste all over the front of my bed-smock.

The drawing things are put away and Myma turns to me, her grin sharp. She points with her charcoaled finger.

I know what you're going to pick, she says.

Dancing, we say in the same blink.

We laugh. Wyn twists his mouth.

I don't dance, he says.

You've got arms and legs, don't you? Myma says.

I don't dance, he says again.

We'll show you, Myma says. Daughter, take his left side.

Together we move Wyn's arms about and make his knees flex. Myma holds his chin, loosens his head on his neck. At first Wyn's limbs are stiff as branches. He grumbles and tries to push us off but we hang on. We tilt him and bend him until he loosens. When our hands let go, Wyn carries on moving. We join with our stomp and skip, our whomp and whirl-about.

The light dims as we dance. Orange streaks come through the window and set Wyn's hair on fire.

Myma does a leaping turn, arms held out. Her hand strikes Wyn in the back. He is on one leg when it happens, and he falls, his arms still dancing. He lands with a yelp and a cough. Stays on the floor, breathing loud. We are all still. Wyn is staring hard at Myma and I wonder if he will shout or hit her in return.

Then he opens his mouth, tips back his head and laughs. Myma begins to laugh too, a deep rich belly-laugh that slops against the walls. Her laughing plucks up my own. I yip-yip-yip and clutch my arms around myself. All three of us laughing together. Howling up to the ceiling where Myma's flock of starlings stab at my wonky crows.

*

We each get a small strip of dried meat and two thin roots. Even at First Frost we must be careful with our food. There is not much meat left. Myma's fingers flutter at her left sleeve where the worry is itching away, but she doesn't say anything. And then it stops mattering about the dwindle of meat because there is pudding. I have been wet-mouthed with thoughts of it since waking to the frost at light-come. Myma's lips tilt up at my excitement.

Go on, Grub-Daughter, she says.

On my hands and knees beside the row of tins. I already know which I will choose but I read all the labels anyway to make the moment stretch. Creamed Rice Pudding. Sliced Peaches in Syrup. Sweetened Condensed Milk Full Cream. Pineapple Slices No Added Sugar. Pitted Prunes in Juice. Caramel Treat Ready-To-Use Dessert Topping. Reach for this one. Fingers twitching nervous and hardly believing I am finally allowed to have it. Both hands around the tin and tight to my chest. Myma chooses Pineapple Slices No Added Sugar. She likes the ones I don't, those with slimy chunks that set my stomach clenching. She says the others are too sweet for her taste. She says I am the one with the sweet tooth. She says this is one of the reasons we exist well together, Myma and Daughter.

We bring our stools and Wyn's log close around the fire. Wyn looks at us sitting with our tins between our knees. He smiles small and does not ask for a tin for himself. I am glad, I don't want him to have one. Pudding is a thing I do not want to share with him.

Your sixteenth winter, Grub-Daughter, says Myma, her eyes on me.

I nod, impatient. My thumbnail flicks the metal ring.

Every winter comes about even sooner than the last when Daughters grow fast as dandelions, says Myma. How quick it comes. How you grow.

There is a little fog of sadness in her speaking, but my mind is full of Caramel Treat Ready-To-Use Dessert Topping and I am hardly listening.

When's yours? asks Wyn.

I look at him, distracted for a moment. He is looking at Myma.

Mine? Myma asks.

Yes, he says. Your birthday. When is it?

Myma pulls her lower lip between her teeth. I wait for her to laugh or to say, What're those not-sense not-words in your mouth, once-Rotter? But her eyes hold Wyn's and they are serious.

I don't remember, she says. It's been too long since I had one. Yours?

April, he says. Spring.

They both are quiet then and I am beginning to quiver, the hunger for Caramel Treat Ready-To-Use Dessert Topping growing desperate in me. My throat readying for a whine. Myma brightens her eyes and looks at me.

Alright then, she says. Yes, Greedy-Guzzler Grub-Daughter, it is pudding now.

Peel back the lid to the thick yellow-brown so sweet that the roof of my mouth buzzes with it. Try to eat slow but it is too caramel-treat, too ready-to-use delicious to pull myself back. I scoop with my fingers, lap where it spills.

Hold a moment, Daughter.

Lift my sticky muzzle from the pudding. Myma is holding an empty tin and a spoon. Pineapple Slices No Added Sugar unopened in her lap. She reaches for my Caramel Treat Ready-To-Use Dessert Topping. I almost snarl her off. Mine. But she gives me a look that warns and I let her have it. Watch anxious and unblinking as she spoons a glob of my pudding into the empty tin. She opens her own and scoops out a pale yellow ring. Then she gives my tin back to me and I clutch it tight. The spare tin goes to Wyn and I bow myself low over my pudding, hunch my shoulders and bring my knees up high so it will not be taken from me again.

Hear Wyn's slurp and swallow as I lick the dregs from my tin and suck the stickiness from my fingers, eyes shut. Pudding-dizzy when I look up. Myma is still eating. Small mouthfuls, chewing slow. Wyn hiccups. His cheeks are wet. He is crying. I stare at him until Myma has finished eating and his cheeks have dried.

Myma peels the labels off and tucks them behind the row of unopened tins. We will read them when we get hungry for the pudding we cannot yet have. Only four tins left now and next First Frost I have already decided I will have Creamed Rice Pudding and after that there will be only two. Unless next winter Wyn is allowed his own. If Wyn is still here next winter. If he stays.

The sweetness has made my head hurt so I lie down beside the fire and sleep.

The arms that carry me to the bed are not Myma's. These are longer, stiffer. A different kind of warmth to them. Then the bed is underneath me and the arms are gone. My eyes open to the red back of a head going towards the doorway.

Wyn, I mumble.

The head turns.

Grub, it says.

This was, I begin to say, but the words I want struggle from me and I have to start again. First Frost, I say. You, Myma, me, This-and-That, pudding. All of us. All of it. This First Frost. This one was the most.

The most what? Wyn asks.

Just, I say. The most.

A dimness to his smile. A look in his eyes that pierces, like they are seeing something in me I can't, the way I can't see the back of my own head, or the inside of Myma's. But he doesn't name the thing. Just dips his chin at me.

I'm glad, he says. I'm glad it was the most.

17

Not until her daughter spat out her last milk tooth did Maya allow her into the forest alone.

'Checking the traps is your chore now, yours only.'

She had given her daughter the other half of the shears, the handle wrapped with birch bark for gripping. She had been saving it for this moment.

'Put your last tooth into the hole on the post when you go,' Maya told her. 'That way there'll be a bit of you kept safe here to lead you back. If you're out alone and the hole is empty, that's when I'll know to worry.'

Of course her daughter would not really be alone. That first time, Maya followed at a distance, barefoot and silent. She watched the girl among the trees. It was strange, seeing her this way, when the child thought herself alone. Maya was disconcerted by the sudden, jolting sense of her daughter as a separate creature. It was like seeing one of her own limbs severed and moving about on its own. Her daughter's fingers at work were deft and sure. Her hands when they snapped the necks were quick, unflinching.

The girl came to the furthest trap and Maya felt herself stiffen. Through the trees she could see the boundary and she knew her daughter saw it too. A cold fist clenched her as the girl walked towards the fence, the rabbit dangling from her hand. Maya saw her neck straining to peer at the forest on the other side, the bird-like bobbing movements of her head. For a moment Maya allowed herself to imagine how it would feel to watch her daughter walk away. Her breath shallowed. At her side, the grey woman began to chitter. If the girl left, Maya would be alone. She saw an image of herself dried to a husk on the bed, her hair piled around her like dead leaves. The grey woman's chittering became louder.

Maya felt a shout gathering behind her teeth. She wanted to scream, Do not go, I cannot follow, I cannot follow you there, do not leave me alone here. But the girl had already turned away from the fence, and now Maya watched her running fast in the direction of the hut, the rabbit swinging about in her fist. She noted the fear that had pinched her daughter's face as she fled from the fence. She looked after the retreating shoulders and saw the tension in them. She was relieved.

The next time, Maya did not follow. She went about her own tasks and allowed the tugging cord between herself and the child to stretch, though its tether yanked every moment at her navel. Even when she felt the itch of anxiety under her skin, she did not go. The sun began to dip, and Maya sat on the step to wait. Beside her sat the grey woman.

'You'll lose her,' said the grey woman. Her voice clicked and scraped. They were the first words Maya had ever heard her speak.

'She is safe,' Maya replied.

Just to be sure, she checked the hole in the post that marked the grey woman's grave. Her daughter's tooth was still there, milk-white.

An Ache

An ache in my gut from pudding. Always I forget the sick pang of it until the First Frost comes again.

Roll onto my side to ease the aching. My belly hard with it. A buzzing between my ears from all the sweetness. Stretch an arm for Myma but her dent in the bed is unwarmed. See through the dim, Wyn's drawing staring back from the wall. Wyn's voice then, on the other side of the sheet.

Sixteen, he is saying. She hardly seems it.

I move to cover my ears, then stop. I am the thing they are talking about. So I listen. Creaking of Myma's stool. Glass clink, pour.

Ah, says Myma. That's the last of it. Well.

Probably for the best, says Wyn. Damn shame though.

Two throats moving to swallow, mugs set down. Then a sound of glass again, trickle and drip.

Might as well get the dregs, says Wyn. Yep. Gone now.

He coughs.

What was I saying? Oh, yes. Seems a hell of a lot younger than sixteen somehow. She's tall, sure. But in everything else, well.

Myma does not respond straight away. When she does, her

speaking is careful, like feet stepping through a patch of thorns. Something in Wyn's talk that has poked at her.

She's young for her age, she says.

You've made her young.

Meaning?

Wyn makes a throaty sound, then coughs again.

I mean, he says. It's like. I don't know. It's like you want to keep her that way.

What way is that? Myma asks.

Hear her stiffening. Her teeth coming together.

Like a child, Wyn says. Not really knowing anything.

She is a child, Myma says, sharp now. That's what she is. She is still a child.

Not really, says Wyn. She might act like one in some ways but you can see she's past that. I just— I mean, what will it do to her? If she carries on the way she is. If she never knows anything else.

Do to her? She's fine. She's healthy. She's strong. She's got me. She doesn't need anything else.

I don't know. The things you tell her. The way you keep her. It doesn't— It doesn't seem right.

I turn my head then to open up both ears for listening.

Shhh, Myma hisses.

Squeeze shut my eyes. Feet padding, sheet lifting. Myma's breath in the room. Then gone again. The voices return, lower now. My ears straining like reaching fingers.

I don't keep her, Myma whispers, her voice barbed. Just keep her safe. There's nothing to stop her leaving. If she really wanted to. But she doesn't. Like I said, she's happy here.

My heart quickening. Mind clenching around Myma's words, not understanding. Me leaving where? To go where? Leaving how? She cannot mean going over the fence. That is not a possible thing. I have heard wrong. Or Myma is making a joke. Wyn laughs then, so it must be a joke, even though it is a flat, cold laughing.

Dog shit, he whispers back. How could she? With what you've made her believe. Rotter, she called me. The way she looked at me. Like I was the first other person she'd ever seen.

Pause. I become tangled trying to pick apart the joke that no longer sounds quite like a joke.

That's right, says Wyn, isn't it? I'm the only other, ever. There's something wrong in that. She's – I don't know. Stunted.

Myma's reply is taut.

I have kept her safe.

It's not right, Wyn says. It's not – it's not normal. The way you two are. I understand something happened to you, and I understand you won't talk about it, but don't you think she at least deserves—?

Myma's turn to laugh now, and hers too is flat, cold and hollow. I have lost grip of the joke's tail and am not sure if the joke was even there to begin with.

You, she snorts, understand. No. You can't understand. Not the same for you.

I've had struggles of my own, he says.

It's not the same, Myma repeats. Not the same as what I – what they – I can prevent that for her. She doesn't have to go through anything like what I – any of that. I can protect her here. Things are different here.

My brow furrowing so hard in my concentrating that the tiny muscles begin to twitch. Things here that Myma has never spoken of. Happenings before Daughter. Things angry and painful inside her, hidden away.

But what about her? Wyn says. The girl. Grub. She's got no say in it. Not in any of it. What happens when she realises?

Myma doesn't speak for a long while. When she does, her voice is low, dangerous.

I told you, she says. I told you there were conditions to you being here. Not getting into her head, not messing with it. She wouldn't understand. It would only confuse her. Upset her. There's no lie in what I've told her. It's a Rotten, Rotten world.

I'm not saying it isn't hard, he says. Living, it's hard. I never was good at it. But I believe in having choices. She doesn't have that here.

She doesn't need choice, says Myma. I've chosen the best thing for her.

You underestimate her. She's smart. She's already wondering, you can see that. The questions she asks. I think she would want to understand why. I think she would listen, if you told her. I never got an explanation from my mother. You can give her that.

What's to explain?

Maya, he says, come on.

Me listening in the bed. Wonder at his strange saying of Myma's name. Mouth it to myself. My–uh. It stirs something uncomfortable in me, this difference in naming, as if Wyn is speaking to a Myma I do not know. A Myma she has shown to him and not to me. For a while there is only the quiver of Myma's breathing. Then Wyn asks a question that fills my pudding-sick belly with fear.

What about if something happens to you? What about when you're gone?

All of me folding and folding around that word. My heart stuttering gonegonegonegonegonegonegone. I wait stiff for Myma's answer. Not going anywhere, am I? she'll say. Silly. Silly thing to ask. Silly Rotted question. Silly Rotter-Wyn.

She'll be fine, says Myma.

Mouth pressed to bed to stop the whimper that wants to

come. Bloodthump so hard inside my skin that I think they must hear the pulsing of it in the other room. Wrap my arms around myself to deaden the sound.

She doesn't know how to be by herself, Wyn is saying. You won't be here for ever, Maya. How do you think she'll cope, alone? And what if she does decide to leave? What then, if you don't at least prepare her?

I've given her all she needs. She can survive here. She won't need to leave. What I've made here, it's for her, all of it. I've given her that. You can't – you can't understand.

In the following silence I can think only that one word. Gone. Gone. Howl of it through me. Wyn coughs and speaks again. Quieter now, even quieter.

It's not just about her, he says. I'm your friend, Maya. We've become that to each other, haven't we? I care about you. Is this the only place you'll ever be? Hiding, for ever? Maya.

Pause.

If I'm hiding, what are you doing?

Pause. From Wyn, a long sigh out.

I don't think I'm a good person, he says then. But I've always tried to be honest. If we can't be honest with each other, what's the point? If we can't – open ourselves. If you can't be honest with her, if you never let her understand, that's not love. That's pretending.

Protecting, Myrna says. Not pretending. Your own mother would have wanted that for you.

Wyn laughs again and I wish they would both stop laughing because it is confusing.

Well, he says, I certainly wasn't protected where she left me. And not knowing why. I was so frustrated by that. So angry. I can see that happening in your girl too. She senses something. It'll go inward, that. It'll get twisted. You say it's for her, all this. But maybe keeping her here is more about your own shit.

There is a clatter then that makes my legs kick out under the blankets, fingers and toes flexing in alarm. Stool hitting floor. Smack of flesh on flesh. Wyn gasping, a scramble of limbs. Me rigid, listening, trying to sort the sounds. I think Myma's hand has struck Wyn, but I don't understand. A backward kind of Lesson. How can he learn anything if he's the one being hurt? Myma's voice then, hard between her teeth.

Man-boy Rotter done with its life came crawling into my place whining for food and shelter. Talking like it understands, blaming its mother for all the bad it's had. It's the grey one that stopped me killing you but that doesn't mean you have a place here. All it means is she's mad. Mad old ghost, she, to want to keep a thing like you living.

She is speaking strangely, and loud. She seems to have forgotten that I am here, behind the sheet, in the room where we sleep.

Mad old ghost, you are, she shouts. What was it for?

These words are not for Wyn, nor for me. There is a feeling of the air tightening. The darkness clotting in the cold hollow of Myma's sleeping space. I slide my hand across the bed and dip my fingers into that thickened dark. Myma's second shadow and I, we listen together.

Maya, Wyn says. Maya. Please. I'm speaking as a friend. Want to help.

Him sounding like a crumpled broken-legged thing. Weak and wounded as when Myma cut the Rot from his belly with her glass shard.

Myma makes a small noise in the back of her throat.

That word again, she says. Is that what you are? Last friend I had turned me inside out. I don't think I want another.

Wyn doesn't reply. Feel myself curled and ragged, a torn-off ear. Myma's second shadow moves off the bed and across the room to stand stark in the doorway, the long-haired Myma-shape of it against the sheet. Hear Myma getting up. Knuckles on tabletop, heels on stone. Scuff of her feet towards the doorway. The outline of her lapping into her other shadow. She stops behind the sheet and her voice comes taut, a stretched skin.

It's not your place, she says to him. I decide what story I tell. It's my place. Mine.

She yanks the sheet aside and the shadow is flung sideways into the other blacknesses at the edge of the room. I close my eyes. Inside my own dark, Myma becomes all sound, padding towards the bed. She doesn't slip into her own sleeping space but climbs over me to wedge herself beside the wall. I am nudged into the unwarmed half of the bed. Myma faces away, all scrunched.

Myma? I whisper.

She is quiet and I wonder if maybe she has already fallen asleep. But her breath comes in quivers, not in long deep sleeping sucks.

Myma?

The hard lump of her beside me feels so small. I know she is frightened and that frights me too. I want to tell her that she can trust me with the fear. That she can tell me and we can share it, we can take it apart together. More Keep-Safes, more branches in the fence, whatever will shrink it, keep it out. I swallow. Make a curve of myself around her.

I won't let it in, I tell her, even though I'm not sure what it is, only that it's worse than anything else, maybe worse even than Rot.

Hear the sound of a stool being lifted and set on its legs. Drag of feet. A rattling. Soon after, Wyn's low rumble. I listen until I notice the bed trembling. Myma's back, shaking. A sound coming out of her.

I have never heard Myma cry. Yet she is crying now. Wyn has made her cry.

The knucklebones of her back press in a line down my

front. Her crying lengthens and loudens to an animal groaning that goes all the way through me, from the stretch of skin between my eyes to the base of my spine. Me wanting to help but not knowing how. I pull my arm from the blankets, reach to stroke her jaw.

Myma flips over and her arms shoot out. The heels of her hands thud into my chest. I am jolted backwards, tumbled from the bed. I lie on the cold stone a moment, curled on my side. Hot tingle in my chest. In my left hip, a dull purplish pain blooming. I breathe steady, my mind quiet and sort of blank. Lift myself to hands and feet. The floor is gritty. In the light it will be one of our chores to sweep it. I dust my palms on my bed-smock and stand up.

Through the dimness I see Myma's body spread out like a hand. Perhaps she is asleep. Perhaps her pushing me was an accident, her arms moved by a dream. I wait for her to shift and make a space for me. She does not stir. I go to the doorway and look behind the sheet. The shape of Wyn in the corner rises and falls, unwoken by Myma's crying. I think about the way he said Myma's name. My–uh. How she answered to it as if she had always been named that way. I imagine going to Wyn's corner and lying down beside him.

I stand between the two rooms. Throb in my hip, the draped sheet bunching in my hands. Wyn and Myma numb at either side of me. My blood pulling in two directions. My two feet pointing away from each other.

I slide down the door frame onto the floor. The sheet pulls from its nails with a loud rip that wakes neither of them. Cocoon it around myself. Fold myself tight.

18

Once they had made dens in the empty steel pig arks and sealed pacts by slapping palms with spit. They had written each other notes and swallowed them. They'd plaited the brown and blonde of their hair together. They'd whispered to one another the words sprayed on the bus shelter. Maya had taken her mother's cigarettes and they had smoked them together until they could do it without coughing. Kitty had stolen sweets from the shop and they had eaten them and felt ill and guilty.

Now they sat apart on the bench. Their eyes looked past each other.

'Kitty, I—'

'All over him, he told me.'

'That's not what happened.'

'You said you didn't like him that way.'

'I don't. I never—'

'You— You kiss me and then you go after Darry too. Don't you think that's a bit messed up?'

'I didn't—'

'What? You were jealous?'

Yes, Maya thought, but not of you.

'I haven't told anyone,' Kitty said, 'about that kiss. I don't care if you're—I won't tell anyone. You were drunk, whatever. You didn't have to kiss him as well to make a point.'

There was a splinter in the bench. It pushed into Maya's leg and she pressed against it so she would not have to think about what had happened with Darry at the rim of Devil's Dip, the thing that had felt like the opposite of a kiss. Her jaw ached. When she had returned home that night she had been sick again and again but she had not been able to rid herself of the feeling of his hands, the hot panic dripping down her throat. She could not tell Kitty what had happened because she did not know the right words for it herself. He had not left any marks on her. Perhaps it had not been as bad as she'd thought. Perhaps it had been a joke. Because it was so unclear in her own mind, she was afraid that Kitty would not believe her. Maya already knew that she had hurt her. She did not want to cause her any more pain.

Kitty bunched her hands inside her sleeves and let out a long breath.

'I know it's not really him you want,' she said.

They sat for a while and did not speak. Then Kitty stood up.

'Me and Darry,' she said, 'it won't last. Not with me leaving soon anyway. But you've not been honest. I think it's best if you and me don't see each other any more. I can't be part of it, Maya. Whatever it is that's going on with you. I'm sorry. I can't do it.'

And Maya nodded, because she understood, because she did not want to be part of it either, this hurting thing. She and Kitty looked at one another. The wind lifted their hair and dropped it again on their shoulders.

Kitty said, 'That's all there is then.'

Maya did not watch her leave. She listened to the going of Kitty's feet. Then she lay down on the bench and closed her eyes. There was a rich and oddly sweet smell of something that must have crawled into the hedgerow and died. She wondered how long it would take for somebody to find her if she too dragged herself into the undergrowth and covered herself with branches. The air cooled. The light dimmed.

Maya heard footsteps again and her heart lifted. Kitty, coming back to her.

'Hey. Are you okay?'

Her eyes opened to the face of a man peering down. Something touched her elbow, warm and wet. She lurched back.

'Come away, Flick. Sorry. She doesn't mean harm.'

The brown collie sniffed at Maya's knees.

'I said away, Flick.'

'That's okay,' said Maya, 'I don't mind.' She put out a hand for the dog's tongue.

'Not planning on sleeping out here, I hope,' the man said.

Maya shook her head.

'Got somewhere to go?'

She nodded.

'Right.' The man swung his arms. 'Hadn't you better be going there then? Dark soon. You don't want to stay out here alone.'

The collie's soft tongue had put a hard lump in Maya's throat. She scratched the dog's ears and did not reply. The man carried on looking at her.

'Sure you're alright?' he asked. 'You've not been hurt or anything?'

'I'm fine,' she said, and her voice teetered.

'It's just,' said the man, 'I worry when girls like yourself are out alone. Not everyone's friendly, you know.'

At that, Maya laughed. The man looked alarmed and the dog beat a worried tail against the leg of the bench. It thrust its muzzle into her palm. She pushed it away and looked up at the man. The concern in his face brought a heat to her eyes, a stinging. She felt the beginning of tears, and this made her angry.

'Why don't you fuck off?' she said.

'I— Sorry?'

'Pervert. What are you talking to young girls for then?'

'That's—' said the man. 'No, I wanted—'

'Didn't ask for your help,' Maya said. 'Pervert.'

The man opened and closed his mouth. He ran a hand through his thinning hair. His expression was strained, unhappy. His eyes moved about.

'Come on, Flick,' he muttered.

Maya watched the man walking away, the drop-tailed collie close at his heels. When she could no longer hear the rattling of the dog's collar, she got up off the bench. Night was blurring the sky. The man was right, Maya thought. The dark was not a good place to be. She walked home, quickly.

The Deepest Rags

The deepest rags on the bed have not ever been washed. Whenever the space we sleep in turns dark and greasy with the clag of our bodies, we peel off the topmost layer of rags and sheets and boil the dirt from them until the water glooms. Then we put them back on again and tamp them to a snug nest, packed down like the hair and moss and feathers in the bowls of twigs where the blackbirds keep their eggs.

Somewhere in the bed must be the cloth strips that used to wipe my mouth of Myma's milk. I do not remember how it tasted. I once tried squeezing drops from my own nipples but they only reddened. When I lie face-down in the bed, I imagine I can smell Myma's milk still, some sweetness turned sour.

I wake in the doorway and it is the first light-come of my existing that I do not wake in the bed. Sore click of my neck when my head lifts. Turn to see the empty bed. Turn the other way to see the two bumps of Myma's knees under her bed-smock, her standing close beside me. Blink up towards her face. Her hair is plaited tight enough to tug the skin from her forehead. Red under-rims of her eyes, tender-skinned and swollen. We look at each other. Her mouth moves like it wants to say something but before it can speak she turns around and carries it away on her face.

My numb feet stick out from under the wrapped sheet. The house is cold, cooking fire and wood burner both unlit. I stand up and the hurt spot where I fell makes me remember it by beating down into the top of my leg.

Myma's beckoning arm scoops the air, draws me to the table. Wyn lies still in his corner, his back towards us. Myma sees my eyes dart at him and her face closes up tight. She goes to the shelf and comes back holding two tins.

Pudding, Daughter, she says.

Her voice too bright, too sharp, like the shimmery bit at the edge of a scream. I want to say, What do you mean, Myma, no, that is wrong, we already had pudding, but Myma is pushing the tin towards me across the table and the look of her is urgent.

Eh, Daughter? she says. Eh? Pudding for us, yes?

Me sitting unsure, my shoulder blades pinching together at my back.

Is it an Exception? I ask.

An Exception, she says. Yes. Yes.

Her words falter, crumble at the edges. I want to hold her by the shoulders and shake. Instead I nod.

I like pudding, I say.

Her sudden smile alarms me.

You do, she says. I know how happy it makes you. It makes me happy to see you happy, Daughter.

I nod again and her smile widens. I take the tin she thrusts at me. Creamed Rice Pudding. I love Creamed Rice Pudding. I want to eat the Creamed Rice Pudding but I know this would not be right, and I know that Myma knows this too, but she is watching my face close. Her smile straining. I open the tin because I want to give her the thing she wants, because she cried in the dark.

The Creamed Rice Pudding is sweet and cold. Swallow in big chunks without chewing. Myma opens the Pitted Prunes in Juice. They look like shrivelled rabbit kidneys. She works them to a mushy pulp in her mouth, lifts the tin and gulps the juice. Brownish droplets stick to the hairs at the edges of her lips.

There are stirrings from Wyn's corner that Myma ignores. She stares into her tin, fingers fiddling at the stain of the worry-itch on her left sleeve that never washes out. Maybe now she will make Wyn leave, after all that snarling in the dark. Or maybe Myma will be the one to leave. What about when you're gone? Wyn said. My stomach closes tight around the Creamed Rice Pudding.

I get up and light the fire. This is one thing I can do that feels normal. No wood left inside so I go out to the woodshed. Slight throb in my side as my hip rolls. In the dim of the shed I peel up my bed-smock to probe the hurt part. The skin is blotched dark.

Myma is standing in her boots when I step back inside. The boots are on the wrong feet. I set the logs in the hearth and the wood steams. Myma speaks behind me.

Won't let it happen.

She whispers but the sound of it is like a wail. It shakes me to the marrow. Want to run to the bed, stuff my ears and eyes with rags. I turn towards her.

Let what happen, Myma? I ask.

She smacks her forehead with the middle of her palm. The crack of it jolts Wyn awake. He sits up, his plait undone and face all rumpled.

What? he says.

Myma doesn't respond. Wyn looks to me. I stick out my jaw and stare back with thorny eyes. This is his doing. The words he spoke in the dark, his bad water, they have done something to Myma. Wyn stands slow and straightens his smock. In all the while he's been here he has only had this one smock for doing chores and for sleeping. Realising this makes me suddenly very sad.

Scritch of nails on skin. Myma's fingers have found their way under her sleeve to the worry-itch. I face her and grin my mouth wide and toothy so she knows she does not need to worry, and that everything is okay. Even though it isn't. Even though this Exception is not the good kind. Myma turns around then and walks straight out through the door. My heart thudding anxious in my stomach. Scramble into my boots and follow with Wyn stumping out behind me. Myma stands midway between the house and the trees. She is facing away from us, legs wide and braced as though about to dance. Her fingernails drag back and forward.

We're doing This-and-That, she says into the air.

This-and-That is not for now but I say okay because I do not want to bring out the scream poking up under the thin skin of Myma's speaking.

It's a new This-and-That, she says, still speaking away from us. One we haven't done before.

What is it? I ask.

Fending, she says.

Fending?

It's a This-and-That you can't do unless you are strong.

I am strong, I tell her.

Not before. Not enough. But sixteen now. Sixteen.

She turns around and the hugeness of her smile jolts me behind the navel. Wyn rubs his chin through its red tangle, his eyes nervous.

Daughter, Myma says. Stand there.

She points at a spot on the ground and I go to it.

You, she says to Wyn, not looking at him. You stand there.

His eyes follow her pointing finger but his feet do not.

Maya—

You, she says to him. You'll do the pouncing. Daughter, you'll do the fending.

I do not understand what it is we are being told to do.

Are you doing This-and-That too, Myma? I ask.

No, she says. Only two do it. You and him.

Wyn's head flicks between us.

Pouncing? he asks.

Yes, says Myma, still speaking away from him.

I'm not attacking her, he says, if that's what you mean.

A force in his voice. His eyes wide on Myma.

I'm not going to do that, he says.

It's This-and-That, she says.

It's This-and-That, I say.

I'm not attacking you, he tells me.

You said you want to help, says Myma. Prepare her. That's what you said. This is how you help.

Fingernails deep in her worry-itch. Her voice almost cracking open and I know that if it does the scream won't ever stop. Wyn flexes his long fingers. His hands go into his hair and clench.

This isn't what I meant, he says. This isn't it at all. Drop this, Maya. Let's go back inside.

She looks at him then and her mouth opens wide, wider than it should. I wait for the surface to break. For the scream to come and for everything to shatter apart. But her jaw clicks shut and when she speaks it is low and quiet.

We are doing This-and-That, she says. We let you stay. We let you be part of This-and-That. And if you want to keep staying you have to do This-and-That. That's how we do things. How I do things. My place.

Wyn, cornered.

I won't do that, he says. I won't – pounce. This won't help anyone, Maya. Just leave it now.

Myma's eyes go to slits.

That face you keep picturing, she says. No wonder it turned from you.

Wyn's cheek twitches like a stone has struck it. His shoulders go up. Caught and blinking he looks to me. I am cold in my bed-smock, belly tight with pudding and not knowing what to do.

How do you do fending, Myma? I ask.

She speaks past me, not quite to me.

You stop him, she says. You get him off you. You win when you throw him off.

The start of fending is like the start of dancing. Wyn and I stand facing each other, arms at our sides. Myma claps her hands and the clap means we must start. Step forward and stop when our knees are almost touching. Myma claps again and shouts, FEND. Wyn puts a light hand on my shoulder. I shake it off. He does it again and I bat the hand away, irritated. His mouth is moving, he is whispering something.

Not going to hurt you, he says.

Properly, says Myma. Do it properly.

Wyn grimaces. He grasps my wrist. I break his limp hold and grab his chin. Rough red in my fingers. His hand finds my jaw then and tries to push me off. Us fumbling at each other's faces until Wyn's fingers slip into my mouth and I bite down. He yelps, stumbles back. His face disappears from under my hand and my balance swings forward. I fall onto the ground with palms and knees. Glare up at Wyn, him panting and shaking my bite from his fingers. There is no blood. Something leaps in me, wanting to see my toothmarks in his hand leak red.

What help is that? says Myma. How can she fend if you won't do your part? If you won't pounce?

Wyn looking down at me, his face all worry.

Are you okay? he is asking. Not hurt, are you?

His question does something inside me. All of me seething to anger. I am angry that Wyn has never done things quite right, always scraping and grating with his words and his clumsing about and his never really trying to understand. I am angry that he made Myma cry in the dark. That he does not speak to me the way he speaks to Myma. My anger is for Myma too. I am angry that she shoved me from the bed. I am angry that all the things I know are getting chewed up and pushed out of place. And I am angry that Wyn won't do his pouncing properly. Him thinking me easy to hurt, not strong enough. Him and Myma both, how they think me helpless, unable to fend for myself. Between themselves, making me a weak thing.

A snarl ripples from me. Heel-spring and slam my body against Wyn's chest. Feel the thump of the ground and the breath on my face as it coughs out of him. My hands hitting and clawing. His fingers scrabbling at my shoulders. I yank his wrists over his head. I am the stronger. Me that has been Claw, Sting, Thorn, Nail, Splinter, Prick, Tooth, Flint, all my tearing sharpnesses. I spit into his eyes and try to bite through his clothing to get at the flesh of him beneath. Him yelling, spluttering under me.

Then Myma's hands are in my armpits, dragging me backwards. I grasp at Wyn's smock to keep myself from being hauled off. The seam rips up his left side. Rough of the cloth tugging through my hand. My heels scudding in the dirt.

Good, Daughter, says Myma behind me. That's good, that's good. Again. We'll do it again.

Her second shadow is darting about, a darker patch on the ground moving from me to Wyn to Myma and back to Wyn.

And you can just stay out of it, Myma barks at the shadow. It's nothing to do with you.

Wyn on his feet now. He coughs and spits red-white on the ground. Smock flapping open where I tore it. See the Rot-scar on his bare flank, the red-brown clump of fox hair under his arm.

Daughter, Myma says, stand up.

I do, my legs trembling. Wyn still panting, hands spread.

Maya, he says low and shaky, I told you, this isn't the way to do things. It won't help. Nothing good will come of this. Please. Let's go inside. Let's talk about it.

We're not done yet, says Myma. She can't learn to defend herself if you won't do your part in it.

And I said I'm not going to do that, says Wyn. This needs to stop, Maya. You're acting crazy. It's crazy, this. Fuck.

A belch comes sour into my mouth. Spit between my feet, the glob cloudy with Creamed Rice Pudding. Neither of them look at me.

Fine, Myma says. I'll do it. You can go away. We don't need you.

Wyn blinks. He looks more hurt by these words than by my clawing and biting. He looks the way he looked when Myma first bellowed at him in the clearing.

Myma puts her back to him and stands opposite me. She claps. Then she is pelting towards me, her small body hitting mine. I am knocked to my back and pinned to the ground. She is on my chest, her knees pressing on my arms.

You have to fend, she pants into my face. Try to push me off.

But the breath has been thumped from me. I let my head drop back and make no move to fend. Myma yanks me upright by the wrists.

Again, she says.

Her hands clap. Again her body hits mine and again I pitch backwards, trees and clearing and Wyn all swinging away into sky.

Fend, Daughter, says Myma's voice, fevered, urgent. Fend me off. Do it.

Myma has always been the stronger of us. I do not want to bite her or kick her or try to hurt her so I lie still. I want to close my eyes and sleep. Myma pulls me to my feet. I sway. I look for Wyn and find him by the step, his head hidden in his hands. He is not watching. I shut my eyes for a moment and in the dark behind my lids hear Myma clap.

Open to see her lunging. Lurch myself sideways but she catches my wrist, swings me round and puts a foot into the base of my spine. I fall on my knees, a wrench in my shoulder to make me cry out.

Myma.

Her face appearing in front of mine, puckered up and anxious.

Didn't hurt you, did I, Daughter? she says. Wouldn't hurt you. Won't let anyone hurt you.

Her fingers probe my shoulder. Hear her muttering into herself as her hands feel for the hurt.

I keep her safe, she is saying. I keep her.

Her cheek close enough to my mouth that I could poke out my tongue and taste her. Surge then of a sudden strong feeling I have never known before. A needing to be away from her. Wanting her no longer touching me. Wanting her away.

Get off me, I say.

Myma's hands go still on my shoulder but she does not let go. Her eyes shift sideways to mine.

Get off me, I repeat.

Tightening of her fingers at my collarbone.

Daughter?

I throw her hands from my shoulder and she stumbles back. Look to her eyes for the anger but it doesn't come. She watches.

She waits to see what I will do. Her second shadow a dark stain between us. Wyn's hands have come away from his face. He watches too.

I turn around and run. Across the clearing and into the trees. I do not stop to put my tooth into the cleft post.

19

The tooth behind Maya's left canine cracked away when she bit down on a shard of bone in the stew. She spat the broken chunk onto the table. It skittered and stopped beside her daughter's bowl.

Her daughter picked up the tooth, a frown pulling her brows together. She touched the bloody edge and asked if Maya would grow new teeth now, too.

'Like I did, Myma?'

'It's not like that for me,' Maya told her. 'I have no more teeth waiting underneath.'

'Why?'

'New teeth are for Daughter.'

Maya's tongue probed the tender gap. When her first few milk teeth had fallen out her father had swapped them for coins but later his coins went elsewhere. She never asked him what he had done with the teeth. It always disturbed her to think of those pieces of herself lying in some unknown place.

Her mother had once had two wisdom teeth extracted. They were put into the bin in their small see-through bag. Maya pulled the bag from among the eggshells and emptied the teeth into her palm. These were much larger than the ones that had fallen from her own mouth. They were brownish-white and stumpy, with ridges and twisted roots that made them seem like things pulled from the ground rather than from her mother's gums.

Maya kept the wisdom teeth under her bed in the bottle of her father's that also contained the rolled-up photograph of the three of them together in the garden. When she woke in the mornings to stinging wet sheets, she would peel the covers off her legs and go on her stomach between the bed and the floor. She would lie under the low roof of lint and mattress springs. She would shake the teeth from the bottle and hold one in each hand, the prongs denting her palms. Maya would stay there under the bed until two bony ankles appeared in the gap beside her, and she heard her mother sigh.

Her mother was thin-mouthed as she stripped the bed. She pulled off Maya's wet pyjamas with her face turned away. Maya moved as little as possible while this happened, her fists tight around the teeth. She let herself be stood in the bath and scrubbed. She knew that she was too old to be wetting the bed but she also knew that when she stopped, it would mean giving up this closeness. Her mother's hands washing her. Her mother's ashy breath at her neck. She held on to these moments the way she held the teeth.

'Myrna.'

Maya blinked. The sharp-chinned face across the table from her came back into focus. Her daughter was holding up the broken tooth.

'What?' Maya asked.

'I said, now you can put your tooth in the hole with mine. Then we'll both be safe.'

'Yes,' Maya replied. 'Yes. That's why I spat it out.'

The Last of My Small Teeth

The last of my small teeth fell from my mouth when I was Bark. New teeth grew in the holes and the ones that had fallen out were hung on the fence. Except for the last one, which went into the hole in the cleft post. My tooth has always seemed small next to Myma's. A little white pip beside a snaggy yellow nut.

If your tooth is gone and so are you, that's when I'll worry.

Cold air in my lungs as I run. I knock a pile of stones and send the marker toppling but do not stop until I reach the ash copse. I stand under my scratching branch. A spin in my head. Sit on a stump and breathe slow to ease it. Myma's voice in me, telling me to put your head between your knees, Daughter. I ignore the voice and close my eyes. Clenching and unclenching of my stomach like a fist. I think of Pitted Prunes in Juice, the sticky sound of them in Myma's throat. A surge and heave. Bend forward and empty my belly between my feet. Maggoty white of Creamed Rice Pudding in the leaf litter. Wipe my mouth and nose on the back of my arm.

Wyn, Myma, fending, pudding, This-and-That, the wrongness of all of it. Lean and retch again but only a string of spit comes out. Clasp my hands at the back of my head and rest my elbows on my knees. I let out some of the angry words I have gathered since Wyn-come.

Shit fuck and hell, I say. Piss shit. Jesus.

I hear footsteps and know by the lurch of them that it is not Myma's always-careful feet that have come following after me. Wyn appears between the trees. Remember that moment when he first walked into the clearing, before I knew he was Wyn, when I thought him Rotter only. How hollow-seeming and strange he was then. How he asked me to give him my name. How pale his eyes through his red hair. Those same eyes watch me now. I glare back.

I don't want you here, I say.

Why's that? he asks.

It was all good, I say, we were all good. Then you let out your Rotted words and broke it. It's your fault she went like that. It's all your fault.

He says nothing, just stands there with his smock gaping. I think about the cold air touching his side and pricking his skin to tiny dots, how I would like to touch him there too and feel the little bumps under my fingers, the warmth of him. I drop my eyes to a blob of Creamed Rice Pudding on the toe of my boot. Stare at the snotty fleck until Wyn's boots appear beside mine.

The way she loves you is wrong, he says then.

I look at his boots instead of his face. Strange, I think, a strange way to use that word. Love. I love dancing. I love potatoes and pudding. I love not wearing clothes. I love apples just before they ripen. I love the smell of woodsmoke and hearing ants go pop when we cook them on the shovel head. Myma loves arm-stroking. She loves having her back scrubbed clean. She loves pushing her hands deep into soil and she loves sucking marrow from bones. That is not what she feels for me. I am not a thing for loving and enjoying. I am a thing for worrying about. I make her scratch and scratch and sometimes I make her hurt and sometimes there is a wild staggering joy in our being together but none of that is love, such a small word. I do not know what it is. No word big enough for the thing between us that is both hurting and holding. I think about what Wyn has said and I wonder if it is true, that Myma's way of holding is not always right. How sometimes she holds me too close to her chest, grips too tight. As though I am a rabbit she is about to snap.

I lift my heels onto the stump and stand so that I am taller than Wyn.

I threw up, I tell him.

He looks down at the crusting mess.

Oh, he says.

A pulsing in me. The itch of it between my legs. There is a swelling just below one of Wyn's eyes, a darkening. I did that. Maybe later I will say a sorry for it. Or maybe I won't. Maybe I am done with sorrys. Turn and jump to the ground with bended knees. Now I am on the other side of the stump. I walk a few paces away then stop. Wanting to be alone but also not wanting that at all. Turn back to Wyn, the stump between us. He lifts his hands, palm out.

I didn't mean to upset her, he says, stepping around the stump. You either. Didn't mean for you to hear things like that. You don't understand.

I am not the one that doesn't understand, I say.

He rubs his hands over his eyes and winces at touching the swollen one. His face tired and creased. Glower at him, a throb in my belly, in my groin. I press my hand into the cleft where my legs meet. I scratch. Wyn's shoulders going tense then. All of him stiffening. I scratch again, harder.

Stop that, he says.

He crosses the space between us and grabs my wrist, not loose like in fending, but hard. I scratch with the other hand.

Close, Wyn smells like the ground, like the sweetness of meat on the edge of going bad. The itch worsening. Wanting to scratch on him the way I scratched on the ash branch. I move myself against his legs and feel a knot that nudges between.

Hey, he says, letting go of my wrist. Hey. Stop that.

He holds me away from him, his hand rough on my shoulder. I am open-jawed and panting. Shivery all over. Feel myself shiny and pointed like a knife, a flint, or a sharp tooth.

No, he says. Not that. That's not for me, you understand?

One hand firm on my shoulder, the other fumbling at his smock, pulling the cloth straight over the knot bulging there. His face pained, unhappy and confused. I rub my mouth against the hand on my shoulder, nibble my teeth at the long fingers. Wyn slaps my cheek. He does not do it hard, but it is enough to sting and stun me into stillness.

Jesus, he says. Jesus. Didn't want to do that.

His hand lets go of my shoulder and reaches behind his ear to grasp a red hank. He looks up at the sky, then back at me with those eyes the colour of air.

Won't do that, he says. No. Won't do that.

Do what? I ask.

Doesn't even know, he says. Jesus. Course you don't. How could you know?

The frenzy of my itch ebbing to a stooping, shrinking feeling. Like I have done a thing I shouldn't.

Barely sixteen, he says. No. I won't do that.

His hands flap about. Fingers going up to rub his chin, tap his teeth, tug at his hair. I wait for his eyes to return to me. When they do, I see the small head and shoulders of me inside them. The black lines of branches behind me. And something else in his gaze that does not quite fit into anything I know.

The top half of Wyn's body lurches forward, as if I have reached inside his chest and pulled hard at his breastbone.

His mouth touching mine shocks me rigid. For a moment I am completely still, stiffened by the warm and wet and hair of him, his close scent. I taste pine and rust, my own sourness of sicked-up pudding. Then Wyn is rearing away, and he is staring at me with a sort of panic, and there is a feeling rising in me, unswallowable, then the splutter leaves my mouth and I am laughing. Wyn's startled look makes me laugh harder. I bend and smack my dirty knees and howl. Wyn spits on the ground.

No, he says. No, of course not.

He wipes his mouth. Opens and closes. He does a sort of huffing half-laugh and nods his head, looking around at the trees, the forest. Then he turns and walks away in the direction of the house. I drop to my backside in the leaf litter and laugh until the tears run down into my bed-smock.

Come dark-come. I am alone in the forest and I am not afraid. Lightheaded with laughing and the vomited-up empty of my belly but not afraid. Lie on my back in the dead leaves and watch the bare fingers of the trees rubbing against the stars. The steadiness of my bloodbeat. Firm ground cold under my back. Laugh again remembering the fright in me when I was alone in the dark before, when I ran from the red-haired not-yet-known. Frightless now. Something in me has shifted. New folds in skin, new tightnesses where slack before. New muscle, rippling.

I tumble upright. Weak-sighted in the starlit black, cold too but prickling now with the thrill of it, no Myma-voice chattering in my head to scare me back to the house. The new muscle sends me running, leaping. I know the forest, my forest. I know without seeing where to jump and where to scramble and where to belly-low. I pick up sticks and hurl them, hear them break. Tip back my head and send a sicky burp up to the moon. Find something decaying, roll myself foul and delicious ultimate creamy in its reek. I skip and scurry and flurry and crawl and hurtle and howl about the forest. I am every name I have ever been. I want to snap the living from something with my teeth, so I take Myma's words and mash them with my own.

There is no Rotter that creeps in the dark, like us at the front and Rotted behind. Its hair is red and it eats our bread, Rot, Rot, bring us another, Rot, Rot, where is its mother?

Things flap and dart from my noise. Shout my song at their fleeing, my not-scared screech into their silly fear. No orange flicker-light comes to fetch me back. No voice calls Daughter. Under the bony rattle of a Keep-Safe dangling from a tree, I glare up and say out loud, It is me that keeps myself. Then climb to a branch and scratch against the trunk until the itch shivers out of me like water shaken from a pelt.

After, a yawn. A belly-whine. The dark is good but food and warm are good too. Slip myself from the tree. Walk through the good dark towards the house. My going to it now is a thing chosen by me. It is me that decides where I want to be, and when.

I do not have to think about which direction to take through the darkened forest. My newly muscled body knows the way like my finger knows the veins in my wrist. Soon comes the open, the wide starred circle of sky. I am back in the clearing. Thin glow of the fire in the gap around the door.

Step inside to Myma stirring the pot, Wyn sitting on his log at the table. He is bare-chested, stabbing a bone needle at the ripped edges of his smock. A normalness here that irks me. I snort. Neither looks up. I move towards the fire. Lift my hem high to warm my backside. I sense Wyn's eyes darting at me, taking in the smeared dirt of me, then away. Myma sets down her stirring stick. Dried blood on her sleeve sticking to her worry-itch. Twinge of guilt in my gut. Must have been a bad one, that worry, to itch it so deep as to drag the blood from it. New muscle in me struggling against the tight tendons of the old guilt. The changed parts of me knowing that the worry-itch is nothing to do with me, that it has never really been anything to do with me, that it is hers only.

You are filthy, Daughter, says Myma.

Her voice high and strained.

Yes, I reply. I am.

She reaches out a hand and puts her thumb under my chin. The scent of her the same as it has always been. See her smelling the changed scent of me and think yes, I am different now, I carry the stink of the dark. Slight flinch of her. She breaks the hold and grips her head with both hands.

Myma?

You'll be hungry, she says, dropping her hands and turning away.

I am, I say.

I watch her a moment but she has gone back to her stirring. I sit on my stool opposite Wyn. Clatter my elbows on the wood to make him look up. His eyes flicker. His hands make big clumsy stitches.

You stink, he says to the needle.

I like it, I tell him. It's the dark I stink of.

It's something, he says.

A wonky stab brings a red pricklet to the pad of his thumb. He puts it to his mouth and sucks. I look at the wetness of his lips and my own mouth tilts in remembering the ridiculous bumping of his jaw against mine, his nose pressed to my cheek.

He pulls the smock over his head. A bad mend. He has left a big hole under the armpit and the stitching is all bunched on the outside, not tucked away neat the way Myma does it.

From behind comes a short, high laugh. I stare at Myma. She is still stirring the pot but her head is flicking to one side, like she is trying to dislodge a fly. Wyn gives me a look. He leans across the table and whispers so quiet I have to watch his mouth for the shape of the words.

Since you went off. She's been – strange.

The swill then of liquid being poured.

Stew's ready, says Myma.

I am very hungry after emptying my stomach but I cannot smell what it is that Myma has cooked. She sets the bowls and Wyn's eating tin on the table. Her head twitches again.

Rabbit and potatoes, she says. Our favourite.

I look into my bowl with a lurch in my belly that is nothing to do with sick or hungry. Wyn opens his mouth, a frown beginning on his forehead, and I kick him hard under the table to stop his tongue from stumbling into saying what I know it wants to. Because the bowl before me is filled with water. Clear water. Nothing else. No chunks of rabbit, no potato, not even the dark green of boiled herbs. Glance at Myma. She is hunched over her own clear bowlful, and she is dipping her spoon, blowing, slurping. I look to Wyn. His jaw is gripped. He makes a downward movement with his eyes towards his tin. I understand, pick up my spoon.

It's good, Wyn says.

Yes, I say.

There is no fun in this pretending. There is a danger here, some threat lurking under the clear water that none of us can see. Myma doesn't say anything, doesn't look up, just keeps lifting the steaming spoonfuls to her mouth. She is no longer even blowing on the hot water. It must be scalding her tongue to blisters. Perhaps this is a Lesson. Don't roll about in the dark, Daughter, or Myma's mouth burns and none of us get fed. I lower my eyes and stir the water in my bowl.

The clatter jolts me like a slap. I look up, see Myma's dropped spoon on the table. Her left hand holds her head, the fingers digging at the scalp as if trying to claw something out.

Agh, she says.

Her right hand bats clumsy at the spoon. The spoon falls to the floor and the hand goes after it, slides right off the table. The sudden limp weight of the arm pulls Myma sideways. It is like something is yanking at her hand, hauling it down towards the floor, dragging the whole right side of her body with it. She speaks a word I don't understand and when I look at her face I see it is sagging on one side. The corner of her mouth trailing loose. Right eye half-closed, the other gaping. Left hand scrabbling at the table. Her bowl tips and hot water splatters around our feet. Her body leans and leans, tilting the stool to two legs.

I am up and round at her side of the table with my hand under her head a moment before the cold stone smacks her skull. I have caught her and I am holding her, but it is not her head I feel. She is already caught by another hand. My palm cups around the fingers of it, the sharp knuckles. Long hair sweeps over me, throws its shadow on Myma like a blanket. I look up, expecting Wyn. And I see him still sitting at the end of the table on his log, staring. His face gone the yellow-white of a dull moon. His mouth is open and I can see all his teeth.

Part III

Imago

20

There was a woman, she had a child, a boy. The man came home each night and took off his shoes. He put the shoes on his hands and clapped her head between them. Sometimes he did it so hard that the world went black and in the days after she would wander teetering through a fog, out of balance. When the man began taking his shoes to the boy's head too the woman knew it was time to leave.

She carried the boy in his blankets. She took food, two chipped mugs. Her coat wrapped them both. In her chest a weak bird beating and she knew it as hope. It flew her to the woods. There was a place there where a forester had once lived, and later where men had hung their guns and drunk from small glasses after putting bloody holes through warm pelts. Now the landowner had left the woodland to itself. Now the place stood empty and forgotten.

The woman and the boy lived a few safe months in the hut. In that time she gave him the sounds of birds and began to let the wings spread in her chest. Her son ran laughing in the woods. She called him her little red fox and let his hair grow past his ears. He laughed and brought her the clumsy things he made with sticks. She saw how it could be, and she wondered how she could keep it that way.

While the boy was sleeping the woman would rise and in the darkness walk the miles of woodland to where it thinned and opened. She stole from cellars and larders and outhouses. She dug beets and potatoes from the edges of fields. She carried what she stole back through the forest, sacked in dewy sheets pulled from washing lines. One morning, another woman walking early with a dog saw her digging in the ground, the clunking weight bundled in the sheet on her back. The woman followed with the dog to the place in the woods. She saw the skinny, dirty boy, his uncut red hair. The dog began to bark.

They came and took the boy. They brought with them the heft of words like 'welfare' and 'neglect'. The woman tried to tell them that there was only one safe place and that was her, but she was taken too, somewhere else, where the boy was not. She asked for him but they shut their mouths, and eventually she began to think they could not understand her. So instead she called for the boy using the bird signals she had taught him, hoping that wherever he was he would hear her. They told her that the bird sounds meant she was unwell. They told her they would make her better. A long time passed and she grew silent and the bird in her chest died. Eventually they said her silence meant that she was cured, and she could go now.

She walked out with her empty chest and empty hands. She went back to the woods where she had last seen the boy, back to the hut. She found it as they had left it. The bed took her weight, and she lay in it, and she lay in it, and she waited, and she did not get up, and the forest closed itself around her like a pair of arms, clasped tight.

Once I Found a Rabbit Sitting Hunched

Once I found a rabbit sitting hunched over itself in the middle of the path. It didn't move when I stepped towards it, just sat there, legs tucked under its body. I thought it must be dead until I saw the swell of its rabbit lungs. When I tried to wrap my hands around its middle the back legs kicked out like it was trying to jump away. Only it didn't jump but fell sideways stretched-out twitchy. White-brown belly arched, teeth clicking. I called for Myma and when she saw the rabbit she said, There's something wrong inside it, something wrong in its head. She said, It's going to be dead soon. And as she said it the rabbit stopped moving.

Myma lies lopsided in our bed. It's the blood in her brain, Wyn said, it's leaked where it shouldn't. After Myma's falling I had to yell his name over and over to unstiff him from his sitting-staring. Then he was down on his knees and trying to scoop her up and saying, We have to go, we have to go now, we have to get help, she needs help, I'll take her, we can go, grab some stuff and let's— And Myma was making an awful mangled sound, her left side struggling against the right, one eye open and wild, and I was clawing at Wyn's arm because I couldn't bear to see her head flopping about like that, and I shouted that he was making it worse, and finally he said,

Okay, Maya, okay, I know I know, I wasn't thinking, I won't, okay, take it easy, you're okay, we've got you. And we did have her, and we carried her between us like a crumpled sheet, held her in the bed until she calmed, and her breath quieted, and her sweat cooled.

The floor hurts my knees but I do not move from beside the bed. My boots still on my feet. Both my hands gripping her left one, the twitch of its fingers that tells me it is still a living thing. The right hand has not moved at all. She sleeps, and her face seems less wrong in sleeping. Both eyelids drooping together, mouth loose. Dread in me for her waking because I know that half of her will stay asleep. Wyn stands silent.

She'll get better soon, I say. Won't she.

I don't say it like a question.

Won't she.

Wyn coughs, speaks quiet.

You should rest.

Sore blink at him. I am more tired than I can ever remember being. I am dirty and stinking still of my forest rolling and I need a wee but I shake my head.

No, I say.

I do not say I am afraid that if my hands stop gripping Myma's then the other half of her will slip too and all of her will be lost. I do not say I am afraid that what has happened is my fault, that when I wrenched myself from Myma in the clearing I tore something out of her. That the shift in me is what has caused the shift in her. I do not say these things because then they will be true.

Come on, Wyn says.

His voice falls in on itself. He wraps an arm over his face for a moment, eyes pressing into the bend of his elbow.

Come on, he says again. Bit of sleep. With a bit of sleep we'll figure out what to do.

I only agree because of the cramping in my bladder. Tug a

tuft of hairs from my head to give to the fingers of Myma's left hand, so that they will have something of me to clutch when I let go.

The long-held wee comes painfully. Body-warm outpouring of it into the cold earth. At the edge of the clearing, the cleft post is a long torso with two up-reaching arms, whitened to bone by the moonlight. Behind, the forested black of the dark where I have reeled alone and unafraid. Turn my back on it.

Wyn is heating water. He passes me a strip of dried meat.

Got to eat something, he says.

Chew and swallow without tasting. Through my mouthful I say, Myma—

She's still sleeping, Wyn says. Nothing to be done just now.

Us looking at each other then. He is filthy too, his badly mended smock streaked with the dirt of our fending.

Earlier, he says. In the woods. What I— I won't do it again.

The memory of his mouth on mine no longer sets me laughing. It seems now like a sad and desperate thing.

Okay, I say.

You shouldn't do that with me, he says. I can't be that for you. I won't. Somebody else, maybe. Not me.

What body else? I ask, and there is pain in his look.

I do not want to disturb the sleeping sprawl of Myma so Wyn drags his sacking through for me to lie on. Huddle down under Wyn's blanket in my stiff and stenching bed-smock. He says he'll use the sheet from the doorway. He says he's slept in worse conditions. He brings a log for the burner. Then goes back through the doorway, back to his cold corner.

Wyn, I whisper.

His head reappears.

Yes, he says.

Stay.

Okay.

We lie side by side in the dark. Reek of me but he breathes

it without squirming. We touch foreheads instead of mouths. No itching in me now. Only gladness at his being here, so I am not alone.

Thank you, I say.

Sorry, he says.

Wyn falls asleep before I do. I hold my eyes open on the glow of Myma's face for as long as I can. Feel how everything has shifted, the order of things shook about and tipped out in a scrambling mess like a tin of cherry stones. I watch Myma's slack mouth and imagine what it would say about the change in me. The question it would ask.

What are you now, Daughter? I murmur to myself.

Reach then into the insides of myself, fingers stretching right into my corners. And I realise that I do not have a name.

When I say, Myma, Myma, she does not respond and the fear in me says she is dead, she is not making noise and she is not moving and so she is dead, she is dead like a dead rabbit, and she will not speak or move again.

Myma.

Her left eye flicks open. It looks at me leaning close over the bed. At Wyn standing behind. Then her left hand begins grappling with the blankets, pushing them off. Surge of hope. Myma will get up and pad through to the other room on solid feet and all that has splintered since the First Frost will become whole again. Her mouth makes a buzzing sound as she hooks left arm under right knee, tries to drag it from the bed. The leg flops to the side and she lies still. Only the heaving of her ribs, the flickering of her eyes. Black of them rolling about in the white, catching on my face, Wyn's face. The searching finger of her tongue comes out, thin and pointed. She tries to speak but her mouth cannot hold the words. They spill down her chin. Something shatters in me as I watch her struggling tongue, and I want to gather up all the fallen broken words and fumble them back into her mouth so that she can tell me it's okay, there's nothing wrong, nothing has changed, let's get on, we have many chores to do. But the words have already sunk away into the bed like the drool of Myma's milk from my small mouth, and I cannot suck either of these things back up.

Medication, I say to Wyn, and he shakes his head.

It's not meant for something like this, he says. I don't know what it would do. It might make it worse.

I try lifting the drooped edge of her face. Pinch the skin between finger and thumb, draw it upward. Her lip and lid slump when I let go.

At least she's no worse, says Wyn. Rest is the best thing. All we can do now is just get on with it.

So we get on with it. It is this way now. Every light-come I am up with Wyn while Myma stays in the bed. If she is dirty I clean her. I change her from bed-smock into chore-smock, then at dark-come from chore-smock into bed-smock. She makes this difficult. Her left leg jerks about. Her left arm snatches at the clothes and the good half of her mouth makes irritated sounds that louden when I can't understand them. When I feed her she is twitchy and impatient. Her one eye looks wary at me as I lift the spoon to her mouth, like it is a trick. Sometimes she lunges sudden for the bowl, trying to grab it from me, spattering the blankets with thin stew.

Why do you need to put her in the other one anyway? Wyn asks one light-come when he finds me panting to pull the chore-smock over Myma's head, her good arm flailing, a groan in her throat.

Because, I tell him, it's what we do.

A strong feeling in me that this is the only way to set things the right way up again. To pull us out of the terrible Exception. To mend the broken parts in Myma's head, stitch the torn-away halves of her together, and pull everything back from where it has tumbled to. What we do, what we have always done, we must keep doing. Chores. This-and-That. Sorrys and thank yous. These things take us through the lights, the darks.

The bruise on my hip yellows, fades. The dried grub goes into the Museum and nothing takes its place in my pouch. I remain only Daughter with no other name to call myself. The new muscle I felt growing in me stays unused and slack, a small exhausted bird with wings pinned together.

Somehow Myma seems to fill more space since she split down the middle. There is no longer room for me in our bed beside the spread of her so I stay on the sacking and Wyn stays beside me. We sleep this way now. Sometimes I see Myma watching us in the gloom but no snarl comes from her mouth to tell me to put the Rotter back in the other room, Daughter, and I am grateful at his being here with us, in this room that is ours.

Sometimes Wyn and I hold each other's elbows when we sleep. Or he tucks his face under my chin, hair draped warm and scarlet across my shoulder. Or I lie with my ear on his chest to listen to the trickle of his blood, the snag and burr of breath as it whistles into his lungs. His smell of pine bark and blood. Feel no urge to scratch against the hard lump of groin that sometimes prods my side when he is sleeping. I prod it back once and he grunts awake and hisses, Owfuck fuck ow whydyoudothat dontdothatagain. After that I leave it alone. He was right. We are not mouth-on-mouth scratch-the-itch for each other. Wyn is something else, something closer than itching. He is like me.

Are you awake? he whispers one dark.

I am awake, I whisper back.

I'm worried about her, he says.

Myma is going to get better.

She might not.

I am asleep now, I tell him. Stop talking.

For a long while he is quiet, only the crackling breath of him. Then he speaks again.

When she fell, he says. When she fell, I saw – I think I saw something.

Saw what? I ask, turning my head to his.

Our noses are close. His moves side to side with the shaking of his head.

I don't know. It was late, we were all so tired. Everything was mixed up. It was only a moment. But I really thought it could be – her.

His hand holds something close at his chest. On the wall, the eyes of his drawing are open and in the dim they seem to look at me.

Winter quicks into the forest. The come of a deep cold without the bright and sharp of snow or frost. Rain freezing to grey streaks. Air scraping our lungs. I knot rabbit pelts around my throat by the legs and start wearing Myma's coat under my cloak to do my chores of gathering wood and checking the empty traps. Wyn cloaks himself in a fur blanket. From Myma's pocket I have pulled his folding knife, and now he carries it in his rag-wrapped hand. We wrap our feet in rags too. Stuff fur into the gaps in the roof, under the door. Wad dead leaves around the window to keep out the rattling chill. Wyn and I take it in turns to feed the burner through the dark.

Comes a light for washing. From the window I watch Wyn stumping out into the clearing with the bucket, as he must always do when we wash. His place for washing is outside. How hard he shivers when the smock comes off. How he grimaces and grits his teeth. I glance at Myma, asleep in the bed. Then I go out after Wyn, I go to him, I take him by the hair and tug him back inside.

He is shrinking and uncertain at first. When I lift my bed-smock over my head he turns away and covers his eyes.

His fear is one I do not understand. I pull his hands from his face, prise apart his lids. He squirms his mouth and nudges me away but when I take the soaked rags and begin to wash my underarms he seems to untighten, to settle. He steps out of his trousers and stands uncovered. Him the tall red animal, naked in the house. His all-over fur. His extra flapping part, wrinkled and soft-looking like a new mouse. In our bare skins we are different but we are also the same. Nothing about his body surprises me. I do not itch for any part of it. It is all just Wyn, the way he is.

With a rag I clean away the grime behind his ears. He lets me take each of his hands in mine and scrub the dirt from the wide palms, the long fingers. I wash his back, and he washes my back, and I wring the water from his hair.

Myma stops fighting the sleeping half of her body. She becomes a still and silent point we move around. It is like she refuses to split herself in two, to stir one half of herself without the other. She is limp when I clean her, both arms and both legs drooping.

One dark, I choose copying for This-and-That. I put the copying crown on Myma's head and wait for her to move but she doesn't so I lie on the floor and stare like her, blink when she does. I do it for a long while and then Wyn, standing over me, says, We should probably do something else. When we dance, I lift her slack limbs and move them about. And when we draw, my fist holds her fingers around the charcoal to scrawl shaky leaves on the wall.

I watch the knots and ropes of muscle in her arms and legs shrivelling up like the tops of the potato plants when their stems wither. Something else going from her too. It is not just her body that has been pulled in half. Some halfness on the inside. The whole bright Myma of her, not quite here. Her eyes hardly flickering when I speak her name, the black of them clouded, dark water scummed with ash. Her tongue no longer scrabbles for words but sits dull behind her teeth. I only see the floppy muscle when she lets it hang from her mouth so I can spit onto it the scraps of dried meat I chew for her.

Keep her here, I say into the hole of the cleft post when I drop her tooth in.

I leave the tooth there. For a tether. For a piece of her kept safe, like when she goes off into the forest. Except it's herself she's gone off into and I do not know how to call her back. When I was smaller Myma would sometimes hide up trees or under bracken, then whistle for me to find her. I was not afraid because I knew that she always kept her eyes on me, whistling when I strayed. The fizzing joy in me at seeing her eyes peering from the undergrowth, her elbow poking from behind a tree. How it seemed like everything in the forest would swing suddenly around and point towards her. There you are, Myma.

Now I am afraid because I am not sure how to find her. No whistle for this kind of hidden.

I bring her pieces of my Museum. Hold each object close under her nose, tilt her head forward to see. I speak the names of them, the names of me. Grub, Bone, Root, Flint, Mud, Tooth, Sycamore, Foot, Wing, Woodlouse, Rib, Prick, Berry, Hoof, Apple, Splinter, Walnut, Snail, Bark, from the last name of me to the first of me, Pip. I do not set the objects back behind their glass but place them around the bed, around Myma. I do it so she will not forget the words, the names. I do it so she will not forget all the Daughters I have been.

Know as I speak slow and clear the name of each thing, each Daughter, that I am also doing it so I will not forget myself. Yet in my mouth the names no longer feel solid and steady. The weight they carry seems to lessen. When I hold the objects to my ears the sound of them is faint, as if covered over with earth. I listen and listen, owl pellet and alder catkin pushed right into the holes of my ears, but they hide their voices from me. I begin to think they can somehow sense the hollow that has opened inside me where there used to be a name, and they shrink from it.

Tooth, I say to the fox tooth. Tooth.

But its sound moves further and further away, a yowling distant and unhappy. Nameless and hungry for a name I grip these things and feel them withdrawing, growing strange to me.

Something in Wyn drawing away too. He is hunching into himself but in a different way to Myma. A trouble in him that I can't quite grasp. The twitching-about of his eyes, the way they seem always to be looking for something. He unscrews and rescrews the lid on the empty bottle that held the bad water, as if by doing this he might make it fill up again. Only a few white seeds of medication left rattling in his brown container.

I find him holding the fox tooth, frowning as if he too is trying to hear something from it, then putting it back beside the bed when he sees me watching. Or I find him standing in front of the tins, just staring at them, at the pictures. He shuffles through the stack of labels, his lips moving. His finger goes over and over the patterns of flowers on Myma's mug, the R and the rabbit on mine, his face screwed up as if grappling with some knotted thought. When I say his name, he jumps. His voice becomes small with hardly speaking. During the lights, he takes himself off chopping logs in the forest, or he fiddles with his knife and bits of wood in his corner, which I still think of as his corner even though he sleeps in the room with us now. Hear him crying in the dark beside me, the quiet fox-cub whimper of him.

Me unwhimpering, dry-eyed since Myma fell. An emptiness in me that I stuff to the edges with doing. In all the silence that has filled the house, I become a clattering thing. I bring my feet down harder when I walk. I breathe louder. My mouth begins talking as soon as it wakes, and later sends itself muttering to sleep. It talks about what chores need doing, about This-and-That and what it will be, whose turn it is to choose, about when we should next wash, when we should cut our toenails, and how good it will be when we are through the winter, how then the traps will be full of rabbits and the ground will turn green and smelly with garlic leaves and maybe there will even be a muntjac again and Myma will go outside and bring the flowers in and fill the empty bottles with their colour. Sometimes Wyn shakes me awake from dreams where I stand bent over in the forest with my mouth open, words flopping out of me like wet moths.

Stop jabbering, he says.

But my jabbering is what keeps the other things from spilling. All the questions inside me that sit half-formed and sticky like the middle of an egg. Questions of how long we can exist this way, how long an Exception can last, how long Myma will stay like that, and of Myma's other name, of Wyn and his carved head and his lost mother, of all the overheard scraps of speaking between Wyn and Myma, the words I did not understand, the hurts they showed each other, things done and seen and felt before I existed, a place not this one, a place beyond the fence, what it really means to be Rotted, what the point is in all our Keep-Safes if the worst thing isn't outside the fence but inside the skull waiting to bleed and change the colour of everything, and most of all IS SHE GOING TO GET BETTER IS SHE but no I ram it tamp it squash it down and think only of what needs doing.

Wyn is in the other room and I am kneeling beside the bed spooning watery rooty stew into Myma's mouth, talking about planting the saved potatoes after the cold has gone, when Myma's second shadow peels itself from the small blanketed mound of her body. I haven't seen it since she fell. It must have clung close to her all this while. A gap in my speaking as I watch the shadow moving across the wall. Anger rushes into the gap.

Why can't you lift her feet too? I ask it. What's the good of a shadow that dances about by itself anyway?

I want something hard to hurl so pick up the fox tooth and throw it. Click of it hitting the wall, then floor. Myma's second shadow carries on moving towards the doorway. See the long hair, how it trails. Wyn comes through into the room where we sleep just as the shadow passes into the room where we eat. He stops. His eyes close and his breath sucks in and for a moment he stands swaying. Then he blinks back into the room. He looks down at the fox tooth next to his rag-wrapped foot.

We're out of meat, he says.

21

Maya was glad to leave school. Kitty and Lauryn went travelling together, Darry moved away to work for his uncle, and Maya stayed with her mother, who only left the house now for church, her scarf knotted close at her neck.

Maya took work that came in pieces. She hacked cabbage heads from their stems and tossed them into trailers. She stood at the conveyor belt to pick out damaged, green and rotten potatoes from the crop. She packaged carrots and loaded boxes into the backs of lorries. She laid hedges. She mended the wire fences and patched the splintering barns and outhouses.

She found she did not mind the way her muscles ached. It was good to have full hands, to lift and haul. At night the exhaustion in her body kept her from dreaming. Because the work was always temporary, she did not have to open herself to anyone. She was paid in cash, which she brought home to her mother along with the defective produce she was allowed to take. The lumpy vegetables disappeared but Maya never saw her mother eating.

In the garden, the ermine caterpillars sheeted the spun gauze of their webs across the bushes. From the kitchen window, the leaves seemed hung with ghosts.

Maya was peeling boiled eggs. It was a Sunday. It was her birthday.

She and her mother sat almost together at the table, their chairs at angles. Her mother wore her church clothes. She kept her cloud of smoke close around her.

Maya's father and the local news had always called the moth larvae 'pests'. Under the webs the hedgerows became gutted and whole trees were stripped bare. Maya found them beautiful and eerie. The larvae were clever too, she thought, to make their cocoons under the cottony swathes that protected them from predatory birds. When she was a child Maya had stood at the end of the garden and watched the adult moths shucking their cases, the damp bloom of their wings. There were always a few that did not hatch at all, and the cocoons eventually fell away with the webs.

Maya picked shell from rubbery white. Her mother spoke.

'When you were born,' she said, 'it took you two days to come. They had to cut you out. You were too small and you weren't breathing. They wouldn't tell me if you were alive or not. I hoped I would die instead.'

Her face stayed turned towards the window. The bones jutted in her neck and a deep inhale lifted her chest.

'Then you got this infection when you were a baby. I couldn't understand where it had come from. I thought I must have given it to you. I was afraid of touching you after that.'

Maya put the peeled egg on her mother's plate. It was perfect and whole. She thought about the two wisdom teeth from her mother's mouth which she still kept under her bed, the photograph that sat with them in the bottle.

'Were we happy?' she asked, like a child.

Her mother's eyes stayed fixed on the white netting where the larvae were doing their changing. Maya was startled by the wetness that spilled into the scoop of her mother's cheek. Crumbs of ash fell from the end of the cigarette.

'He did love us, Maya.'

It was not an answer. Her mother said nothing else. The tears trickled into her scarf and darkened the collar of her shirt. She did not wipe them away. Her face did not move at all.

Maya felt a raw space opening and contracting. If she had let the words come bloody from that part of herself, she would have told her mother that she was wrong, that love was not something you hid like a stone in your fist. It should be held out in an open palm, not heavy but light, no more than the weight of a moth. She would have said, One day, I hope to love something with lightness.

Instead she spoke from somewhere higher up, from the lump in her throat.

'I think I've always felt alone.'

Her mother looked at her then. She took the egg from her own plate and placed it on Maya's. Maya caught her hand before it could draw away. She gripped.

It would not be long before the moths would emerge and mate. They would lay their eggs and the eggs would hatch into caterpillars which next year would drape the branches with the pale ghosts of their mothers before wrapping themselves in their mothers' shrouds to birth themselves all over again. The inevitability of it was crushing, Maya thought.

Over the coming weeks she watched the web thicken. It became opaque, the leaves underneath no longer visible. When the moths flew, the shroud remained. In it Maya found a spun casing hanging unhatched. She put it under her bed with Darry's sweet and the rabbit bone, the scrap of sleeve smeared with Kitty's lipstick, her father's bottle, the photograph, her mother's teeth, all those other containers for the things her mind struggled to hold.

I Hunger

I hunger and am unfed. I listen and am unhearing.

22

Sometimes in the hut Maya dreamed of hip bones at her back, the warm press of a mouth against the skin behind her ear. She dreamed of a tongue that searched for hers. She loosened and unspooled in the darkness while the child slept.

In the years after Kitty left, Maya had buried the part of her that wanted. She thought of that part as a stunted thing, forced to grow in a small, dark space. It led nowhere, a cut string.

Sometimes Maya went to the pub with the other workers. She recognised how the men's eyes changed when they drank. They looked at her and she looked back. It was easy then to stand and leave and go out to the back where the bins from the butcher's shop next door put a sweet and rotten stink into the air. One of them would always follow like a dog with his head slung low and hopeful. There was no need to speak. Maya felt the simpleness of their hunger and how it made them vulnerable. She wanted to understand the quick urge of that hunger so she cracked the men open like eggs. Her shoulders and back had grown strong with hefting. She put their hands where she wanted them. The men sighed and she heard things dying in their throats. Sadnesses came off them and trickled past her in the dark, and she wondered where it was they poured themselves to. She thought, There are places in me that you will never see. Out by the rank bins she searched for the opposite of something.

Then Georg came with the potato harvest one year. She had a broad jaw and when she spoke her name it sounded from under her tongue. She stood beside Maya at the grading station to pluck out the stones and clods of earth. Maya watched her fast hands as they tossed the waste. During the midday break those same hands wrote cramped black words in a small book. At the end of the day Georg would meet Maya's eyes and nod briefly, and the something that Maya had tried to numb would stir.

Georg and the other seasonal workers avoided the pub where the looks and slurs that were flung at them said there was no room for them there. So when Georg turned to Maya after a late shift and asked, 'Will you come for a drink?' Maya followed her back to the grid of static caravans where the workers from overseas were housed for the harvesting season. The caravans had grey roofs and lace curtains. Washing hung between them. Across the fields Maya could see the grain silos of the plant where her father used to work. They passed other workers sitting outside in green plastic chairs. Georg spoke greetings in more than one language.

On the leaf-patterned sofa in the close space they sat and drank from cans.

'At home,' Georg told her, 'I write for newspapers. But there's no stability in it. My father came here every year until the pain in his back stopped him. I'm not sure I will come back. The managers, they are bastards. They call us gypsies like they're not the ones who give us these shit places to stay in.'

'I don't plan on staying here either,' Maya said.

Georg drew one leg up onto the sofa so that she sat with her torso angled towards Maya. On the shelf behind her Maya saw a framed photograph: Georg, younger, standing grinning with a man around her age who shared her eyes and jaw. She felt the reach of Georg's gaze like a searching hand.

'Everyone here keeps their faces hidden,' Georg said. 'Like they are wearing them on the inside.'

She held Maya's chin and Maya was struck by how much she did not want that finger and thumb to be taken away. The surge of feeling made her dizzy. She groped for a stopping place, somewhere to draw breath.

'What do you write in your book?' she asked, her voice stumbling.

Instead of replying, Georg put her mouth on Maya's. Her taste was fresh and yeasty. She stood and shrugged off her clothes like it was the easiest thing, like there was no fear in being seen by another person. Then she took what Maya had tried to deaden and she set it pulsing.

For some weeks it was like this. They worked in silence at the conveyor belt, then they lay on the floor of the caravan where Maya felt herself unfolding. Her hair slid through Georg's fingers. Georg spoke guilelessly and seriously. She told Maya of the brother at home whom she missed. She read Maya the poems scribbled in her book.

'They don't translate well,' she told her. 'It's hard to make them mean the same thing.' So she read them in her own language and Maya thought how sometimes sound was more important than meaning, or that perhaps all meaning could be carried in sound.

What went between them was brief and bright. They were two lines crossing over for an instant. Seasonal, Maya thought, means belonging to a moment – it means coming to an end.

Because she knew this, there was only a little ache in the parting. She tucked away the potato Georg nudged into her workspace on that last day, the rooted shape like a lumpy shrunken heart. Georg had been looking forward to returning home and seeing her brother. She did not look back as she left.

Only in the quiet sleeping dark was Maya able to slip again into that short season where wanting had not been shoved down to lie sour in the dirt but had sprouted green and vigorous. She could never stay there long. Soon, always soon, would come the murmur from the child curled at her back, the tug of her daughter's sleeping fingers at her hair. And they would be two in the bed again, the only two. Across the room the stirring shadow of the grey woman, keeping watch.

You Are Looking Fat

You are looking fat and full, Berry-Daughter, Myma said. That's very good.

I grinned through my mouthful of dock and bark bread smeared with a mash of strawberries and yellowy pigeon grease, and I rubbed my hands over my stuffed stomach, pleased.

You are looking fat too, I told her.

She smiled back with big cheeks, her teeth spotted with seeds. It was our fattest summer ever. We still had meat left from the muntjac, and our snares caught so many rabbits we did not know what to do with them. The foxes got plump on our leavings. The ground was swollen with potatoes that we pulled up in heavy clumps, each tuber almost the length of my hand. My shorts strained. Our sacks split. Rain gushed warm from the sky and we ran out into it, our skins bare and our mouths wide.

I was Berry, round and firm and sun-flushed like the ones that thicked the bushes, like the hard little blood-bead of the redcurrant I carried in my pouch, its full sound like the swell before a burst.

Myma called it our Summer of Feasting. Then the winter came and even with all the food we had saved I still had to tie my trousers tight and become Prick-Daughter, the thin needling spine I plucked from the dead hedgehog, and I haven't been quite as fat since.

Myma and I always prepare for winter by putting extra meat on our bones and storing up our food. Only this winter all the food is gone and our bones are almost naked. Wyn and I take turns trudging the forest. Wyn finds what he calls some likely-looking holes, spends a whole light digging them up but unearths only caved-in burrows, a scatter of dirty bones. He comes back panting, the bones rattling in a sack. We boil them for broth even though they are dry and brittle and all we can wring from them is muddy water.

We stew thin roots with the pulpy white inner bark of pine. We boil the skin from old pelts, cut tough strips for chewing. One piece of hide can last for ages if I gnaw slow. Wyn swallows his when he is done with it but I feed the mush of mine to Myma. Spoon chunks of my own small food share into her mouth because I know that when she gets better everything will be better. She will make it better.

One dark, we cook the potatoes meant for burying after winter. Sadness in me as I eat because without any kept for planting we won't ever have potatoes again. I crush the last potato to a pap for Myma.

Wyn says we should open the last two pudding tins and to hell with it but I tell him no, they are for the First Frost and that has already passed, so we have to wait for the next one. To open the tins now would be too much wrongness in all the wrong. If we did, there would be no pudding left as well as no potatoes, and that would mean the end of something, some vital thing that keeps us. We read the labels out loud instead, to each other and to Myma. The words cramping our hungry bellies. Enjoy hot or cold. Serving suggestion. For a delicious dessert, serve heated custard over a fresh slice of your favourite pie.

When I fetch water in the early light I listen for birds and hear only feeble chitterings. The few I see perched in the trees are scrawny like us. No bait to bring them close. They stay above the reach of my arms, flapping higher when I climb up to snatch at them. The rabbit snares are untouched. Once, I see a ribby fox skulking the fur and bones of itself along the edge of the clearing.

You can't have our leftovers, I snarl at it. We haven't got any.

I have never known the forest like this, so stripped and quiet and still. I cannot help feeling that Myma's falling is the reason for it, that the forest and everything in it has fallen with her in some way, that if she does not get better then this winter will never end.

We are ragged and unwashed. All three of us bone-skinned. If I stand too quick the blackness swarms and I have to lean over my knees. Shadows like smears of charcoal between my ribs. Wyn's trousers gape wider and wider at the waist until he needs twine to keep them up. Deep grooves appear under his cheekbones. The cold puts its scraping in him and he coughs and coughs his red clots into rags I later find dried brown and brittle like my own blood-rags.

Mostly he sits in his corner setting his knife to lumps of wood, making eyeless faces and half-creatures, carved and rasped and pared down until he is left with only chippings, which he sweeps into the fire. Only the first wooden head stays. He holds it in his fist to sleep.

I watch him becoming less of himself, less solid. Worry that if he keeps thinning and coughing up chunks of himself then soon there might be nothing left of him, and it will be like Wyn-come never happened at all. He still sleeps beside me on the floor but he faces the other way, his spine knobbling towards me. Don't disappear, I want to tell him, but my own flesh is falling off too and I hardly have the energy for speaking any more, the outpour of my words made thick and sluggish by hunger and exhaustion. I clamp my teeth against the fear piling up in my throat, hold my arm firm over Wyn's chest in the dark to keep him pressed here. Grip the jut of him.

The strain of all there is to hold at the moment. My arms tiring with it.

We wake to snow. Not the dry white powdery kind that falls like flecks of skin brushed from the heel of Myma's foot, but a snow that is grey, heavy and wet. I glare at it from the window. Snow makes everything more difficult.

I pile Myma with blankets, draw them right up around her ears. The water tank is frozen so Wyn and I pack the bucket with snow to melt in handfuls in the cooking pot. Taste the shadow of the sky in it when we drink, the haze of clouds mixed with the root-tang of ground.

The snow keeps us close to the house for the whole light, gathering sticks for kindling and digging around the edges of the clearing for roots.

Anything for the pot?

Some.

Me too. Some.

Lots of bark.

Yes, lots of bark.

We speak this way now, Wyn and me. It is like Myma took all the important words with her wherever she has fallen to, and the only ones our mouths can make now are the ones that carry the least amount of meaning. Or maybe it's just that we both understand if we haul up the words that sit heavy at the heart of us, the weight of them will be the thing that shatters us.

There are four wishbones in the crate. They have not been boiled for broth because they are for This-and-That. And we must carry on doing This-and-That. Myma told me once that This-and-That is the one thing we do that we don't have to do, so that's why we have to do it. Now I think I know what she meant. We need This-and-That like we need laughing and thumbs under the chin. Those things won't keep us fed but they will lift our heads when we are tired. And when we fall on our backs in the grey snow they will cover us like a blanket of warm hands.

This dark it is my turn to choose This-and-That and I have chosen wishing. It is a silent This-and-That, so Myma can still do it. Wyn sits knee-bent and facing me on the sacking. With thumbs and fingers we pinch the flat branches of bone.

Onetwothree, I say.

We split the bone. Wyn's branch holds the crest. His head lowers as he makes his wish and I stare at the top of it where the hair parts. I had wondered if Wyn's hair might turn from red to yellow, then brown, then drop from his head the way the leaves drop from the trees. But the strands have stayed as bright as when I first saw the blaze of them in the forest.

Wyn's wish is a long one and I grow impatient, pick at the skin around my thumbnail until it rips and bleeds.

You and her now, Wyn says finally.

I grip Myma's fingers around the bone, onetwothree and pull. The wish is mine and I make it fast, scoop the wish floating nearest to the surface, the one that feels most urgent. I wish for everything to go back to the way it was.

A strange flatness in me after I have made this wish. I watch Wyn curling Myma's hand around the next wishbone. Look at the skin of her left inner arm, the lumpy heal there. With her right hand always sleeping, she has not been able to scratch at her worry-itch. I think about what it would mean to go back to the way things were. How maybe not all those things were good. Myma pricking and pinching and digging at herself, me wrapped tight in all her worry. And I think of my tumbling-leaping-shouting in the dark forest, of the fence and of the doubts in me that have been growing since Wyn-come. Wonder then if going back to how it was would even be possible after all that has happened, after all I have thought and heard. Wonder if going back is even what I want.

The snap of bone brings me back into the room.

Your wish, says Wyn to Myma.

We both watch her. She breathes and blinks. This hardly hereness. Her hair drapes dull and limp. Imagine under all that grey-brown, the wish forming like a shoot under snow. I used to think that we were two parts of the same body, that our heads, split open, would look the same, filled with the same stuff. But really I have no idea what fills her head. She has always been able to tell what I am thinking, and I have never been able to tell what she is thinking. All of it hidden from me.

The last wishbone sits between us.

You take it, Wyn tells me.

So I grasp it with myself, a bone-branch in each of my hands. Onetwothree pull. The wish I make with the splitting of bone is the opposite of my first wish.

Then something. A light-come with less cold in its breath. Sun bright like the snap of ice on the puddles. Pale yellow-blue splintering the grey.

I find Wyn standing on the step outside, his eyes closed and his face turned upward. Sunlight fills the hollows under his eyes and cheeks. It puts the brightness back in his hair. I stand looking at him, and I think how familiar he has become, how known. I know he feels me there but he does not open his eyes.

Pissit, I say.

The first word I heard him speak. Back when I still thought

him Rotted. No longer sure that he ever was. Wyn's lips twitch, then spread. And then his eyes do open, and they look at me, and he is smiling, and I am more warmed by his smile than by the chilly sun. I stretch my lips back at him, feel the tight muscles in my cheeks.

Pissit's about right, he says.

His smile dims slightly then, and his eyebrows dip. He opens his mouth as if to say something else. Then the sun slips behind a cloud and the shadows reappear on his face. His mouth closes. He coughs and jerks his head at the door.

I'll get her cleaned up, he says.

I'll look for food, I say.

The forest drips when I walk into it. Plapping of snow as the trees shake it off. It is still cold enough to keep me shivering and touching my nose to make sure it hasn't dropped numb from my face. Something stops me on the path and in my groggy hunger I have to stare a while at the thing before I can remember what it is.

A pigeon. There is a pigeon on the ground. There is meat. Stay very still, watching it. The bird flaps in a circle. It seems injured. One wing beating while the other drags, stirring the slush to mud. Tread closer. White-rimmed orange eye seeing me. The pigeon beats its wing harder then tips onto its back, scaly legs thrashing. A laugh spurts from me. The sound strange in the forest's quiet trickling. Once the laugh has come it is hard to make it stop. It gasps the air out of me. I have to force myself to breathe slow. Pat my cheeks with rag-wrapped hands and remind myself that I am supposed to be gathering food, that the bird on the ground is food, that I must catch it and take it to the house so that we can eat and Myma can get better.

The pigeon does not struggle when I lift it. It must be tired from all its flapping. I am tired too. As I pin the bird beneath my elbow I think about Myma and her worst Lesson at the ash tree, her saying, If I step off my neck will snap and I'll be dead.

If being dead means not making noise and not moving, then does it mean half-dead to only move half the body? And what kind of being is it if Myma refuses to move at all, if she does nothing but blink and breathe? The pigeon's breast beats fast under the feathers. I am gentle as I grasp the neck.

Don't worry, I say to the pigeon.

I tug. The feet scrabble then go still.

Wyn looks up frowning from his corner as I fall through the door and fold over with panting after running all the way back.

What's happened? he asks.

I thrust the sack at him. He tucks away his knife and bits of wood and comes to look. When he sees the pigeon at the bottom of the sack his whole face lifts. He makes a whooping noise, pulls the pigeon out by the neck.

Oh, he shouts. We'll have a right feast.

It is not a right feast. It is a single chunk each and the rest saved to be eaten over the coming lights. But it is meat, and it is good. Myma swallows a whole bowlful of broth and I am pleased.

A dizzy dark-come energy in us then from the scraps of meat lining our stomachs. Wyn chases me round the table, blows a spray of pigeon feathers from his fist and howls laughing when they settle in my hair, real belly-laughing like I have not heard from him since the First Frost. I grab up the feathers, blow them back towards him and yip my own laugh. The laughing makes our heads light and it makes Wyn cough himself ragged but it is the best thing, better than potatoes, better than the first taste of pudding after a season-cycle of stew.

Then another sound comes rasping from the bed. A word, scraped and pinched but here, in the room with us.

Bird.

Our laughing stops.

Myma?

Myma's left hand grips a pigeon feather. Her mouth is scrunched, chin pushed outwards.

Bird, she says.

23

The man held the wall with one hand. His spumy stream puddled around his feet. Maya saw how he leaned, how his head rolled about on his shoulders.

She carried a bag that carried the eggs that were too small, too large or too warted with calcium deposits to be sold to the supermarkets. The treads of her boots were thickened by straw and chicken shit. She had taken work on the poultry farm her father used to roll grain for. When she gave the hens their feed she thought of him, of his scooping hands. At the end of each week Maya took the potato Georg had given her out of her chest pocket and washed the overalls before returning the potato to the pocket. Georg had left no address, no phone number, and Maya had not given her own. She supposed she could have asked at the potato farm but she didn't know what she would have said, had she made contact. I miss you. Can I come and stay? Can I come and stay for ever? The static caravans stood empty. The potato, misshapen souvenir, was a reminder of something. One day it would moulder, and perhaps that was best.

The man's urine moved along the cracks in the pavement. As Maya approached the door of the pub another man came out and saw her. He stood in her way and grinned.

'Just going to buy cigs,' he said. 'You'll be here when I'm back? It's been a while.'

Maya recognised his voice but not his face.

'Not tonight,' she said. The man's arm caught her waist as she made to move away.

'We had fun, didn't we?' he asked. His breath was meaty and his grip was sloppy. Maya pulled herself from him easily. The man snorted.

'You have her, mate,' he said to the other man's back. 'Stinks worse than you do.'

He walked away. The other man lurched around and Maya found herself looking at what used to be her father's face, blotched and hanging loose under the eyes. His open trousers showed a wilted brownish cock. His eyes slipped about and caught on Maya's. She stood stiff and waited for the widening of recognition. But her father's gaze slid off her, his face slack and impassive. His feet shuffled back towards the door of the pub. He went after them, stuffing himself away.

In the house, Maya put the eggs into the fridge. Then she went to her room and reached under her bed for the cold and certain shape of the bottle that held her mother's teeth. Her hand moved in the empty space. She looked and saw only the floor, cleaned of dust and of the things she had kept there, the fragments stored up against her spilling. Even the sticky lump of boiled sweet and rabbit bone was gone.

Maya's mother appeared in the doorway.

'Don't be angry,' she said, and Maya was unable to speak.

She did not sleep that night. The space beneath her felt too vast. With nothing left to grip, she felt herself untethered. The things she had tried to shut out now came into the room and stood around her bed, a circle of faces peering down. She went downstairs when she could no longer bear them.

The only light came from the open door of the fridge. Her mother sat at the table in the yellow shadow and stared at the eggs. Her shoulders were sharp lines, her cheeks two empty cups. Maya saw the underside of her chin swelling, as if something were gathering there.

Her mother said, 'I— I hoped it would make you leave,' and Maya said, 'I know.' Her mother said, 'Forgive me,' and Maya said, 'Mum.'

They looked at one another a while. Though neither spoke again the silence that went between them was teeming.

Every night after that, when Maya came downstairs unable to sleep, her mother would be sitting there at the table. Sometimes Maya sat down too. Sometimes she cooked eggs and ate them. Sometimes she stood looking out at the dark garden, or she went back upstairs and lay under the bed. She came down one early morning when the sky in the window was just beginning to pale. There was her mother at the end of the table. Her head had fallen back against the chair. The blood to her heart had stopped flowing. The cigarette was a column of ash between her fingers and her body was cool and stiff.

Words Fall Differently

Words fall differently from different mouths. This I learned after Wyn-come. Words familiar as my own skin turned strange in his mouth, came back to me heavy and lumpy with new meaning. And the other words, the ones I didn't know, carried here in the pouches of Wyn's cheeks. Boy. Girl. Dog. Family. Mother. Medication. Hell. How those words sat like stones, cold and hard and unknowable until I picked them up and felt them beating. Still I do not understand them all.

Myma's speaking returns in patches, stretched and strained slow by the drag of her mouth. She spits out single words that flit like bats about the room. Bird. Am. Fence. Both. Smoke. Spoon. And others that sound like words but that I only understand as clusterings of sound. Pig. Kitty. Darry. Farm. Mirror. Candle. Georg. Kitchen. When her mouth does manage to join words together, the sense of them is lost as they struggle out into the air, and they collapse into not-meaning. Grey one cut black underneath. Culled it dirty. Hundred big wet. Red thief bled the milk. Rotty barn. Now cold I am full of rustling wings. Daughter-Bird. Pig-Daughter. Savage Pig-Daughter. Them all underneath. You with teeth till it doesn't bite. To Wyn she says, Fox-bird her one, her little red. Her eyes thrusting eager into ours as she speaks, prodding us to understand. But when I repeat the words back to her she frowns and jerks her head side to side, as if that was not what she meant to say at all.

Between the broken-up chunks of Myma's speaking, I think a lot about mouths and words. I think how one fits into the other, how they shape each other. I think of a sinewy cord, something like a long plait of hair, tying the speaking part to the thinking part. And I imagine this cord snapping in Myma's head. Then the bloody ends clotting together in a bumpy scar. A crookedness in that mending, like Wyn's badly stitched smock.

Something of her coming back to us, or at least wanting to. I do not know if it was the pigeon meat or our laughing that reached in and plucked her from her lying-still-staring. See the try in her now. She no longer leaves the left side of her body to wither like the right, but bends and stretches her left arm and leg as if afraid of letting them stiffen. She throws the good half of herself into This-and-That. I put a stick of charcoal into her left hand for drawing. The charcoal shudders when she holds it to the wall beside the bed and the pictures jumble like her words. Each thing turning into another before it can become itself. I watch as her three-legged scrawl of a rabbit grows branches from its head. Above it flies a flock of Daughters with huge flapping moth wings. Below, a faceless Myma-shape lying flat, with hair that spills downward like roots. Next to it stands another Daughter, small and squat, the neck ending in a fox head. The drawings unsettle me but they seem to put energy in Myma, so I grin wide and nod when she points at them, when she taps them over and over, saying only, Grey Rot. Grey Rot.

Then, when I am biting short the nails of her right hand, a flicker. A twitch. The tiniest shivering flex of her finger. I draw back, see the very slight straightening in the tilt of her eyes, her mouth. And I think how that is a good thing, even as a pang shoots through the unused muscle in me. Even as I feel a tightening, like twine around a toe.

She is getting better, I say to the back of Wyn's head as he lies beside me, and he says nothing, so I lie looking at the birds on the ceiling and think about my wishes, about what two opposite wishes might make when they come smashing into each other. I picture a grinding-together of everything-back-to-the-way-it-was and everything-changing, and wonder what I have done.

The strips of meat we saved from the pigeon do not last long. We boil the carcass dark after dark until nothing more can be wrung from the bones. There are still the two tins, Sweetened Condensed Milk Full Cream and Sliced Peaches in Syrup. We mustn't open them. Not yet.

I am at the final set of snares, about to turn towards the house with my empty sack, when I see the movement. On the other side of the fence, a swaying of twigs, a shuffling. I move to the edge to look. Four legs appear between the trees, stepping careful. The muntjac is round-backed, small-headed and brown. It does not notice me standing behind the fence. It noses between the dead leaves, then raises a hind hoof to scratch its shoulder. The coat on it is thick. The animal is not as large as the one we caught before, but it would still feed us for many lights. I stand silent at the fence and watch it. It has not seen me. Come over, I think to it. Come over. In my head I am already pouncing with my knife and the blood is spurting warm onto my cold hands and I am hefting the body over my shoulders and carrying it back to the house where Wyn and Myma are waiting for our right feast. The muntjac does not come any closer. It stays on the other side, where I cannot go, where I must not go. I do not realise how hard I am gripping the fence until a branch breaks under my hands. The muntjac flicks up its head, lifts its tail high, and then it is bounding fast away, the white rump of it disappearing among the trunks.

I do not tell Wyn about the muntjac. Knowing it is there, the meat of it walking about somewhere beyond the fence, fills this dark-come with more difficulty and aching than all the dark-comes I have known. We drink what Myma would call a restorative brew but it is hardly enough to restore us. The last of the dried herbs, sprinkled into boiled water for something to fill our stomachs. Wyn and me on the sacking beside the bed. Me kneeling up between mouthfuls to tip the gritty brew onto Myma's tongue. Cloth spread under her chin to catch the spill.

I try to feel happy in this moment, to grip the goodnesses. Us three together. Pieces of Myma returning. Heat on my tongue. But I know that these are scraps, that so much is still missing, still wrong. Exception, meaning not planned for. And how could we have planned? How could we have planned for any of it? I watch Wyn, unspeaking behind his hair as he slurps, and I think he will surely be the next to crumble apart. And me, slipping a little further from myself with every light-come of hungering and worrying and wondering and trying and forcing myself and holding in, and even though the snow has melted there is still a cold in the forest that threatens to skin us of what little flesh clings to our bones.

We have not had the energy for chopping and our stock of firewood is dwindling. Wyn's log has already been given to the fire. Myma's stool will be next. Then mine. Then the table. All the parts of us, our existing here, turning to ash.

Myma chokes on her swallow and goes on choking. It is Wyn who scrambles up to tip her forward and thump the flat of his hand between her shoulder blades. The choking brings herb-flecked spittle stringing from her lips. It hacks her, shakes her whole body. Remember once making myself laugh while eating an apple, the sour green bite sucking backwards into my throat and sticking there. The panic of it, all of me closing up around the choke. Myma's fist pounding into my back until the chunk hurtled from my mouth and I gasped and gasped.

If I wasn't here, she told me, you'd be dead.

I always thought I needed her more than she needed me. She was the first one, the one I came from. Me the fruit of her, needing her leaves, her roots. But I have stood alone and unafraid in the dark. It is Myma now who cannot be alone. Maybe she could never be alone, and that's why she grew me. Me her swollen potato, bursting with my own shoots but nowhere for them to go, shrivelling in her tight-packed earth.

Hey, says Wyn.

He has smoothed the blankets over Myma. She lies back, exhausted. Wyn goes into the other room and I follow. A coughing grips him as he turns towards me. He bends over, sleeve pressed to his mouth. See the red mottle on it when he straightens. He reaches for his brown container but the rattling it once made is gone, the white seeds all eaten up.

Fuck, he says, and flings the container from him.

He closes his eyes a moment, hand on chest. Then he takes my arm and tucks us round the door frame so we are hidden from Myma's seeing. The sudden nakedness of his expression as he looks at me makes my mouth taste bloody. He presses his tongue to his lower lip.

She's still really bad, he says. Not well at all. She is not going to get better here.

She is getting better, I say, my voice flattened.

He just stays looking at me, his face so wretched that I want to pull the red tangle of his hair over it and bundle him away into his corner.

I have to tell you something, he says then. Show you something.

I shake my head.

No, I say.

I am not ready for what he has to show me. I do not want to look at whatever it is. I do not want to hear it. Wyn's hands are on my shoulders then, shaking me. My head rattles.

Do you think about what will happen, girl? Do you? She could die. Then she'd be gone. Do you think about that?

Myma's voice reaches round the door frame, speaking a word that sounds like Daughter. Daughter, not always my name but now the only one I have. The one that wraps me to her. Before, when Myma called me Daughter, it did not feel like there was a gap before it. My other name, the one I carried in myself, that name was always there, not said but meant. Now, an empty space. A silence. A wound. A hole. I teeter on its edge. To keep myself from falling into it, I grip the only thing left to grip.

We have to do This-and-That now, I say.

Wyn's brow ruckles. He opens his mouth but I have already pulled away from him. He follows helpless into the room where we sleep.

It's my turn to choose, I say. I choose dancing.

Think of Myma standing solid in the centre of the room, hands on hips, saying, I am going to dance well, I have a lot of energy. See her now, crumpled in the bed we used to share. There is a shaking in my hands and I can feel my teeth wanting to chatter. Wyn and Myma are both looking at me. Myma's second shadow squats like a damp patch under the window.

We have to dance, I tell them. It is This-and-That.

My voice jerks about, too high, too loud. I stand trembling in the middle of the room. Set my hands on the poking bones of my hips. Wyn is shaking his head.

It's done, he says, and there is something like a sob in his voice. It's done, girl. None of your This-and-Thats or Keep-Safes will help.

This-and-Thats. Keep-Safes. The way he speaks them, like a gutting.

A tightness in my chest. I straighten my back. Lift my chin. And because there is nothing else I can do, I begin to dance. My feet slap the floor. Juddery beat of them. My arms whirl and my head reels about on my neck. My bed-smock flaps. Wyn and Myma and all three of their shadows, unmoving, only watching me. I spin to make them blur. The pressure growing on my chest. I try to throw it off by hurling my limbs from my body in sharp thrusts and jabs. I am afraid of what will happen if I stop, so I dance faster. Feel my ribcage shrinking, the air squeezing from my lungs.

Something struggling there, behind my breastbone. Something nameless and terrified. Flutter and squirm of it. Then it heaves itself free, hurtles up into my throat. I open my mouth wide to let it out and it comes, all at once. A wordless, dark red howl. My knees crunch into the floor as my throat tears itself apart.

24

The men stood in a circle and kicked the hen between them. They had tied the wings and feet. The bird was white and grubby like a balled-up shirt. A babbling came from its open beak.

They were lit from above by a bulb strung over the rafters, bare and flecked with droppings. Cans tilted to mouths. Two empty cans set a few feet apart made a goal. Someone scored and the others cheered. The hen screeched. Its head struggled like a red-tipped limb.

Some of the men stood at the sides and though they cheered along their eyes were troubled, uncertain. The sound coming from the trussed bird clawed at them. They found it uncomfortable. They wanted to cover their eyes and plug their ears but they were men not boys. One gave himself away by cringing back when the hen was kicked towards him. A crowing went up from the others.

'What? Scared of the cock-pecker? Worried she'll peck your cock?'

The man looked down at the bird, which had stopped screeching and begun rasping. He felt a cramp of pity and an impulse to smooth the broken feathers, so he picked up the hen and with the toe of his boot sent it soaring between the cans. Feathers sprayed white from his kick. They drifted down around him. They settled on his shoulders but he felt only the hands that clapped his back and reverberated in his chest even after they were taken away.

The hen's panic was shapeless. It couldn't understand why the pinioned wings would not respond to the flurried terror in its mind that told it flee, flee. There were wrenchings and tightnesses of pain. The hen knew the straw below and it knew the grain-feeding hands but it did not know the meaning of the hard jolts that sent the ground spinning up around the air. It knew the sound of the voice that spoke but not the words that were spoken.

'Let's make the cock-pecker fly.'

One man had taken up the string that bound the bird's feet. He stood in the centre and his arm went round and round his head. The hen became a blur of white, its crown a red streak. Its cry was strained and glottal. The man let go. There was only a slight thump as the feathery body hit the wall like a flung bag.

Booted feet came close and prodded. There were murmurs, a few laughs and low whistles. Liquid swilled in cans. No sound came from the bird now. Some of the men were disappointed and blamed the end of their sport on the one who had done the throwing. Others breathed out, relieved that it was over.

The warmth of violence faded and left them cold. They went back to their homes, their wives and children, carrying this coldness like a rock, heavy in the hand.

Under the feathers, the body stayed warm a while longer. The heart was still beating, though faint and stuttering. The filmy membrane of the inner eyelid slid back and forth across the golden iris. Then the living part of the bird spread its wings and flapped from that place.

All Red

All red but not a red that comforts, not like the back of an eyelid or the soft secret place under a tongue. A red that burns and suffocates, scorched palms pressed to eyes and mouth. I am falling into it and there is no bottom to catch my falling. My hands find the back of my skull, hold it. I feel the sound coming out of me, how it strips my throat like hot vomit. Heave and strain, almost retch. Push my fist into my mouth but still the sound pours. It wrenches me, splits me. It turns me inside out.

I howl until there is no sound left in my body. My mouth gapes, tongue hanging. Under my armpits, two hands. They try to lift me but I am heavy, so heavy. The hands pull at me. I want to tell them to stop, that if they pull any harder I will snap at the tendons, but I have forgotten how to speak. I hunch myself small, squeeze myself tight.

After a long while, the ragged edges of me begin to pinch back together. After an even longer while, I am able to lift my head. A rawness in my throat. My chest in tatters, stinging when I breathe.

Girl, a voice says. Daughter.

Hear the words as if through a strong wind. Struggle to connect them to myself. I am not a named thing.

A face surrounded by red hair swings down into my vision. I shut my eyes on it, hating it. But when I feel the arms around me I do not shove them away. Let myself be held.

I know, says the voice beside my ear. I know.

I open my eyes and see that I am clutching a body, and I remember that this body is called Wyn. Under us, the stone floor. These things are solid. They hold me up.

I know, Wyn says again. I know you're angry.

It takes me a while to remember I have a voice.

I'm not angry, I say to the body that is called Wyn, the voice of me scratched to a painful whisper. I don't know what I am, I say.

You are angry, he says. You're angry with her. I've seen it in you. I know because I've been angry too. Because I didn't understand. But I do now. I remember.

He is big around me, big-armed in holding. But something of him seems to shrink then. He pulls away and stands up suddenly. I am left sitting on the floor with loose arms and this raggedness in my chest. Myma has made no sound in all of this. Her eyes on Wyn. His hands holding each other. Him looking lost and afraid and somehow so small. A sense of something readying itself to come out of him, something like my red howl, or something redder, more terrible. Too exhausted now to look away or cover up my ears. I wait, and I listen.

When I came here, he says, I didn't know I was returning.

His hands begin to wring each other as he speaks.

I think I needed to be here. To remember. It was her. It must have been her. She called me back.

I try to make sense of what Wyn is saying but my mind is slow, stumbling around his words.

Back? I ask in my new scraped voice.

I didn't know, he says. I didn't recognise any of it. But I remember now. It was ours.

Ours?

Mine. Hers. This place. Ours.

I look to Myma. She is silent and very still, watching Wyn.

She brought me here so we could be safe, he says. That's what she wanted. To keep me safe. I remember now. I remember her. I remember here.

He is talking about the she that is neither me nor Myma. The her he calls Mother. His Myma. He is talking about her and him, the two of them, here. Somehow here.

And I remember why, he says now, speaking faster, hands twisting and twisting. I remember why we came. I remember him, and the way he was, and what he did to her. To me.

He fingers that spot below his lip where he showed me the thin, silverish scar, the one he said he didn't remember getting.

I remember her saying I was hers, he says, only hers. She said he was far away now, and we would be alright here, just us. I remember her speaking my name. My name. Wyn. Ro-Wyn. Rowen. Red-haired, it means. I remember her telling me that. I remember her calling it. I remember her calling it when they took me away.

His face puckering then, like a closing-up fist.

I think they wanted to help us, he says. I think they did. But they didn't understand. She was scared. I was scared. She tried to keep them out. There. There used to be a door there.

His finger pointing to the empty doorway.

I remember hearing them on the other side of it, he says.

His hands coming up to press over his ears. His breath shuddering.

I remember it breaking when they rammed it. She was holding me so tight. Then someone else was holding me, carrying me away from her, saying it would be okay now, they were going to take me somewhere safe.

These words come gasping out of him. Each gasp pushes out his back as if he is falling again and again from a great height onto a thick branch. Crumple of his body around an awfulness too big to hold.

They took me, he says, and I couldn't understand why she didn't come. I waited and waited for her. They told me she'd been a bad mother, that she hadn't been looking after me properly, and I knew they were wrong, but I was so young, and soon I got to believing it. I shut out everything from before. I forgot this place and what it meant. I forgot everything that had happened. She was a bad mother and she had left me. That's what I thought. My whole life, that's what I thought.

Rotters? I rasp. Rotters took you? From here?

Wyn coughs and spits on the floor. The spit has blood in it. He is quiet for a moment, his chest going up and down. Then he makes a sound that is almost a laugh.

Too easy a name for it, he says. No Rotters, girl. Just people. Like us. There's Rot and good in all of us, that's certain.

That same hollowness to his voice as when he spoke about This-and-Thats and Keep-Safes. Rotters, Rot, the thrust of those words cut away. I swallow and it hurts. Wyn spits again. He turns to Myma and she holds his gaze, unblinking.

You did what we couldn't, he says. You stayed. I think that was her, too. I think she's the reason nobody but you has come here. It sounds strange, but I think she did something to this place. I think she made it so nobody else could come and take it. But then you needed it. You needed it, Maya. She let you in.

Myma's mouth moves.

Grey one, it says. Grey one under. Grey with the red.

See her eyes on his, the look they hold and the water that spills from them. Wettening of my own cheeks. I look at the face Wyn has drawn on the wall. I look at Myma's jumble of drawings beside the bed, the long-haired lying-down shape I thought was Myma, the small fox-headed shape I thought was me.

That other shadow moves to where the Museum is splayed out around the bed. Beside the fox tooth the shadow quivers. Wyn bends, picks up the tooth.

This was mine, he says. I remember. I remember finding it in the woods and bringing it to her. She made a hole and put it on her necklace for me. I was her little fox. I remember, I was playing with it when they came. I must have dropped it.

His fingers move over the tooth, the hole that pierces it. Hear how, in his hands, the tooth hums loud through the air the way it did when I first found it at the edge of the clearing. Calling a name that was never mine. Wyn reaches up, unfastens the silver cord from around his neck and slides the tooth onto it. The humming stops, an insect pinched silent. The tooth settles, goes still and quiet on his chest. He presses the pad of his thumb onto its point.

Every way I walked, he says, I ended up at your fence. It was her. I know it was her. But then, where is she? Where is my mother?

He swings his face between us, his eyes huge and wanting. Peering from them, a frightened creature. I can only stare back.

Myrna does not speak and neither do I. After a while, Wyn nods. He pulls his shoulders around himself. Exhausted hunching slump of him. His thinness. Try to imagine him stub-limbed and short, his hairy face shrunken, him running about unsteady. Him with a laugh like a cub. Then he coughs again and it goes on for ages and we just watch him, we wait for it to finish. When he speaks it is in a whisper so quiet I have to strain my neck forward to hear.

It's not your fault, he says. What's happening. Can't carry that guilt with you, when you go. Not the anger either. Leave all that here, girl. Only carry what matters.

The whisper is for me. Me he looks at now. He stretches to a grin and his teeth are bloody at the edges.

I wasn't good at living, he says then. But you. You are so good at it. You will be so good.

His grin buckles. He begins to cry. Tears and snot running into his open mouth, dribbling into the hair that covers his chin. He folds to the floor. His hands press their heels into his face.

There was home here, he says. We were home here.

I do not know what the word means and I do not ask. Shuffle closer until my knees touch his. Then, because I do not know what else to do, I lift my hands and stroke his jaw, his red jaw.

Myma is silent, breathing. Soon Wyn quietens too. He sags sideways until he is lying curled on the stone floor, one arm outstretched. The shadow that drapes itself across him is not Myma's.

At some point I must fall asleep too because I am woken by Myma's voice.

Daugh–ter.

Still dark. The stone cold under my ear. Wyn's ribcage rises and falls beside me. His hair spills like blood across the floor. Move my head and see Myma's one and a half eyes beetling through the gloom. Hear the cling of her lips as they part around the thing she is trying to say. It takes a while for her mouth to make the words. They come slow, dragged up thick like clots of mucus, one by one.

Thank. You. Sorry.

For what? I whisper.

All, is all she says. All.

25

If she had not taken the late shift. If the rooster had not cut up the hens' backs. If her mother had not left the fridge open and spoiled the milk. If she had swallowed her mother's wisdom teeth before they could be taken. If her father had looked up at her window as he left. If it had not been a Friday. If the devil hadn't dug the gravel pit. If the moths had made their webs elsewhere. If Kitty had not said 'screwing'. If Maya had just eaten the sweet Darry had given her. If she had worked harder at school. If she had followed Georg. If it had been raining. If the foxes had kept away. If she had stayed under the bed. If she had been called a different name.

She sprayed the salt solution on the raw flesh where the rooster's spurs had dug. The hen flinched and shook its feathers at her.

Some weeks had passed since her mother had been buried. The older woman from the church had stood with Maya at the graveside. She had put a dry arthritic hand on Maya's arm.

'Your mother was a very clever person,' the older woman said, 'though I think she was not always happy. She spoke of you often.'

And Maya had smiled, unable to reply.

She set the hen among the others. The naked patches on their backs wept into their feathers. Behind, the door swung open and a face looked in.

'Locking up now,' it said. 'Are you done with these?'

She said, 'Yep,' and threw a handful of grain. The man in the doorway shook his head at the injured birds.

'Dumb cock-peckers,' he said.

He did not move aside but stood in the frame. Maya had to brush against him as she stepped out under the overhead light that turned the flat grass yellow.

'Sticking around?' he asked as he clicked the padlock. 'We've got some cans. Other stuff too. Might make a night of it.'

Maya could hear the laughter from the disused building where the men sometimes gathered to sluice their throats. There had been an incident in there with one of the hens last week. She had heard them speaking conspiratorially about it the way children might whisper together about hiding some foul-smelling thing in their teacher's desk.

'I'm alright, thanks,' she said.

'Maya, isn't it? One drink, Maya?'

'Thanks, but I'd better head off.'

'Too good for us, is it?'

She felt something shift in the air between them, as a licked finger feels a change in the direction of wind. He leaned towards her.

'You act like you're better than us,' he said, 'but everyone knows you don't really care who you give it to. You'll even give it to the gyps, I heard. So when's it our turn?'

Close to hers in the yellow light, his face seemed altered, as though the bones had been prodded out of place from the inside. Then he straightened. His face settled back on its skull.

'Next time then,' he grinned.

As he walked out of the light, Maya's eyes were drawn to something on his back. Between his shoulder blades and down his spine, a rift opening onto a black and empty cavity, like the split trunk of a tree. Then he passed into the next light and the slice of darkness she had seen became a rip in his overalls.

In the dirty bathroom behind the laying barn, Maya splashed her face and stood looking in the mirror. She peered into her eyes, so dark they appeared black in most lights. Her reflection had always made her uneasy. She did not like knowing there was this outside to her that others might grab onto in a way that did not fit her own understanding of herself.

She had already handed in her notice. The house was paid for up to the end of the month. She had no plan other than to leave.

Outside, a door banged. Feet and voices came around the concrete walls. In them Maya heard something furtive and restless.

'That her in there?'

An open palm hit the door. Maya's fingers held the edges of the sink.

'Come out, cock-pecker.'

'What are you hiding for?'

'Maybe she's not decent.'

'Doesn't matter to us.'

'Show us what's under those baggy overalls.'

'Why don't you show us?'

'Why don't you?'

The handle rattled. Maya remembered how the boys at school would stand waiting by the door to the toilets, and when a girl came out they would crowd around her and ask if she was in heat. They would sniff at her, they would say they could smell it on her. They would press close and thrust their hips and moan and the girl would stand still so the humiliation would be over more quickly.

She put her fist into the mirror. It broke the glass and split the skin. A shard clattered in the sink. Maya scooped it out and held it. The edge was sharp. She stuck it down the side of her boot.

The voices outside had quieted. Maya heard a hissed word, bodies shuffling. Her fist had spread branches across the glass. Between them she saw more than one of herself.

'Why don't you?' she said to the reflections.

She opened the door to whistling. They seemed tense and agitated as they moved around her. Tongues came out to touch lips. Maya's eyes flicked across the men. She knew some only by sight, others by name. They sometimes made small talk with her on their breaks, or offered her pieces of flapjack, homemade biscuits.

Some stared back while others twitched their heads away. A few stood apart, talking and leaning outside the disused building, glancing over occasionally. One of these called out, 'Go on and leave her be,' but when the others only laughed he shrugged and shook his head and turned away.

As if she was in on the joke, Maya threw a quick smile at those closest. She made to move past them. The one who had stopped her earlier spread his arms.

'Don't be like that,' he said. 'Stay a while.'

She felt tired and bitter. The bitterness filled her mouth and she thought of Darry, whom she'd heard was now married, with two young boys who shared his face, and she thought of the men behind the pub with their sad-dog eyes and their hunger. She recognised it, that smell coming off the body that blocked hers. Overhead, the light buzzed.

Maya spat. The glob hit the man's cheek and slid down. The others were quiet then. She pushed between them and they did not stop her and they did not follow. She could hear the crackling of blood in her ears.

The night had dragged itself further along than Maya had thought. She had missed the last bus. The walk would take her a little over an hour. Two fields to cross, then she would reach the road that led in one direction to Devil's Dip, and in the other to the town, its houses. The moon hung like a dim bulb above.

At the edge of the field she heard a whimper. She saw a long, struggling body, a dirty orange pelt. The snared fox was thrashing against the wire that had pulled tight around its neck. Its scrabbling had gouged the ground to furrows.

The fox made a noise in its throat as Maya came near. She spread her hands and thought towards it, I am no threat. The fox growled again and snapped. They would find it here, Maya thought. They would tie shut the muzzle and swing it round and round by the tail.

An eye rolled back in its white to watch her as she went to the back end. The wire had rubbed away the fur behind the fox's ears. Maya looked down at the animal. She saw the wide barrel of its body, the teats slung low. She reached down fast and gripped the muzzle. The fox jerked against her but she held it firm. She loosed the snare and in the same moment released her grip.

The fox shot immediately into the dark. Maya heard the rustling panic of birds and small mammals fleeing its path.

Then, from behind, another sound. The darkness at her back no longer empty but thick and bodied, all panting breath and hot stench.

She did not turn around but started walking, a sick ache in her stomach. They walked behind her, unhurried. She felt her t-shirt sticking. She thought, Across two fields then along the road. She thought of the underside of the bed, of the slicing shard beside her ankle and of all those gathered fragments her mother had thrown away. They were coming around her now. When the press of them forced her to stop, she felt an awful kind of relief. She was so tired.

She thought, It happens like this. She thought, That fucking fox.

If she had not if she had not if she had not if she had.

Somewhere a Fox

Somewhere a fox is screeching. It wakes me.

Light pales the dark window, turns the air in the room a bluish colour. A blanket has been put over me. It is heavy like a body, sweat-soaked. I slide from it and slowly stand. Myma is sleeping, her blankets tucked close around her chin. Her breath makes a haze. The room, cold. Wyn, not in it.

In the other room, the fire is out. A blackened hunk of wood that used to be Wyn's log. His smock lies like a skin on the floor, the sleeve stained red by coughing, like Myma's by her worry-itch. His boots stand empty. Tiny hairs all over my body bristling at the air that comes through the half-open door. I take my cloak and pouch from their hook, pull my boots on. Push the door wide.

Grey frost coats the ground like mould. See the thawed tread of bare feet making a trail across the clearing. I go after them and among the trees without leaving my tooth in its hole. Sun sliced apart by leafless branches. The flicker of it, sore behind my eyes. My stomach a stone as I move through the forest. White fog of my breath. A shiver on my skin that raises little bumps and a fuzz of hairs, the shiver nothing to do with cold. Follow the prints under my feet the way I followed them when I tracked the Rotter through the dark. Follow all the way to the ash copse where Myma taught the rope Lesson, where I came to scratch my itch. Follow to the bright blot of red ahead of me. Then I reach it. Then I reach him.

He sits at the foot of the tree, his head tilted back against the trunk, his eyes open, looking up. They do not flick towards me. His hair the only part of him that moves. No. Is moved. It's the wind that does the moving.

His legs stick straight out in the trousers Myma stitched for him. Feet and torso bare. A purpling to his heels. Rot-scar gone pale on his belly where Myma's shard cut. Frost crusting his lashes like the scabs of sleep. Frost whitening the hair on his jaw too, his eyebrows, the red fuzz on his bare chest where the fox tooth nestles. His mouth half-open but empty of words. Blood in the cracks of his blued lips. No sound in him, not even a cough. Nothing left in him to speak and no movement in his tongue to speak it with. Because he is dead.

Everything sounds, even the air when there is no wind in it. But Wyn's sound has stopped completely.

Being dead means no noise, no moving. Only now, looking down at the cold still silence of Wyn, I think that's not quite right, that dead must also mean other things. Like no longer being there behind the eyes to look out and see. No longer sitting at the rim of the ear to listen when a noise goes in. No longer stretched out under the skin to feel when something strokes it, or pricks it. No hunger and no thirst, no difference between light-come and dark-come. I think of it, that blankness. Once, I would have found the idea of it frightening, or lonely, or boring. But I don't think dead would be any of those things. I don't think I would even know, or care.

Imagine the cold-foot walk here in the not-yet-light. The red head leaning to rest against the numb bark. The pricking stiffening beginning at the fingertips, the warm breath of the body pouring out. The see-through of his eyes clouding over.

A part of me wants to touch him, to see if he is frozen solid like the water tank, or if there is a give to him, like snow. Instead I shut my eyes. On the inside of my head, uncrack the stiffness of his limbs, warm him until his body softens. Blow air into his chest, squeeze his heart to pump the blood. Wet the stones of his eyes, blink them. Stand him upright, then walk him through the forest, towards the fence. The ground greening under him as he treads it, winter to new growth and bloom. Leaves swelling the trees as he passes. Roused shufflings and smells of animals. At the fence, fit his heel into the jut of a branch, step him up and over. Send him loping away on the other side. Watch the red of him going.

I see it happen. I make it happen, his uncoming. I make him go.

The cold hereness of him pressing on my lids. I open and look at him. Dead is not gone, like Wyn said it would be when he told me Myma could die. Gone means gone somewhere, like gone into the forest to check the traps, or gone into the other room to fetch a lamp. Gone means being in a place that is not here. It means going-to-come-back. It means a tooth in the hole. Wyn hasn't gone anywhere. He isn't any place but here. He is not Wyn going, Wyn gone, or Wyn about-to-return. He is only his own weight of blood and bone gone still. Still here. Still and here. Moveless soundless breathless here.

Ro-Wyn.

I take the name into my mouth, the way he took Flint into his when he first spoke it back to me. Rowen. Ro, the extra part that makes it whole. R for Wyn. I think of him saying, I know you're angry, and of Myma saying, Grey with the red. Pissit. Boy-girl. Mother. I part my jaws wide and scream at him. The scream is without feeling. The sound a blunted blade, dull and flat. The kind of scream I might do into a sleeping ear, just to see what would happen. Nothing does happen. Wyn does not hear it.

His arms are at his sides, his hands upturned on the ground.

Something lying there, next to the crook of his fingers. I know what it is without needing to touch it but bend and pick it up anyway. The wooden face is cold and quiet in my palm. I hold it until it warms to my skin. I touch its chin, its cheeks, its sharp nose, the blind knots of its eyes. I stroke the wooden jaw with a fingertip. Put it into my pouch. Step backwards. Chew the inside of my cheek and look at Wyn, knowing I will not look at him again, not ever. I will not come back here to this ash copse of Lessons and itch-scratching and dying. It is too much bruising here.

Once, I might have cut hunks of Wyn's hair to keep in my pouch, pulled the fox tooth from around his neck to return to the Museum. Somehow that doesn't seem right to me now. The tooth is not my name to take. I think of unfastening my cloak and putting it over him. But then I would be cold, and he doesn't need it.

My bed-smock flaps against my shins. Somewhere a blackbird is singing. I stand here until I am no longer sure why I am still standing here.

I walk in the direction I made him walk in my mind. Through the forest, away from the clearing, away from the house, towards the fence. I do not look back but I feel Wyn there, behind me. His being dead is heavy, like a full sack. It pulls at me, makes my neck ache. Heavier the further I go from his body. Until it becomes so heavy that I am panting. Thrust my shoulders forward, bend myself in half like I am walking into the strongest wind. My lips grinning towards my ears with the effort. Teeth grinding. When I think I cannot go any further, when I wonder if it would be easier to let myself be pushed to my knees by the weight of all the uncovered truth and the awful heft of Wyn dead, when I think I might lie down on my side and let my heat drain into the ground too, my outstretched hands meet knotted branches, sharp bones.

I stop. The ground on the other side of the fence is frozen like the ground on this side. Its trees are leafless like ours.

Blood beating thick between my ears as I stand looking over the fence. Sweat slicking me even while the cold stings my throat. I used to think that if we did everything like we were supposed to, then nothing would change. I believed that chores and This-and-That and Keep-Safes would protect us in the same way as the fence. That all badness could be kept out with a barrier of bones and branches and plaited hair.

In the dark beyond the fence creeps the Rotted thing. Sleep you sound now, little Daughter, safe from everything.

Safe. Keep safe. I do not really know for myself what the word means. I have only ever been told. Myma's meaning for it comes from a fear that is not mine. And what about when safe changes from the inside? When the thing that makes it not-safe isn't out there in the dark beyond the fence but close, and still here when the light comes. The blood breaking in Myma's head. Wyn's naked grey-blue feet.

I sway in my boots, at the very edge of what I know, looking towards what I do not. Feel a rippling then, in the muscle I have kept cramped-up tight since Myma fell. An almost-itch.

And I know that it is now, that it must be now. I do not think. I put all of myself into my feet. The one lifting, bracing at the heel, the other swinging up, over. Beaks and ribs and thorns tear at my bed-smock but I pull it free.

One by one, my two feet lower onto the ground on the other side of the fence. My two hands hold tight to the woven branches behind me.

In the animal part of me that knows only freeze and flee, my first instinct is to stiffen against the expected danger. I wait for the seep of Rot into my lungs. Rotters rushing to pull me apart. I wait and I wait. When nothing happens, I let my breath come. The air here is the same as the air there. I am standing there. Only now, there is here. Here and there, muddied together. I feel no shock at finding it to be this way. Since Wyn-come the know of it has been growing in me. Since the strange red thing loped into the clearing and held my name in its mouth. Here the answer to the question I didn't allow myself to think. Yet here it is. The mangled truth. The thing that everything else hangs upon. It doesn't feel good or satisfying, the way an answer should. Instead, a dull pain. The slow well of blood when the thorn stopping up the wound is finally plucked out.

Lick my upper lip, taste salt. Sharp of my own sweat, the most familiar thing besides the taste and smell of Myma. The inside of me goes quiet and calm. I take my hands from the fence. I stare straight ahead. Move my legs to make them walk and feel how the space opens up around me, the endless stretching of it, no fence to contain it. It is like falling into the sky. I begin to run, dizzy, breathless. When I stop and turn around, the air catches in my throat. I have come further than I thought. Through the trees I can still just see the fence, the way it curves like an arm around what it holds, the place where I have lived all my lights and darks.

I look the other way, towards the not-yet-known. All around me there are trees I have never climbed, ground I have not trod. I could go further. Run and then go on running. The ground will hold me up, the way it always has. I cannot lose myself if I know where my feet are. New muscle tensing me to move. Realising that I could do it. I could go. Wyn's body and Myma and the house and the clearing and the Keep-Safes and all the achings would stay there, in one place, and I would be – not there. A different there. What comes after forest if not fence? Another place. Other faces, perhaps, ones I do not recognise. Wonder how many. Wonder what they sound like when their mouths open, what words they carry.

Sense it then, the coming of a name. It does not come from outside me. There is no object attached to it, nothing that could be carried in my pouch or placed into the Museum. I do not hear it, but feel it. It stirs with the new muscle I have grown. It swells me like a breath. A sounding too low for hearing, but somehow loud, thunder without the crack.

Name, this thing I give myself, this thing that sticks me to myself. A name that is me and mine. Not a name to be called by. I will not speak it out loud. It is enough to know how to call myself. Feel it surging in me as I stand with lifted heel, leaning towards all the where that I have never been. Knowing nothing can haul me back. Nothing to stop me from putting it all down, all this weight I have held, shucking it off like my old names. There is nothing to keep me here. Only. Only.

26

Once there was only Myma. Then the dark came and so did the Rotters, so Myma built the fence to keep them out. When Daughter came, Myma gathered things that were strong and she fitted them together to protect them both. They lived in the house and they were safe.

It was the only story she knew now. The other one felt distant, a thing told to her rather than lived. A name she had heard once.

She lay in the bed with the hut around her. At her side, her daughter breathed. The girl had grown taller than her. She was long-limbed, lean-muscled like a hare. Her body had learned about time and it marked it by bleeding. She sprawled beside Maya with her mouth open and her arms above her head, the fine hair beneath them damp with sweat. The child would be sixteen in less than a year.

That whole night, Maya had lain restless. She turned about in the bed, unable to find a comfortable position. Something was jabbing into her hip. Her hand dug down among the rags and met a hard, cold edge. She prised it free like a splinter from skin.

It was the length of her palm, heavier than she remembered. She held the shard of mirror carefully. Without waking her daughter, she stood and walked out on bare feet.

Outside, the darkness had begun to pale. It was late summer. The air was already warming. She sat on the low step with the mirror in her lap.

Maya had avoided her reflection for so long that when she bent her head she did not recognise the face looking up from the glass between her knees. She saw the high ridges of the cheekbones, the two brows almost meeting in the middle, the left parted by a scar. When she turned her head the mirror showed her the slight curve to the bridge of the nose. Fine lines traced the edges of the mouth. The hair that fell around the face was streaked silver. Maya looked at the eyes last.

'Sort of creepy,' Kitty had once said. 'Like a crow.'

'They are raven eyes,' Georg had said later.

Maya saw that the comparison was true, but not for the reasons she'd thought back then. The corvids that had flocked the fields and pecked at roadkill had seemed to her ragged and desolate things. Yes, she had thought, I am like that, I perch at the edges, my eyes are those of a carrion bird, dirty, dull. Since coming to the woods she knew those birds differently. She admired their intelligence and the strength of their beaks. She had eaten their tough meat and in plucking them she had learned that their feathers were not black but iridescent, shifting blue to brown to violet to green to red. The eyes blinking up at her from the mirror shard were that colour.

She felt the weight of the trees belted thick around her. Beyond them, the boundary she had drawn. When she sat still like this, she could feel all the slivered parts of herself that she had scattered through the wood. She knew where every speck of herself lay, every hair and scab and fingernail. She sensed them as if they were still attached to her, as if the place were a collection of nerve endings, herself at the centre, a body grown vast beyond its skin. In this small place, she thought, I am larger than I have been.

A sleeping murmur came soft through the open door at her

back. The sound opened like a colour. Her bright yellow-green child. Her trilling, chittering daughter. The previous day, she had turned to Maya and said, 'I think we are always making trails of ourselves, but they're not the kind we can see or smell, and we leave ourselves behind in them, all lined up like ants behind the us that is here at the front, only the us we are now is different every moment because the now is always moving, so how do I know that I am me if I am always stepping away from myself?'

Maya had replied, 'It sounds like it's your thoughts that are making trails of themselves, Daughter. You are always you and I am always me. Daughter and Myma, the way it will always be.' But in truth she was not at all sure of her answer. It tripped her when her daughter spoke like this, which she did more and more often recently. Maya was used to knowing what her daughter would do or say almost before the girl had grasped it herself. Yet there were things in the girl's mind that Maya had not put there but that came from somewhere else completely, somewhere Maya could not go. She envied and feared it, that place in her daughter that was nothing to do with her but was all the girl's own, expanding every day. That will outgrow me, Maya thought.

Sitting now on the step with the face she hardly knew lying flat in her lap, she took a strange kind of comfort in what her daughter had said. As her hands gripped the mirror she imagined what her trail would look like, the rings of it in the woods and the long arm stretching off and back, the crisscrossings and the places where it faltered, almost broke.

And she breathed out, and she let herself remember. It was painful, the remembering. It bled like a fresh wound, as if she still lay split open on the ground where they had left her. It was a grief. She knew there were tears coming from her when she could no longer see her reflection through them.

A blackbird whistled. Maya wiped her eyes on her wrists

like a child and saw the grey woman sitting beside her, thin fingers making knots of her hair. She was different. The long hair she twisted was not grey but red, like the clusters of rowan berries Maya would dry to make a sharp tea. The grey woman looked at her with eyes turned pale blue.

'Tell me,' the grey woman said. Her voice was full of clicking.

Maya let her mouth name it. For the first time she named it.

'They raped me,' she said, 'and they left me. And I thought I would die. And I didn't.'

She had expected the words to be unbearable but they felt instead like a release. The release was followed by a flatness. Such unremarkable words, she thought.

'Well?' said the grey woman. 'What else?'

'I think,' said Maya, 'I think I am happier here, yes. But I didn't want this. If I could change what happened, I would. Even if it meant not having her. Even if it meant giving her up.'

She thought about the child sleeping behind her in the hut and she knew this was true. The grey woman's blue gaze held hers.

'There is nothing that matters more than her,' Maya said then.

She knew this was also true. She would never be grateful for what had happened but she had made something from it that was good and important. She had done this despite what had happened, not because of it. By herself, she had done this. For the first time, she wished she could show it to someone else. Look, she would say, look what I have grown here.

'I do think about it,' she said. 'About leaving. I think about leaving with her, going somewhere else.'

The grey woman said nothing. When her arms went around Maya, there was a warmth.

'Myrna.'

Maya straightened. Her hand released the mirror piece. She had not felt the skin break but now the blood trickled from the cut across her palm. She stood up. It was time to go back inside. Time to be Myma. She slipped the shard of Maya into her pocket. She would bury it again in the bed. The blood was pooling in her palm but Maya would tell the girl that she had sliced the skin on purpose to strengthen the protections she surrounded them with, and the girl would believe her, as she believed everything Maya said. And Maya would daub the boundary branches with the red, and so make herself believe it too.

She tightened the stitches that had come undone in her mind. She felt the edges pulling back together. She sucked a breath and rubbed her eyes. Then she turned away, back into the hut, following her daughter's call.

The grey woman stayed sitting on the step. She flickered, red to grey, grey to red. Her chin rested on her hands, her elbows on her knees. She listened, and she watched, and she waited.

I Come Back

I come back because I will always come back to her. She is every direction I will ever run. Her the centre I turn around. Even with all I now know, all that has happened, I come back.

Somehow I expected everything to look different. But it is here the way it has always been. The clearing. The cleft post. The house. Beaks above the door. For a moment I stop, try to see it with the eyes I used to have. Eyes that had only seen the fence from one side, and had never known that exact lone shade of red. There has been goodness and happiness here.

In the house, I push the door shut behind me but do not bolt it. All the things I might want to keep out are already inside. Step from my boots, stand at the edge of the room where we eat. Look around for some sign of Wyn no longer being here, something to show me that being dead actually does mean being gone after all. But he is here, still. What has been scooped from the air has left behind something dense and heavy. An empty hole made solid. That muscled lack, a bulk to it. The greasy imprint of him in the shrugged-off bundle of his smock where his body used to fit. Red strands on the floor, on the table, thin and blood-warm in the pale light, the colour so living that I have to blink and blink and blink.

His naked grey-blue feet. The stopped breath of him. His naked grey-blue feet.

I gather each thing of Wyn. His boots and smock, his green sack, his knife, his bad water bottle, his empty medication, the burned remains of his log. I take them to his corner. I place the R-for-rabbit mug on the blackened log.

Myma is shifting in the other room. A murmured sound that might be Daughter. I do not go to her. Not just yet. Instead towards the table, the small round shape that sits on it. I did not notice it before. I peer down and find that I am looking at my own face, carved into wood. Sharp chin. Brows low and close together. Hair tufting around the forehead. The mouth of me neither downturned nor smiling but firm and set. Upper lip fuller than lower. Eyelids pulled back as if in seeing.

When I pick up my own wooden face I half-expect it to be as heavy as the head balanced on my neck. But it is hardly the weight of a rook's egg. Cup it careful in my palm. A barely felt ticking to it that could almost be a name. I turn it over. On the other side, another face. Slight curve of the nose, eyes closer together than mine, lip broader and jutting. Myma's face, the way it was before it slipped sideways. Our two faces growing out of each other.

This the way Wyn saw us. Stuck together. One always pulling the other with it. There was so much he didn't understand but his hands saw how we are joined, Myma and me, the split root of us. We have always been this way. Myma. Daughter. Always we. But I know my own name now. It twitches between my chest and my throat.

I turn the two-sided face back over and look again at my face. Imagine Wyn's hands grooving out the shape of it. When I first saw his hands, the bigness of them, I would not have thought them able to make a thing so small.

Bring the wooden face close to my own, press the tiny hard nose into the fleshy tip.

Yes, I say to it. Yes, I think about what will happen.

The question Wyn asked me. Let it unfurl in my mind. New muscle stretching me towards an answer. What will happen. Happen, meaning not just what is done or what is now but what is coming. Meaning that when the last of the tins are gone there will be no more pudding, not ever. Meaning deeper and longer lines around Myma's eyes and mouth. Meaning Myma getting worse, not better. Meaning one light-come waking and being the only breathing one here. No voice but my own to call me. But I know too that happen isn't a solid and certain thing. I can choose the happening.

Daughter, comes Myma's voice from the room where we sleep.

I put the joined faces into my pouch with the other wooden face. Then go and crouch in front of the last two tins. Sweetened Condensed Milk Full Cream. Sliced Peaches in Syrup. I struggle to remember why, through all our hungry lights and darks, we didn't just open them. Wrap my hand around Sweetened Condensed Milk Full Cream, finger in the metal ring, pull. The ring snaps off so I take my knife from my pouch.

Daughter.

Grip the knife tight, stab the blade at the rim until I can fold back the top. Dip three fingers and suck the sweet thick. It goes all over my chin. I stare at the word Milk and think about Myma feeding me from her breasts. On the cold floor with feet pressed together, knees up by my elbows, I sit and drink until the tin is empty.

I go to her then. Into the room where we sleep. Where we have always slept. Feel myself strong with eating. I carry Sliced Peaches in Syrup to the bed where Myma lies. We look at each other and I feel her seeing me.

Daughter is not always my name. I am also this other thing, separate from what she calls me, a name all my own.

I think of all the things that have been buried from me. And I think of the prickings and woundings Myma gave to herself that have hurt me more than any cut or burn in my own flesh. Her fear that I took as mine.

Her hand lifts, fingers curled, thumb pointing as if to fit against the underside of my chin. Something flares in my chest and I want suddenly to hurt her. To bring the tin of Sliced Peaches in Syrup swinging down between her eyes. I want to shout very loud, I want to tell her that she lied, that she lied to me, that I see all of it now and hate her for it. Lying is a bad and Rotted thing, I want to say. But Rotted no longer means what it used to and I am not sure if lying is even the right word for what Myma did.

The anger leaves me as I look at her. Me seeing her then. She is not only one name either. I never really thought what it meant, her being here before me. The existing of Myma without Daughter. The things she did and saw and felt before I sprouted from her. I still do not understand the whole of it. What it was that made Myma build her den here and fence it against Rot. It is still too big to look at properly. Maybe, one light, when Myma has got all her words back, we will talk about it. Maybe she will tell me the things that happened to her and we will know each other differently.

I do not fit my chin to her reaching thumb but climb onto the bed beside her. Slide my arm under her back and shoulders, lean her up. Peel open Sliced Peaches in Syrup. Low moan from Myma at the scent. Her left hand grasps my wrist as I tilt the tin to her lips. The soft chunks gulleting down. Ripple of tendons in her throat. She swallows the dregs and I let the tin clunk empty to the floor.

Wyn's drawing watches from the wall. No sign of any shadow but our own. A terrible sadness gripping me then. Something has ended. Wyn's being dead has changed this place. Blotted the forest scarlet. No longer any way of things going back to how they were. It is not our place any more.

Myma belches, sighs. As if she can see the colour of my thoughts she speaks a question that is one word only.

Wyn?

I do not reply and after holding my gaze a while she nods. Her teeth bite at her lower lip. Her eyes close a moment and she breathes out long and slow.

I get up from the bed.

It is a light for washing, I say.

She blinks, then raises her worry-scarred left arm to help me. The bed-smock comes off over her head. It is damp and stained. The smell of her strong underneath. She twists her head away from herself, brow crumpled.

I fetch the pot with the little water left in it, a fistful of clean rags. I pull the dirty sheets from under Myma, half-lifting her to haul them free. Bundle sheets and bed-smock into the corner. Then I begin to clean her. Wipe the rags over her skin, beneath her arms and the puckers of her breasts, the hollows at the base of her neck, between her legs, the backs of her knees, her feet. The water is cold. It raises the hairs where it touches her skin. In such a short while she has changed so much. Sturdy beech to bent hawthorn in a single winter. She breathes sharp when the rags pass over the sorenesses on her back from lying still. I am gentle. Dab careful around the tender parts.

I toss the dirty rags into the corner with the rest. Myma is shivering so. I rub her with a blanket until the chatter leaves her teeth. Tug her arms into her chore-smock, grip her under the shoulders and lift her so she is almost standing. Pull the hem to her shins. She is panting when I lower her, but she does not slump sideways as I take away my arm. She stays sitting upright on the edge of the bed, swaying slightly. Her shadow sits behind her on the wall, alone.

I take off my pouch, my cloak, my bed-smock, wash myself in the cold water and dry myself with the same blanket I used for Myma. Put on trousers and chore-smock. The scratchy cloth is good.

When I grasp Myma's foot in my hand, I find it freezing. Her heel an icy egg. The thought of Wyn comes stabbing into my gut. How cold. How cold he must be now. His feet, his feet. His naked grey-blue. I do not push away the awfulness of it. I let it be there, let myself think him, and though the pain is huge and racking I find I am still able to breathe around the red hole he has left, and I know this will scar too, and I must hold the goodnesses as well as this aching, I must keep the laughter and the trust, the way his arms steadied me when I howled, and what he meant when he said that word, friend. Two palms, held out.

I cut strips from the blanket to wrap Myma's feet. As I unbend from her she clasps the back of my neck with her left hand, surprisingly strong, forcing me close. Our noses come together. Her breath sweet with Sliced Peaches in Syrup. Her speaking slow but solid, clear.

What. Are. You. Now?

She can always sense when I have changed. She waits but I do not speak my name. I do not want it to be a heard thing. I do not want to give it away from myself. Myma looks at me a long while before dipping her chin. Her eyes flicking then towards the doorway.

We are. Going.

I nod.

Yes, I tell her. We are going.

Her jaw clenches and as I watch I am gripped by the strangest fear that her face is about to collapse inward, cheeks and chin and forehead folding up to seal her away inside her skull. The fingers of her left hand close tight at my nape. It looks like it takes all her effort not to buckle. Then it passes. Her fingers slacken. She makes an impatient sound with her tongue and swats at her hair with her hand.

Off.

She does it again, slicing the side of her palm at the thick grey-brown cloak of it.

Off.

Her eyes set firm, black and bright.

Okay, I say.

I take up my knife. Her hair twitching when I gather it. Inward breath from Myma at the first cut. It seems like it should take more effort, like going through tendon or cartilage, but the knife slices easy through the strands. The long coils heap up on the floor. I cut away the season-cycles of growth until Myma's hair is as short as mine, standing out from her head in soft tufts. Somehow more brown in it now than silver. She feels the back of her head, makes a sound that might be a laugh.

Like. Daughter.

She turns her head to me and smiles. The muscles in her face working so hard that even the right side tilts upward. There is an anxiousness in the smile but her thin neck holds itself straight. Her chin lifts. How tiring it must have been to carry all that weight of hair around. I gather up the off-shed mass and in my arms it is warm, like something once-beating. I pile it on the bed, where our two heads have lain.

A glint. I look down, see my own eyes looking back at me from among the folds and rags. Myma's reflecting glass. It flickers when I pick it up. I tilt my hand and the glass fills with the room behind me, the upper half of Myma. Jolt at seeing her head small and bare. The sharpness of her edges in the glass. She has kept it close all this while, this Keep-Safe, the kind that wounds instead of warding off, for when the threat gets close enough to show its eyes.

Turn my head then to the real, solid Myma.

Myma. My–uh. Maya. She not mine but still of me. Me not hers but still of her. I have held on to her fear without knowing why my arms were heavy, or what it was that weighted them, not realising that what I carried did not really belong to me.

I drop the glass into the piled hair. Maybe some other light, long from now, another face will come here, and it will look into the glass and find a trace of us.

These the things we will carry. Few the things we need. Strips of bark for chewing. Labels for reading. Resin lamp. Bark rope. Skinshoes. My shorts. The clothing I wear, my boots on my feet. Myma's boots. Our two knives. Our two faces set into wood, mine and Myma's, the touch-memory of Wyn's hands in the grooves and smoothnesses. And the little wooden face Wyn called Mother, we will carry this too, we will carry them too.

Sling the full sack across my back, the pouch across my chest.

These the things that will be left of us. The Museum of my names. Keep-Safes. The This-and-That crate, the things in it. Our drawings on the walls and ceiling. Dirty bed-smocks and sheets. Empty pudding tins. Wyn's corner. His leavings. A heap of hair on the bed, our nest of rags.

We are ready now. Shoulder my cloak, put Myma in her coat.

I bend and scoop her into my arms. She is lighter than the skeleton of a leaf, so small I could almost tuck her up under the hollow of my ribcage. I use the last strips of sheet to tie her to my front, her legs at either side of my hips, her short-feathered head on my shoulder. The breath of her, light at my neck.

Ah, she murmurs at my ear. We're. Going? Now?

Yes, I tell her. Going now.

She sighs and I feel her loosen in my arms. Yes. We are going now.

As I step past the pieces of the Museum towards the doorway I hear the faintest humming, like the thrum of air after a name is spoken into it, so low it seems on the edge of going silent. That echo of the names I carried.

Out now into the cold clearing, Myma warm against my chest. The weak sun at the sky's middle. I pause at the cleft post and rummage in my pouch. My tooth in the crease of my palm, the little ridge of bone that used to be part of me. I tip it into the hole with Myma's. Pieces of us to be kept safe when we go.

I do not walk us through the ash copse with its red ache, but the opposite way. We pass stone markers and dangling Keep-Safes. Myma is quiet in my arms. Her eyes are open, blinking up. Leafless branches slide over their surface.

When we near the fence, she begins to shift against my chest. A moan coming from her. I stop at the boundary of branches and bones and hair.

Myma?

She strains her head over my shoulder and I turn. Our forest spreads out from the place where we stand. Myma's cheek against mine, us both looking towards what we leave. I feel suddenly afraid in a way I did not when I stood alone on the other side of the fence, when I ran on that other ground through the other trees. Still so much I do not know. I am stupid and tiny, barely hatched.

Myma shifts against me again. Her mouth opens. Out of it, a shout. Not like my torn red howling. Not like my hollow scream at Wyn's body. Her shout is low and high at once, a bellow and whistle, and it swells, dark green, glistening, full of stomping feet and clapping hands and clicking bones and splitting fingernails and crackling hair. I glimpse shapes in it, almost solid, spilling over her lips. Half-faced, half-formed things that streak off into the forest and disappear. Others tall and lumbering, spitting from Myma's mouth to stagger away through the trees. Last comes a fox, the muzzle pushing out between her jaws, the tail coughed up. I watch it run, making no sound, before it sheds itself like a wintered tree and becomes leaves, ground.

The shout ends and Myma slumps on my shoulder, panting. I grip her. Always I will hold you, I whisper inside myself. Always for you I will be Daughter.

My new name, secret and shivering on my tongue like a hatching moth. It steadies me.

I clamber us up and over. We hold on to each other as we cross the fence. Tight together as we leave the place that has been ours. Her chest against mine, our heartbeats a single pulse. Our bodies that are one but always two. Mine now the one that carries, hers the carried. And I will carry her oh I will carry her even when she goes still and soundless, until all the trees have fallen and all the red foxes have turned grey.

I make piles of stones as I go. Markers, to help me remember the way back.

Acknowledgements

Heartfelt thanks to all those who have helped bring *Life Cycle of a Moth* flapping into the world. My fearless agent Lucy Luck, for your belief and for untangling the knots with me – I am so glad this book and I met you. My editor Leah Woodburn, for seeing Maya and Daughter so clearly, for your wise insights and endless advice. Anna Frame and Jamie Norman, the best advocates I could wish for. Jenny Fry, Leila Cruickshank and everyone at Canongate, for being so passionate about this book. Rafi Romaya, for your beautiful artwork. My copy editor Gale Winskill, for your sharp eye and sensitivity to Daughter's voice. The team at Curtis Brown Creative, especially Jennifer Kerslake, for the continued enthusiastic endorsements of my work. Jake Arnott, Laura Barnett and Lisa O'Donnell, for the excellent tutelage, and my fellow CBC students for the feedback on *Life Cycle of a Moth* in its larval stages. Stephen James, for your boundless generosity and many formative conversations. My brilliant Ph.D. supervisors, Kaye Mitchell and Frances Leviston, for instilling me with confidence as a writer and academic.

Sophie van Well Groeneveld, for working through early chapters with me at the kitchen table. Candle Hirst, for being a generous reader, friend, feeder, reassurer and all-round good egg. My wonderful writing cohort in Manchester – thanks to Sam Lamplugh for allowing me to ramble and mull until the ending made sense. Everyone at the Broca Cafe, for the laughter and mutual support; the best job and the best people. Sophie Waldron, for all the years, for being staunchly you. My dear friends and family, for cheering me on and keeping me grounded in equal measures.

My grandfather, to whom this book is dedicated, for being the best of men, for the unreserved enthusiasm and support – I imagine your hands holding these pages and the way you would have smiled. My mother, to whom I also dedicate this book, for being the sturdy body I can lean on and the home I can come back to. My father, for your humour and wisdom, your gentle encouragement. My brother, for exploring the woods with me, for your ruthless teasing and immense kindness. And my partner, Dan, for always uplifting, supporting, emboldening.

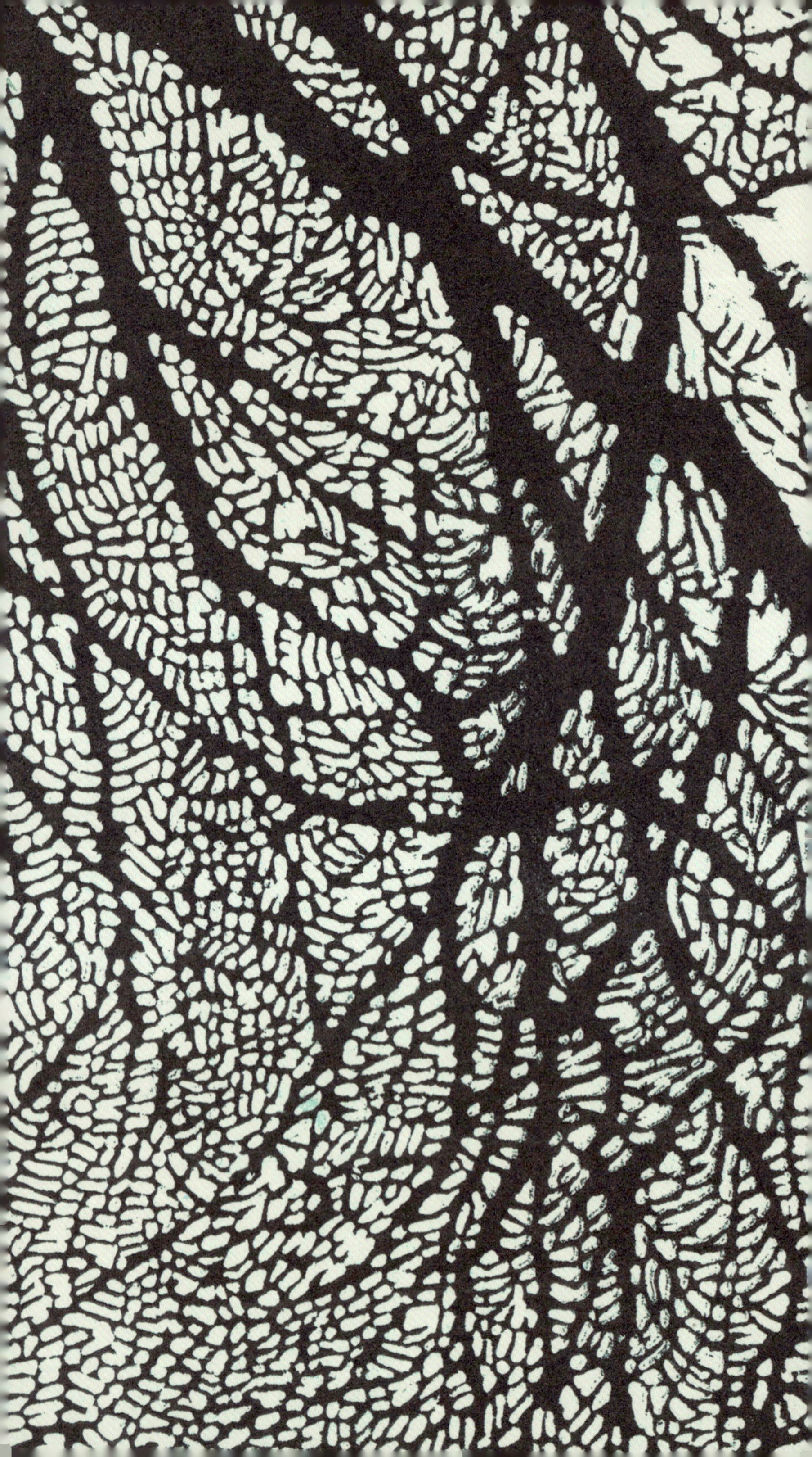